The Pet-Sit

Carol Moreira

Hippie Hill Press

This is a work of fiction. Though I have tried to be as accurate as possible about the geography and landmarks of Portsmouth, I have taken a bit of licence in inventing a few bars and restaurants. All the characters in this novel are the product of my imagination and are not based on real people.

For my sister

Retired Chief Inspector

Kate Firman

A role model and inspiration to many women

Chapter 1

"What a bloody ugly building—all that glass, those weird colours and angles." The taxi driver stares up at the row of flamboyant, modern-art-inspired townhouses. "Warhol Way—daft name." The driver has a deep Portsmouth accent that Marilyn remembers from childhood. "They knocked down a wonderful old inn and pub to build this monstrosity," he says. "The Sailor's Legs."

He chuckles and glances over his shoulder. "I wouldn't sleep there myself. The Sailor's Legs stood for hundreds of years. Some of those bar fights must have ended in murder." His eyes widen. He is enjoying winding them up. "The ghosts of long-dead Portsmouth drunks must be stalking this whole area. Well, good luck to you."

Doug frowns at the driver's ruddy, whiskery face then glances at Marilyn. She sees concern in Doug's eyes. Her husband is worried that talk of ghosts is getting the pet-sit off to a bad start.

"We don't believe in ghosts," she says as Doug hands the driver his credit card.

"Good thing. Goodbye then." The driver gives them a cheery wiggle of his fingers as they get out and lift their bags from the trunk. He drives away and they turn to face their temporary home. Their townhouse, like all the others in the row, looks sleek and modern, decorated in panels of blue, yellow, and red glass and paint.

Not my kind of place, Marilyn thinks as Doug slips his hand beneath a nearby flowerpot and retrieves the owners' house keys.

The bright red door swings wide, and they enter a narrow, gleamingly white corridor. A garage door leads off it. Another staircase winds upward. Clearly the living areas are upstairs.

Marilyn feels the usual tremor of excitement and unease at the start of a new pet-sit.

What will we find this time?

It'll be okay, she tells herself. The post on the website was good. No red flags on difficult pets, no complaints about domestic dirt in sitter reviews.

They manoeuvre their bags inside the front door, close it, and begin to bump their way up the stairs, emerging into a bright living area steeped in natural light that slants in through wide patio doors.

Two dogs lie sleeping in the sun. The pets are sprawled across their beds, deeply unconscious.

"Those sedatives sure work," Doug says with a grin. "They haven't heard us at all."

Marilyn nods. "Better to have them groggy than barking like crazy as we arrive. I'm glad the owners thought of sedating them."

"Hey boys, you gonna wake up and say hello?" Doug is already kneeling by the pets, his wide, friendly face close to their slumbering snouts.

"Doug, get up." Marilyn glances toward the open-plan kitchen where dog treats and kibbles have been laid out. "They don't know you. They could attack. Let me get the treats to distract them."

"Okay, worry-wart." Doug sits back on his heels. "Hurry up. I want to say hello."

Marilyn strides to the counter and chooses the biggest, meatiest bag of treats—dried liver bits. She walks back and hands the bag to Doug then stands looking down at the pets: one a svelte border collie, apparently named Finn, and Winston, an obese English bulldog.

The pets' eyes begin to open, and Doug raises his arm and shakes the treat bag.

"Hello, you guys. We are your new American carers," he says, dropping treats into mouths that are already opening although eyes remain cautious. The dogs scrutinise him then Marilyn.

Finding their stares uncomfortably intense, Marilyn glances out of the patio door that leads to the small enclosed garden. Beyond the glass, crimson koi fish circle a tiny pond. She wonders if the fish feel trapped in their claustrophobic space.

Doug reaches out and pats the bulldog's sturdy head. Winston is enormous. Even lying down, his breath wheezes and judders in his throat. Marilyn feels sorry for him although his drooling is already making her queasy. It's going to be easier to love the beautiful Finn.

"We'll go for a walk very soon, fellas," Doug says, "First, I have to check out the TV and Wi-Fi."

And he walks to the coffee table, picks up the remote and points it at the screen. As Marilyn heads to the kitchen, the TV jumps to life. The kitchen's gleaming granite surfaces look pristine but she always insists on scrubbing a house when they first arrive for a pet-sit. A stranger's dirt is always more disgusting than one's own. And this house does have a faint, unsettling odour—a damp, mouldy scent that suggests something long forgotten decaying at the bottom of a cupboard.

She kneels at the space beneath the sink, is about to reach for the bleach, when she hears Sean's voice. His tone, his accent, make time spin backwards then leap forward, dumping her in the present as her body and mind ignite with a fierce, molten energy. Marilyn breathes deep, rises slowly, and leans against the counter. She observes her hands, motionless, stilled. They feel separate from her, as if someone has placed them there. She breathes and her mind calms with a sudden understanding of how perfectly suited Sean is to the world of politics.

She inhales, turns to the TV.

"I'm not in this race to be brought down by malicious lies." Sean's voice is bright and calm—posh Portsmouth. "I have not assaulted anybody. I'm running again to continue my work bringing jobs and prosperity to the citizens of our city."

He's older, of course, his voice deeper, but he's unmistakable. Marilyn stares. The situation feels unreal. Sean's loomed in her nightmares for so long, and here he is smiling, ivory-toothed on TV, clean and professional like a normal person.

From the corner of her eye, she sees her husband sitting at the dining table where he's perusing the homeowners' printed instructions on how to care for the pets and house.

Doug looks up. "It won't be hard to work this system."

"Good." Marilyn feels dizzy and fears a panic attack. How can this be happening, and why is she so unprepared when she'd known Sean had gone into politics, known she would encounter news of him in her home town?

"But Mayor Adams," says the reporter. "Four different women have accused you of violence, of sexual assault."

Marilyn sees Doug aim a remote at the TV. "Leave it," she says. "Please."

"What do you care about British politics?" Doug's rolling American accent sounds oddly casual after the clipped tones of the BBC. "We've got our own asshole politicians back home."

"I just want to know what's going on." Marilyn returns to the screen.

"As I said, Nigel, these allegations are groundless, levelled by people with political or personal agendas." Sean's face is as grave as the accusations. "My campaign will focus on the issues and how I will continue to help the people of Portsmouth."

“But you saw the ITV interview with one of your accusers? This will hurt your chances...”

“Why would I jeopardise everything I’ve worked for?” Sean’s smooth, seductive gaze is fixed on the interviewer. Eyes like a cobra, Marilyn thinks, too green and steady.

“The fact is, once you become a prominent figure, there are people who want to boost themselves by association, or by taking you down.” Sean shrugs. “They might...hate men...crave attention, money... There are some very sad people in the world.”

Sad people? Anger rages in Marilyn’s veins.

She longs to turn off the TV and forget him, but she knows she’ll Google the interview with Sean’s accuser the moment she’s alone. She should not, but she will.

The picture on the screen morphs to two women playing tennis. “This is Sky Sports.” Doug says, holding the remote and the printout of the instructions. “I bet there’s no basketball or football.”

“Probably not. Can you take the dogs for a walk?” She glances around the spotless home. “I have to clean this place.”

Doug sighs. “Really Marilyn? Here we are in England and you want to waste time cleaning a clean house? The pandemic’s ancient history.”

She nods. “You know me.”

“Okay, fellas. Let’s go.” Doug claps his hands at the pets then turns and strides across the living room toward the stairs. Finn jumps from his bed and scampers after Doug. Winston looks up, levers himself upright, waddles behind.

"Marilyn, stop it." Doug frowns at her from the doorway.

"What?"

"Your hands. You're wringing them, love."

"Oh." Marilyn stills her fingers, hides them behind her back.

"You're stressed out." Doug walks over and grips her hand in his. "It's not surprising. Pet-sits are hard at first, you never know what you'll find." He glances about the comfortable, bright home and the dogs waiting at the door. "But it's nice here. This'll be good."

"Yes." Marilyn nods, glad of the warmth of her husband's fingers. "I'm just tired. I didn't need the drunks yelling in the street on top of jetlag. A nice hotel, but they ruined my sleep."

She frowns to recall the night-time sounds that woke her—beer-infused laughter, shouting and scuffles, thudding feet. Why do the English drink so much? She knows, of course. It's to escape their social awkwardness. English people are born into the past, learning their place in the pecking order along with their first words.

"There's always drunks," she says, "everywhere you go." She pauses, breathes. She'd almost said, 'There's always drunks in England.'

Doug nods. "Lie down, hon."

"Maybe later." Marilyn kisses his cheek, which is grey and stubbly after their journey. She watches him leave and stands, listening for the clicks of the leashes and the slam of the door. She waits in case Doug has forgotten something then rushes to her iPad and opens it with shaking fingers. She connects to the homeowners' Wi-Fi then finds the ITV news site and the interview with Sean's accuser. The picture shows a darkened room. A young woman with long hair sits with her back to the camera. The girl is shadowed, unidentifiable. She describes how she met Sean at a Tory fundraiser.

"He invited me for a walk, in Southsea Wood, said we'd talk about an internship in the fresh air. I thought he was kind, generous with his time..." The girl pauses, and Marilyn reaches out and turns off the recording.

Don't watch, you'll feel worse.

But Marilyn's heart is already pattering. She's hot all over. She breathes deep, into her belly, as her therapist taught, but her skin burns. She's read that nerve impulses can travel at 200 miles an hour. She believes it. Her entire being has lit up in a fraction of a second. She lowers her shoulders, craving a Xanax.

You don't need it. Calm yourself.

She strides to the kitchen and sees a note from the homeowners about the preparation of Winston's raw meat diet.

Gross! Doug can deal with that.

Pulling on rubber gloves, she scrubs every surface then she heads upstairs. Her naked toes sink into the thick white carpet on the steps. She tries to distract herself by focusing on the house. How strange to have white carpet in a home with two dogs. It must get filthy. It's a big, comfortable house and the dogs are going to be manageable, maybe even fun. But she can't shake the feeling her luck has turned. The opportunity to visit Portsmouth disguised as an American pet-sitter had seemed providential, the way it came up shortly after her mother's death—she could never have come while the old bitch was alive—but now the pet-sit feels like a trap.

She reaches the master bedroom that sits like a secret cave at the summit of the last flight of stairs, and pauses, noticing that the stale smell from downstairs also infects the upstairs. Maybe it's the drains, maybe it's the dogs. She sighs and cleans everything, swiftly, urgently.

Leaving, she pauses beside a glass dome beneath which several gorgeous diamond rings sit. She pulls off the rubber gloves, lifts the dome, touches the gems' glistening hardness, and slips a ring—the smallest, least extravagant one—over her finger beside the neat gold band Doug gave her. She admires it, but it feels alien—too brash and showy—and her hands are red and lumpy from washing bottles and changing diapers at the kindergarten. She puts the ring back on its cushion, replaces the dome.

How can people be so trusting? This woman's life must be very different to mine.

Pet-owners are weird, she thinks as she moves down the stairs. It's strange to leave your home and animals with people you've never even met. All we did was answer their post on the website. They didn't even want an online or phone interview.

She wouldn't put her home on a website, have strangers sleep in her bed, however many good reviews they had online.

We have lots of great reviews. But people are often not what they seem.

At the base of the stairs, she stops beside the wide window and sees people standing in the street below. Most are staring at their phones as they wait for a bus or taxi. But a woman glances up and sees Marilyn, then swiftly looks away.

Marilyn frowns. *There's no privacy here.* Acres of house spread over four floors, and not a cosy, homely corner anywhere. Living in this glass house will fuel the alarm that's building in her. It's back so soon, this native fear. It's the way she always felt in her hometown—hyper-vigilant, nerves taut.

It's okay, she soothes herself: Mum is dead, Sean doesn't know you're here. But her mind fills with her mother's voice "You moron, you cretin." She recalls her mum's bright-eyed, exuberant cruelty and shudders. She's been in England less than 24 hours and her defences are already breached. Her mum and Sean have erupted into her mind, and the person she'd thought she'd become is falling away, revealing the injured nub, her broken core.

I haven't changed at all.

In the kitchen, she wipes the surfaces again and avoids the dreadful windows, but Sean's voice resounds in her mind: *I will help the citizens of Portsmouth... There are some very sad people in the world.* As she scrubs the stove top, something scalding and familiar snakes through Marilyn. It is a long-dismissed thirst for revenge. She puts her head down and scrubs harder.

Chapter 2

Paula shifts uneasily in her seat. Stop it, she tells herself. Sit still. Across a polished wooden desk, Deputy Mayor Hugh Walker is flipping through the pages of her CV. Paula studies his high-ceilinged office and the desk photos of Hugh with Tory grandees and Mayor Sean Adams.

Hugh looks up and places her CV on his desk. "We were interested to hear you'd become a private eye, Paula. The word is that you were a good cop, until that one lapse in judgement."

"I was provoked." Paula tries not to sound belligerent.

"The victim was handcuffed. You put him in hospital."

"He kicked my dog. He broke Husky's leg. I saw my dog—and in the dog squad, that's your partner—in agony, and that scrote laughing. Husky will always limp now."

"You used your baton on him, Paula. That's my only concern about employing you—this seeming propensity for violence."

Walker speaks so solemnly Paula wonders if he's taking the piss. Baton. He's making the incident sound comic, slapstick.

She swallows, tells herself to remain calm.

You need this job.

"I'm a dog person, not a violent one," she says. "And I've paid for my mistake. I got sacked. I'm still living with the harassment. Yobs tweeting about 'Chesty Lesbo Pig' gets old, you know."

Inwardly, she sighs. Those people are half-wits, a bigoted mob, and she hates that she's learned to fear them. "Actually, I'm not gay," she says with a teasing lift of her brows. "I'm bi."

And she breathes deep, accentuating her cleavage. She has dressed to look attractive to men in this interview. Her curves are on display.

Gotta play the cards I've got.

Hugh blushes and Paula suppresses a grin. She must stop winding men up but it's hard to resist. They're so predictable. And she's off men, most of them, likes to see them squirm. Bastards won't leave her alone, online or in the flesh.

She turns to look at the photos on Hugh's desk. "Your boss there, Sean Adams. Lots of women accusing him of sexual assault. That puts what I did in perspective."

"The mayor has said there is no truth to the accusations," Hugh says evenly. "The mayor will be vindicated."

"He'd better be vindicated fast. Isn't he running for Westminster?"

She holds Hugh's gaze then lowers her eyes. *You need this job.* "Sorry. The past few months have been tough. I react. . . over-react. Sorry."

"Of course." Hugh does sound sympathetic. "I heard your marriage has ended, Paula. Are you okay?"

"I'm fine," she says too sharply. "Thank you."

Hugh studies her face. "Okay Paula, we'll give you a try, because of your past reputation and your service to the city. But at the first sign of trouble, our relationship will be at an end..."

"Thank you." She means it. "I started out as a detective, actually — CID, long ago, before I realised the appeal of working with animals." She recalls the pride she'd felt on getting into the Dog Unit as the only female member of the team.

All gone now. I fucked up.

"So, what do you want me to do?" she asks.

"I want—we want—you to find a former Portsmouth resident called Marion Taylor. Her brother, David, was supposed to be here actually." Hugh glances at his discreet wristwatch then at the door. "He's very late."

Hugh looks uncomfortable suddenly. His eyes have begun darting like flies at a picnic. He seems upset David is late and nervous about the prospect of him arriving.

"I'm afraid we must discuss salary," Paula says. "My daily rate is £200, plus expenses."

"Fine."

Damn, should have asked for more.

Hugh's eyes shift to the notes on his desk then turn to the window where seagulls swoop and soar.

Paula prompts, "So who is Marion Taylor?"

Hugh picks up his biro and clicks it, the sound loud in the formal room. "As I indicated, she's the sister of my friend and colleague, David Taylor." He glances again at the window, as if he wishes he could join the seagulls swooping beyond. "David wants his sister found. His lateness might be deliberate. It's tough for him to talk about his childhood. Their father died. David's struggled with it his whole life."

Paula studies Hugh. His face is flushed but there's no emotion, no empathy, when he speaks of David Taylor and his father's death. Hugh's getting divorced. Maybe that's why he's distracted.

"What can you tell me about Marion?"

"They were a military family." Paula notes his tone—detached, impersonal.

"The father was a fighter pilot in the Fleet Air Arm. He died, a tragic accident on board an aircraft carrier. His survivors — Marion, David, and their mother, Judith — lived on in Portsmouth for a while, then moved, initially to Peterborough."

"Peterborough?" Not an obvious choice for a naval family. Paula knows it as an inland city north of London. It has a magnificent Gothic cathedral. Paula visited it once, long ago, with her father, a lover of ancient buildings and young women. "Did they have family there?"

Hugh's eyes skitter, he shrugs.

"I presume David has attempted to trace Marion on social media?"

Hugh blinks. "Yes. No luck."

"How old would Marion be, if she's still alive?"

"About forty-five."

An important age, one Paula herself is fast approaching. "What did her mother do?"

"A teacher, primary."

Paula's own mother had been a teacher. It was something women of that generation did, there being few other options. "Teacher, nurse or secretary," her mum once said. "I chose teacher. I was a bloody good one."

"Can you tell me the family's address in Portsmouth?"

"They lived on the naval base."

Paula nods, thinking of those rows of uniform houses. She won't learn much from visiting Marion's government built and owned childhood home. "You have a picture of Marion?"

"Only an old one, I'm afraid." Hugh opens a drawer and gets out a white envelope.

Paula studies the enclosed headshot. It shows a young girl, curly dark hair, her cheeks plump in that blossoming way of kids becoming teens. The girl is smiling, her face acquiring definition, personality. But there's something distant in her pretty blue eyes, as if she's already learned to be wary of life. The picture makes Paula sad, as if the young Marion represents all their long-ago, more hopeful selves.

"Thank you." Paula takes a shot of the photo with her phone then returns the picture to its envelope and pushes it across the desk. "What was the father's name?"

"Jack Taylor. Died 1994."

"I'll look up his accident. And the mother, Judith?"

"She and her kids emigrated to America, but Judith and David returned to Portsmouth. Judith died recently. Her loss has made David realise Marion is now his only living relative. David has a communications company — Tidal Words. He and I have worked together on political campaigns."

Hugh is now barely meeting her eyes. Why is he so awkward? He's accustomed to dealing with people, to giving orders.

"Sorry I'm late." The door jumps wide and a chunky middle-aged man strides to Hugh's desk and pulls up a chair. "Something came up."

Hugh frowns. "You are very late."

"Sorry." David sits, and leans into the desk, steeples his fingers. His eyes meet Paula's with a brightness that aims for honesty, although his hands seem to be offering each other mutual support.

"Hello," Paula says. "Can you tell me when you last had contact with your sister?"

The new arrival frowns. "Oh, it must be... decades. I never liked Marion when we were young, to be honest." His unblinking gaze suggests he is being anything but. "I was into sports, had lots of friends. She was quiet, introverted, stayed in her room brooding."

"Brooding? What about?"

David's eyes falter. "Well, you know, we'd lost our father."

Paula studies David's fleshy face and body. He's probably a beer drinker like herself—she must cut down—although his wide shoulders, the bulging upper arms, suggest he might still visit the gym on occasion.

"Why did Marion remain in the US when you and your mother returned to England in ... 1998?"

David shrugs. "She'd started working in a nursery school, liked it."

He's pretending. He doesn't want his sister found.

"Your mother must have been anxious about leaving Marion. She was a teen?"

He shrugs. "Mum needed to come home. She'd married an American submariner. We moved to Portsmouth, New Hampshire, a submarine base—strange coincidence with the name—but Mum and Chuck didn't work out. Mum said Marion later moved to Bangor, Maine."

"I'm sorry about your mother's death."

"Thank you." David's eyes fill with real warmth.

So, he loved his mother.

Paula stands to leave. "I'll be in touch."

The men stand too and walk around the desk to shake her hand.

"Thank you," David says. He studies her. "By the way, well done for thumping that low-life who hurt your dog. Good to see someone get what they deserve."

Paula nods and smiles but doesn't know who's worse: the civil liberties types who got her fired or the law-and-order fanatics—some of them would bring back public flogging, she's sure.

"Well, I now have a new career," she says. "Your sister's disappearance is my first case."

David nods. "Great."

Paula finishes her goodbyes and walks out through the long, official corridor, down the wide steps of the Guildhall and into the fresh air. As she moves into the late winter sunshine, she feels relieved to be outside. Hugh and David appear to be lying although she could be imagining their twitchiness, maybe transferring her own nerves to them. She's still defining herself as a private detective. She's trying to forget all the male versions of the role. Those characters provide a template she hopes to avoid—cynical, hard-drinking, embittered. That persona would be easy to adopt now Jane has kicked her out. Distress rises in Paula's eyes at the thought of her wife and she decides to take the long route home and makes for the waterfront. She is not keen to return to her drab little apartment near Eastney and needs the cheering sights and sounds of the water and the people it attracts downtown.

The atmosphere by the waterfront is as lively as she'd hoped. Tourists are mingling with runners and students and parents with young children. Everyone is smiling, enjoying the English Channel and the sun. She notices a couple—middle-aged, thin and clad in Lycra sports gear—standing near the statues that commemorate the emigrants who left for America.

Paula smiles as the man's voice reaches her. He's reading aloud the inscription on the plaque below the figures. His voice is loud and unselfconscious, vibrating with emotion. She notes his short grey hair and wiry body, his tanned face. American, for sure. Portsmouth is full of his type, searching for their roots. It's ridiculous. The tourists are no more English than she is American.

She passes a police officer. Automatically, Paula nods, but Officer Yates' eyes slide and Paula realises she's been snubbed by yet another former colleague. Her temperature rises as her phone vibrates. It's an abusive text: *I'm gonna hate-fuck you, gorgeous.*

She should change her number, but this has been her contact for years and it's the one she's attached to the advertising that touts her as a private investigator. She used her own profile picture in silhouette peering through an outsize magnifying glass like Sherlock Holmes.

The haters will soon find another victim.

Removing her jacket, she lifts her face to the sun and wonders about joining the sunbathers on the nearby rocky beach. Her mind returns to Marion Taylor.

Why did Marion stay alone in the US when her family returned to England? Had she fallen in love, or fallen for the way of life? Why didn't David stay in touch with his sister? Paula feels a prickle of interest. The missing woman is her new start.

Chapter 3

Marilyn spins around so fast she almost loses her balance. Her hand leaps to the banister, bracing her against a fall.

"Idiot," she scolds herself as her breath jumps in her throat. "Be careful."

Cautiously, she turns and scans the space behind her. The landing is empty. There is not even a framed photo or picture to disrupt its pristine whiteness. Yet, she'd felt a distinct sensation of being watched. Eyes on the back of her head. Close, as if she was being approached softly, stealthily from behind.

She breathes deep, and sees her left hand still gripping the banister, her knuckles white with strain and fear.

"Calm down," she tells herself. "Bloody hell."

"Are you talking to yourself again?" Her husband's face appears at the bottom of the stairs. "You okay?" He grins. "Did you meet one of the taxi driver's ghosts?"

"I'm fine." Marilyn begins to walk down the steps, her legs unsteady. If only she could confess to Doug: it's not a ghost I fear, it's my past.

"Come into the kitchen," her husband says. "There's loads to see in Portsmouth, the naval history especially." She follows him and he sits down at the kitchen table by his open iPad. "There's *H.M.S. Victory*, Nelson's ship." He grins at Marilyn as she sits. "I'll buy the tickets online, it's cheaper?"

Marilyn nods but her heart thumps.

Dare I go to the dockyard?

"The home-owners said the dogs are good in the car," Doug says. "Do you want to take their vehicle and drive along the south coast? We could get some nice photos of the dogs to send to their owners."

Marilyn shakes her head. "No. The roads are so narrow here. And it's the wrong side. And it's expensive. Brits insure the driver, not the vehicle."

Doug nods. "Well, let's see how it goes. There's probably enough to see in the city anyway." He smiles his wide American smile. "It's a nice day. Let's go now."

They give the dogs treats to console them for being left alone then walk along the waterfront where they dodge construction work. They stop to read big signs that explain how the city's sea defences are being beefed up to protect residents from the warming, storm-prone waters of the English Channel.

"Interesting," Doug says. "Impressive." He shudders. "I can't bear to think about climate change. I wonder if San Francisco will soon be underwater."

The walk to the dockyard is beautiful along the waterfront. There are sailboats, the hover ferry surging to the Isle of Wight, townhouses slanting toward shore. It's a city shaped by water; Marilyn sees that now. The English Channel, that shimmering liquid body that shifts like a bride's veil between England and France, has moulded this place, and so have generations of sailors, of emigrants and soldiers, merchants and vacationers.

They pass the bronze figures of a family of emigrants bound for the New World. The male figure is standing, gazing into the future. One hand is clenched by his side, the other rests on the back of a slight young woman who's perched atop a small trunk. The woman holds the hands of a toddling girl. A boy, slightly older, teases a crab with a stick. Marilyn's eyes mist. She knows how the emigrants felt—the apprehension, disorientation.

Doug turns to her; his eyes bright with tears. "Imagine leaving home and never being able to return, Marilyn."

She nods and wonders what her loving husband would say if he knew how she's deceived him. She's glad to be wearing sunglasses.

Doug stoops to the inscription on the plaque and reads: "*A Permanent Legacy to the commitment of the Europeans who courageously left their native lands to create a new home in America. Presented to the city of Portsmouth on 27th August 2001 by members of The Pioneer Heritage Foundation*.

"Many people must have left from here." Doug glances at the pastel terraces behind them then turns to the red brick wall that separates the street from the beach. The wall is indented with archways long since filled in and occupied by little stores and cafes. Through one, the only archway left vacant, a soft light shines. To Marilyn, the glow resembles the light that beamed through the windows of Portsmouth Cathedral during her father's funeral. A delicate beguiling light, it suggested a better place. This light encouraged the emigrants, maybe, or tricked them.

She smiles at a blonde woman who passes as Doug is reading. The woman is gorgeous, sexy with the curves and pretty cuteness of an old-style movie star. The woman looks sad, but her mouth lifts in a mocking smile as she hears Doug reading the inscription.

She thinks Doug is ridiculous—yet another American searching for his roots.

Marilyn frowns at the woman, but she has already moved on, her hips swinging away from them.

"They likely walked through there, Marilyn." Doug points to the archway. "And onto the beach. Plymouth is down the coast. The Mayflower went from there." His voice rises. "For all we know our ancestors came from right here, Marilyn!" He turns, gazes toward the city centre. "Let's go explore," he says.

Marilyn follows her husband, who is leading, having researched the route online. It feels surprisingly good to let him lead, to stroll along, to admire the old houses and pubs. Like an American, she feels appreciation without attachment.

I will be American here.

But she glimpses Sean's face on the front of a newspaper and memory spins her back to Southsea Wood. His voice, commanding yet wheedling. "Come on, Marion. Relax."

"Come on, Marilyn." Doug's words are a troubling echo of Sean's. "You tired?" her husband asks.

"A bit."

Forget Sean. You can't approach him now.

Her notion that they could meet as adults and talk things through had been a fantasy. She'd hoped for a confession, an apology, but that won't happen. Sean's unchanged. And her terror at seeing him on TV revealed she can't face him anyway. No. The only way to get through this trip is to act, think and feel like the American her husband believes her to be.

They linger on the stone wall built to protect the city from the French. Doug reads the sign that says the round tower was built in the 1490s, replacing a previous wooden one. "Everything is so old here!"

They watch the huge passenger ferries surging away from shore and on to France and the Isle of Wight. They pass The Dolphin pub, a haunt of Lord Nelson's.

"We must have a drink in there," Doug says.

Marilyn copes with all the echoes of the past. It's the security guard at the Historic Dockyard who checks their bags who unnerves her. He's young and vital—the serviceman type, like her dad.

"That's fine, thanks," he says when he's looked through Marilyn's purse and Doug's backpack. "Where are you from?"

"San Francisco," Doug says with a grin.

"Nice. What brings you here?"

Marilyn's jaw tightens. The tension travels up her face, fills her eardrums with ringing distress. Doug smiles. "An opportunity."

"Well, welcome. Enjoy your stay."

"Thank you," Doug says. "Now, which way to *HMS Victory?*"

The young man points. "That way, sir. First, you'll see *HMS Queen Elizabeth*, the largest warship ever built for the Royal Navy. I recommend a boat tour. Then turn right. You can't miss *HMS Victory*, sir."

"Thank you." Doug strides ahead, and Marilyn follows, reluctant now, her steps slow.

Don't think of Daddy, don't.

Soon the massive grey bulk of *HMS Queen Elizabeth* lies before them. "Awesome!" Doug stares. "And look, there's the *Victory*. She's amazing."

She is. Dark and long, Nelson's ship is beautiful, brooding. The ship looks trapped in the past, Marilyn thinks, like me, and her heart jumps in her chest.

They stride up the wooden gangplank, and the sky begins to drizzle as the wind cuts in off the Channel.

On the deck, Doug surveys the information board. "Nelson was shot right here, in 1805, during the Battle of Trafalgar. Do you see the spot, Marilyn? Where exactly did Nelson die?"

"He died below," Marilyn says. "I read it online," she adds swiftly. In her mind, she's a child again. "Where was Nelson hit, Daddy?"

"Right beneath your feet, child." Her father had lifted her like a doll. "Don't stand on the spot where the great man fell, sweet pea."

As her father's strong arms raised her, Marilyn had looked down and seen the plaque marking the place where Nelson fell. Above the plaque, her legs and feet swung in the black patent shoes Daddy bought her for being brave in hospital. "Those nasty tonsils are all gone now, my brave girl." How she'd loved those shoes.

"There, Doug." She points to the bronze sign inlaid in the polished wood.

Doug stoops and reads. He shakes his head. "War, such a waste."

They go below and take the tour. Marilyn stares at the portrait of Emma Hamilton, Nelson's mistress and mother of his illegitimate daughter. She ponders the passion that caused Nelson to desert his wife. She's never felt such passion herself, although with Doug her body has been awakened, stirred.

Soon, I might not have to pretend at all.

In the cramped quarters below the waterline, they hear it took Nelson three hours to die. He asked Sir Thomas Hardy to kiss him at the end.

Like Daddy, dead in the service of his country.

In Nelson's elegant study in the stern of the ship, Marilyn feels her father standing beside her, his warm hand in hers. Young Marilyn had looked from the portrait of Nelson, handsome in his cocked cap and medals, to her father. Her eyes had travelled from her father's shining black shoes, past the pressed trousers and jacket to the white collar and gold braid atop his shoulders. His eyes shone blue within his tanned face. His cap was white, with a shiny black peak.

"You're more handsome than Nelson, Daddy."

Her father had guffawed. "Thank you, sweet pea!" Then he'd glanced at his watch. "Fun's over, I'm afraid. Time to go home." And Marilyn's heart had dropped, as it always did when her special time with her father was over.

"Oh Daddy," she whispers. "Why did you die and leave me?"

"Marilyn, what did you say?" Doug's voice is close. "You're wringing your hands again, love. Are you tired?"

"I'm okay." Marilyn stills her fingers.

Doug rubs her arm. "Let's go. Can't leave the dogs too long."

Marilyn nods, glad to leave.

Back at Warhol Way, the dogs are restless. They both, even Winston, rush them as they ascend the stairs. The animals are clearly used to a lot of attention.

"Okay guys, we're back." Doug shepherds the dogs away from the door then taps his fitness watch. "Eleven thousand steps—we're golden."

Marilyn nods but Doug's exercise addiction is tiresome. Without his exercise, Doug is as twitchy as she is without Xanax. It's annoying, how some addictions are 'good' and some 'bad'. Doug is 'strong and fit', 'health-conscious' while she is 'neurotic', 'needy', 'damaged'. That's what Doug thinks anyway.

It's what I think, most of the time.

"Come on, boys." Doug leads the dogs to the kitchen. "Time for food."

"I'll take them out first." Marilyn says. "They must need to pee."

"You're not tired?"

"I'm fine." Marilyn wants to avoid the preparation of Winston's raw meat diet.

"Have a snack," Doug says. "A few nuts?"

Irritation quickens Marilyn's pulse. Will Doug ever stop treating her like he's still the nurse and she his patient? "I'm all right. I used to be overweight, remember? And then I was bulimic. Let me eat when I'm hungry."

Doug looks hurt, as he often does. His eyes slip away. Marilyn feels bad.

But I'm not his patient anymore.

"Come on boys," she says.

Finn darts down the stairs. Marilyn follows and Winston lumbers behind. Marilyn hears his laboured breathing. She walks carefully, hand on banister—being hit by Winston would be like being tumbled by a boulder.

She slips their leashes around their necks and checks her pockets for poop bags. As they step onto the street, she grips both leashes tight. It's not easy to confine the speedy Finn to the waddling pace of Winston. They proceed down the sidewalk, and Marilyn stops to let Finn pee. Her pulse thumps as she sees a photo of Sean taped to a lamppost. She looks away, down at the dogs.

"Oh. My. God! Those two are so funny together!" A young woman stops, gazes at Finn and Winston. She turns to her friend, rolls deeply kohled eyes. "Aren't they just ... hilarious?"

Her friend nods. "He's soooo fat." She stares at Winston, who stares back. He's accustomed to attention, takes it seriously.

It's odd, Marilyn thinks, how people focus on ugly Winston rather than beautiful Finn. People like a freak show. She knows that from personal experience. *I used to be the fat lady.*

"They're a sight, aren't they?" she agrees.

"Oh, you're American!" the first girl says.

"Yes, from California." Marilyn smiles and is surprised to feel her mind tingle with hope. Here she is in England, and people do not recognise her as one of their own. *Sean won't either.*

"Cool, that's so cool," both girls say. They look at her with big eyes, as if Marilyn has stepped from Hollywood's own red carpet.

"Why are you here?" the first girl asks.

"Pet-sitting. We like to travel."

The first girl crinkles her nose. "I wouldn't leave California for Portsmouth. Would you, Mandy?"

Mandy shakes her head and gives Winston's round skull a tentative pat. Winston gazes at her, his eyes soft. He's a dear, Marilyn thinks. I must pay him more attention.

"Okay, bye," the girls say.

"See you," Marilyn says, although that's unlikely.

She walks on, leads the dogs all the way to the derelict but still lovely old house that's marked for demolition at the peaceful end of a nearby street. The sight of the abandoned home fills Marilyn with a soft pang of sadness, and she wonders if the old pub that used to stand on the site of Warhol Way looked anything like this. There's a developer's sign outlining plans for the new block of flats that will soon stand on the site. She turns away, glad that she'll be back in the US when the work starts, and wondering why she cares about the loss of this small part of her city's complex heritage.

As she returns to the house, she passes Sean's photo on the lamppost and looks away. It's going to be a long few weeks trying to dodge Sean Adams.

"You shouldn't have come back, Marilyn," she scolds, her voice a trembling whisper. "It was a terrible, a stupid mistake."

Chapter 4

Paula gazes at her laptop and swallows hard. The details of Jack Taylor's death are distressing. Marion's father had been landing a fighter jet on the deck of a naval warship when he misjudged the approach. He'd been too low to abort the landing, too low to activate his parachute and eject. He'd landed the plane but hadn't been able to lose enough speed and he and the aircraft had toppled over the end of the ship and into the frigid North Atlantic. The weight of the plane pulled Jack Taylor to the bottom of the ocean along with his unlucky navigator, a man called William Fosse.

What made it all the more sickening was the pace of the tragedy. There was time for the doomed pilot to look from the cockpit, into the eyes of colleagues working on deck. Jack Taylor met the gaze of Paul Williams, with whom he often shared a beer in the messroom. Taylor had nodded to Williams. He'd tipped his drinking buddy a salute, then he was gone.

Paula lifts her eyes from the old newspaper report. She looks to the window and the bright day beyond, then back to the photo of the handsome young pilot standing beside his plane, and the headshot of the equally young and handsome navigator. Her thoughts go to Marion, aged 12 at the time of the accident.

What a terrible age to lose your father. Eleven is far too young to feel the full, weighty cruelty of the world. Paula lost her own father at 13. Which is easier on a kid, she wonders—losing a parent to death or divorce? Marion might have resented her father's tragic mistake but he hadn't chosen to desert her. Paula had known that leaving was her dad's choice. Her mother had made sure she knew.

She picks up her tea, walks to the window, and looks down into the narrow street cluttered with cars and rubbish bins put out for the morning. She feels a surge of longing for her own family house, for its wide street and rooms, its roses and flowerbeds—now all Jane's. Husky pads over and Paula bends to stroke his dear, two-tone head. "Soon, old boy."

He thumps his tail against the lino. She feels guilty. Husky finds life very dull since they were forced out of the police force. Her memory returns to the pain of hearing herself and Husky described as "aggressive" and "out of control."

"At least they didn't lock me up," she tells Husky's eager face. "Of course, I'm gonna react when a creepy toe-rag kicks you. But we have each other, Husky. We have our own space and some peace."

But she doesn't feel peaceful. She returns to the window and watches a boy meander home. The boy's socks have crumpled to his ankles; his satchel bumps his shoulder. He'll sleep soundly after a parent makes him wash away the grime of the day.

Neil used to look like this kid.

Today, Paula's son will return from school and she won't be able to ask about his day, won't hear his curt "fine", or see his eyes slide from hers to the contents of the fridge. Protest swells her mind and body. She's the one who gave birth to Neil. Why does he have to stay with Jane? So what if the house is bigger? They'd promised to be equal parents, to not highlight Paula's biological role. That seemed fair at the time. It doesn't feel fair now.

Her phone pings, and she glances down to see a text: *You won't be gay after you've had my ten inches.* It's followed by another: *I'm watching you.*

Paula's heart skids. Do they know where she lives? Probably not. But there's her former home, where Jane and Neil still live, the home where she's about to drop Husky. She was pictured outside that house; her address was reported. She feels sick at the thought of her son's home being targeted, of her boy being harassed, maybe attacked. Don't be daft, she tells herself, they won't hurt your kid.

They're homophobic crazies, not child abusers.

She sighs and looks down at Husky. "There's lots of assholes in this city, eh boy? Way more than even I thought."

Her phone pings again, and she stiffens, but it's just her former colleague Sue checking in with her daily mental health update.

I'm ok, Sue's texted. *Going to the gym, don't worry about me.*

Paula grins. Good old Sue. She just needs time. No wonder she developed PTSD. Anyone would after years of working traffic accidents. Paula doesn't want to think about the mangled bodies Sue's seen. Kids, young victims, are what's messed with Sue the most.

I couldn't have done it, I could not.

And she sends Sue a thumb's up. *Glad you're ok.*

"Come on Husky. Let's go for a walk and get ourselves a treat." She'll return to her former patch in Southsea, to Salty's, her favourite cafe. She'll ignore her phone, enjoy one of their scones, and plan her upcoming trip to Peterborough.

"Let's go," she tells Husky and he spins to the door so fast she grins. You'd barely notice his limp anymore.

They set off, taking the route by the water.

The waterfront is not as fancy in her new neighbourhood, but the walk is still pleasant with the salty wind in her hair and there are fewer people to get in the way of herself and Husky's eager pace. There is a lad wading out in the water, defying the beach signs that warn of strong currents, large breaking waves, steep shelving at high tide.

Be careful, kid, Paula thinks. Be careful. It must be freezing out there.

She walks, losing herself in her stride, until she nears Southsea. She crosses the road.

"Hey! It's that scrote-bashing cop!"

Paula flinches, keeps walking, but glances at her assailant. It's Brian Muise, a little shit she put away for aggravated assault.

Now he's out and apparently working in a public garden. His gloved hands are folded around the handle of a lawnmower. He's grinning, mocking her.

"Not so high and mighty now, are you?"

She walks, tries not to speed up, as Muise turns to the guy he's working with and loudly relates Paula's fall from authority. "She's cute though," the other guy says. "Sexy Mama. Look at those curves."

"She's fucking gay!"

"So? You never dream of a threesome with a coupla dykes?"

"In your dreams," Paula yells over her shoulder. But she doesn't feel it. She walks quicker, surprising Husky. Some days, she takes the haters and harassers on. Sometimes, she winds them up and swings her wide, beautiful hips at them, but not today. Tears blur her path. She blinks, glad to have Husky by her side.

Don't you dare cry. Don't.

Chapter 5

Marilyn stares at the man on her screen. Her brother's dark hair is thinning. He must have inherited baldness from Mum's dad. But David's also heavy, his features distorted by flesh. She'd expected him to look polished and preserved, like Sean. Her older brother's eyes are pouched and ringed with wrinkles, but she recognises his pale gaze. It's guarded—a lot hides behind the eyes.

She reads the blurb. David has his own communications company, near the Historic Dockyard. *We could have walked right by him, maybe we did.*

David is Sean's campaign manager. He extols Sean's virtues, his belief the mayor is ready for a national role, his pride at being part of Sean's team.

"You always were an ass licker, David," Marilyn tells her brother's even stare. "You and Sean..." Her face heats as she thinks of the woman she saw on TV. Another young accuser has come forward. Speaking in a digitised voice in a darkened room, this woman said Sean grabbed her by the throat when she resisted. He was so forceful she feared he'd kill her. She only got away by kicking him.

Marilyn looks up and sighs. "If only I could scrub the bastards out of my mind," she tells the dogs, who are lying in the sunshine around the patio door. She thinks of a headline she saw: scientists are working on a drug to erase traumatic memories. "I wish it was ready to take," she says, looking back at her brother's frozen features. "I'd swallow it down. I'd erase Sean, and you, David, and Mum. I'd keep Dad. Only Dad." Tears fill her eyes. She won't be able to face her brother either. She won't get that longed-for apology, that cleansing.

Her gaze lingers on David. It's odd that they're estranged and yet so intimately connected. Shouldn't he have sensed she was back in the country? Her presence should have displaced the air around him. She should have seen him in the street, gazing up at the house's wide windows, wondering how to make amends for what he did. She turns her head, stares at the kitchen window and wonders if David is indeed down there. She feels drawn to the glass, to the need to check, but jumps as she hears Doug's swift feet coming up the stairs. She shuts down her iPad.

"Another awesome day." Her husband appears and taps the watch on his wrist. "Twelve thousand steps." He lifts his left foot, grasps it. "I had a great run, Marilyn."

"Good." She looks to the patio. The sun is shining on the garden furniture, on the gleaming koi fish circling their pond. Finn is now lying on the sofa, his snout resting on his paws. He seems to be relaxing, but his deep eyes are primed. "I'll take Finn out."

"You two are getting close," Doug says. "I love to see it."

Marilyn feels a shiver of annoyance. She's always struggled to relax with animals—it's the openness in the pet's eyes, the trust. It makes her feel her own fault lines and her need to remain guarded. She is growing close to Finn, but she doesn't need Doug observing, giving her marks out of ten.

"I'm trying not to leave Winston out, but he doesn't like to move." She turns to the dog she rarely considers, the one only Doug shows any real attention. "I don't want to play favourites."

No, Heaven forbid I should be like my mother and favour one innocent dependant over another.

"Good for you," Doug says. "It's easier to love Finn. He's more beautiful, fun."

Marilyn nods.

Is that what Mum thought? David was a cute lad.

Doug puts his left leg down, grabs the right foot. "I ran by that tableau of the family that left for America. I wonder what the difference was—between the people who emigrated and those who stayed. I like to think the leavers were more adventurous, braver. But I would, wouldn't I?"

"Circumstances," Marilyn says. "If your life was great, you wouldn't risk the ocean, those disease-filled coffin ships, starvation, the unknown ..." Her eyes fill with sudden tears and she blinks hard. So many emigrants never even made it across the Atlantic.

"Come on, Finn," she says. "Let's walk."

"Take a photo of Finn for his owners," Doug says. "And dinner won't be long."

"Yes." She glances at Winston but Winston merely blinks. She walks toward Doug, kisses him on his sweaty mouth. Thoughts of David have reminded her how lucky she is to have a kind man care for her.

Outside, it's colder than Marilyn expects. The blue sky, seen from inside, deceived her. Undeterred, she turns right, opposite the line of bag-laden shoppers waiting for a bus. Finn trots along, light and bouncy on his young paws. The people at the stop follow him with their eyes and she enjoys their assumption that the handsome, healthy animal is hers.

Despite the cold, which is starting to creep inside her clothes, she takes the route that leads to the waterfront. She likes this road. The street is lined with coffee shops and charity stores.

Brits love their charity stores.

She looks in the windows she passes, admires the jackets and blouses. She will check the stores out. Southsea is a prosperous part of town. She'll find bargains. She passes an old-fashioned toy shop, sees Lego, science kits, colourful structures, and dolls—Barbies with long limbs, voluminous hair—and thinks of her mother, of how she grabbed Marilyn's shoulders and shook until her head swung and snapped. Back and forth, back and forth young Marilyn spun, her neck cracking, her ears ringing. I always shook my dolls, Marilyn thinks. I shook them, made their heads and hair toss.

Like Mum tossed me.

She doesn't look in the window of the bakery. Those extravagant cream cakes, the dense doughnuts still call to her, and she feels her weakness. She strides on and notices the sad, drooping facades of old buildings that are being torn down. Her lips tighten. Finn walks ahead. He is rarely distracted by smells the way other dogs are.

Finn is like me. He knows to keep moving.

They walk the path that leads across the green expanse of the Common toward the Channel. Her father said soldiers used to train here, years ago. Finn pauses occasionally to pee or give another dog a swift, assessing sniff. Dog-walkers are chatting all over the Common, standing together in little groups. Marilyn has no wish to join them. They would ask questions she doesn't want to answer. One of them might see through her thin, mature face and body to the plump, shy girl she was. She could be recognised, interrogated. She shudders.

They reach the Channel and she pauses, surprised to find fog on the water. She leans against the stone wall and realises she feels disoriented, as if she's travelled the world only to be startled to re-discover home. Since she and Doug became pet-sitters, she's seen many places but sometimes they merge, and she recalls flashes of life—a city road, long and menacing in the darkness, the laughing face of a street performer—and struggles to remember where she was. Mostly, it's the atmosphere of a place she remembers—the honeyed sunlight of Pasadena, the wind-scoured beauty of Quebec, the friendliness of Toronto.

But now she's home, and Englishness is sinking into her, just as fog seeps into soil and stones. "Don't start using English words, Marilyn! What would Doug think?" she says aloud and she chuckles.

Doug will laugh and tell me to stop pretending to be someone else.

But it does feel strange. As a girl, she'd transformed her accent and buried her alarm at America's intimidating landscape and its frank and noisy people. She'd told herself America was a chance to be someone new. And now ... Fear flickers in her gut. Will she split apart, lose the self she has created? The process has begun. She shakes her head. "Come on, Marilyn, it's all right," she says as panic rises and spreads like hot fingers through her chest.

"No! I won't have a panic attack. I won't." She puts her head up, turns from the water and strides about. She pulls in the clean, cold air and exhales the terror out. She sees an elderly woman approach and something in the woman's rigid gait reminds her of a friend of her mother's. Marilyn spins to the water, tucks her head. She won't be recognised.

I will not pretend I'm sorry Mummy is dead.

She stands motionless until the woman has gone. "Oh Finn, I shouldn't have come," she tells his dear watching face. "I knew it the moment I heard Sean's voice, saw his unlined face. How can he look so ... innocent?"

Finn gives her fingers long, rasping licks, and she chuckles. "Oh Finn, you are sweet." She laughs louder. "It tickles, Finn!" She lifts her wet hand, rests it on the wall, and stares at the looming outlines of the sea forts built against the French. It's hard to believe this place of pain can feel like home. Yet here by the Channel, she feels ... lulled.

She turns, studies the path where she walked with her father. He'd lifted her and plonked her feet on his. Together, they'd waddled along. "Marion, stop being silly. Get off my feet!"

Tears blur her eyes. "Are you here, Daddy?" She stares at the nearby historic building, recognises its severe grey outline as that of Henry VIII's castle. Legend has it that the monarch stood here in 1545 and watched as his flagship, *The Mary Rose,* capsized and sank during a battle with the French.

"Daddy, are you still here?"

She hears nothing, feels nothing—no returning ghostly answer, no warming lift of the heart, just the blasting horn of a ferry sailing to France. Her eyes meet the suspicious stare of a man who is striding against the rising wind.

Why is he glaring at me like that?

So hostile, curious. *Rude Man!*

She glares back then realises she is talking aloud, making others wary of her. Finn is nuzzling her leg and gazing at her with big, uncertain eyes.

"It's okay, Finn, sorry Finn." Marilyn strokes his neck and he beats his tail against the path. She calms, looks out at the water, sees how the sea defences have been widened since her time. The

Channel now glimmers slightly further away across a barrier of densely packed rocks. It is beautiful how they have built these new defences, she thinks, noting how the grey concrete paths and benches mimic the grey water beyond. In front of Henry VIII's castle, the city has constructed rows of rounded stone seating, facing the ocean and evoking the curved defences of the castle itself.

What an amazing job, Marilyn thinks, and she feels an unexpected surge of civic pride.

She walks on, spots a memorial bench purchased by a bereaved family, and thinks of her father still trapped in that plane at the bottom of the cold, dark ocean.

A thought leaps. *Daddy would not have let Sean get away with his crimes.*

She could finish Sean, end him. In England, she's unknown, an American pet-sitter.

I could do it, and be back on that plane.

Marilyn glances down. "I could be a mother to Sean's victims, Finn. I never had my own children, because of Mum, Sean ... But I could have been normal, I could."

She raises her head, gulps air, then stills as the thought reforms: *I could be a guardian angel to those girls, I could be an invisible shield.*

"But no!" She shakes her head. "Doug won't love me if he discovers I've lied. He'll say I should have gone to the police. But what do they ever do?" She puts up her head, squares her shoulders. "What do they ever do?"

She turns from the water and pulls out her phone. "Smile Finn. Great, that's perfect." She calls up the address of his owners now holidaying in far-away Australia.

Finn is an amazing walker, she types, *and a wonderful companion.* Then she sends the message.

"Good boy, Finn. Come on." He leaps up and they head back toward Southsea.

The wind rises, carrying a light but stinging rain. Marilyn puts her head down and remembers how deadening English rain can be, how it can flatten the landscape, and the human spirit. In bad weather, something about England's dark old stones, the weight of its history, feels suffocating. Finn feels it too. He leans into her legs, sheltering.

She turns right at the pier that leads to the hover ferry, away from the tall, clanking, yellow cranes still bending their heads to the task of defending the waterfront, and heads across the grassy Common toward the community that huddles behind the grass and the tightly knit Victorian buildings.

She pauses as she passes a plasticised poster taped to a tree and stares at the smooth face, the smiling white teeth. Her blood thumps but she forces herself to look in those eyes. She reads and learns the mayor will be appearing at a church breakfast in seven days. All are invited to attend and learn how Sean's faith motivates his work. Refreshments will be served.

Marilyn returns Sean's smile. She feels a sudden, tingling sense of possibility. Resolve strengthens her shoulders.

"I will be a hero, like Daddy." Her mind returns to long-dismissed fantasies of revenge, to the plans she formed and discarded. "Come on, Finn. I have a special batch of baking to plan."

Chapter 6

Paula pours boiling water over a teabag in her Peterborough hotel room and splashes in milk. She thinks of Jane. Morning tea is a ritual, a religion, with Paula's wife. Tea leaves must be steeped for three minutes in a warmed pot, and milk poured first. Paula's parents always added tea first, but Jane's family were more refined so her parents' tradition prevailed.

Paula drags the bag through the murky liquid. It's hard to believe she misses Jane's rigidity around tea, especially as Paula only drank coffee until she met her wife. She picks up her drink, moves to the window and gazes at the lop-sided bulk of Peterborough Cathedral that sits like a strange ship at the other side of the square.

She ponders the previous afternoon. A visit to City Hall provided the address of the Taylor family's former home. Paula knocked on the door of the semi-detached. The young mum smeared with baby food who answered hadn't heard of the Taylors. The next-door neighbour, a sweet-faced elderly woman called Gill, had.

"The mother was not friendly, neither was the son," Gill said. "The daughter was quiet, head down, studying the pavement. She sometimes gave me a whispered 'hello.' She was pretty. I saw her brother's friends gazing at her, but she showed no interest." Gill frowned. "That girl seemed scared of the world."

"You don't know where they went?"

She shrugged. "No, one day they just weren't here. I'd seen a man about, heard an accent, assumed he was the mother's boyfriend. Why do you ask?"

"I'm looking for the daughter," Paula said, "Marion."

"Well, I hope you find her." Gill's eyes lingered on Paula. She was clearly hoping for information about why Marion was being sought—an inheritance maybe, a family illness.

Paula smiled. "Thank you for your time, it was nice talking to you."

"You too, dear," Gill said as Paula turned away. She's lonely, Paula thought as she walked through the well-tended garden. It's hard to be old. She thought of her own mother, of the stale sadness that hung about her.

I should visit Mum more. I will.

Now, she looks at Peterborough Cathedral and drinks her flavourless tea. She visited this cathedral once with her father. He'd rejoiced in it, but its immensity alarmed Paula, and the ancient cracked and gaping graves gave her the creeps. She'd hidden her dislike in order to feel close to her dad. That seems sad, given what a wanker he turned out to be, but little girls adore their fathers. Strange that he'd had no religious faith yet always emerged from a cathedral softer, chattier. Once, he even reached out and took Paula's hand.

I've barely thought of Dad since he died.

She studies the building and sees how the cathedral's grandeur is lessened—humanised—by a massive flaw. The tower on the left side is incomplete, lacking the solid inner tower of the other side.

Did they run out of money?

She watches a little girl in the square below. The child is skipping, holding her mother's hand, when a young dog, untrained obviously, leaps on the child, pushing her to the ground. Paula waits for the girl to cry, for her to stretch out her tiny arms and howl. Instead, the girl gets up and laughs, then leans in to pet the dog whose owner has pulled the animal back and is talking to the mother, red-faced and apologetic.

Paula laughs too. "Spunky kid!"

She laughs louder. It's good to hear her voice asserting itself into the empty room. She checks her phone and feels relief—no abusive texts. She discards her tepid tea and decides to go over to that café in the square and find a table outside. No one knows her in Peterborough. There'll be no sliding eyes from former colleagues or insults from scrotes she put away. She'll ignore her phone and people-watch and think about her upcoming trip to Maine. She's never been to America, a fact she did not share with Hugh when she asked him to approve the expense.

She smiles, anticipating sitting anonymously in Cathedral Square with a large mug of coffee.

Chapter 7

Apricot Oatmeal Muffins

1 ½ cup rolled oats

¾ cup flour

¼ cup granulated sugar

1 tsp baking powder

2/3 cup milk

4 ½ ounces apricot puree

1 egg

3/4 tsp vanilla

2/3 cup chopped dried apricots

1/3 cup sultanas

Marilyn stares at the recipe on her iPad. She'll have to modify it, of course. Sean is vain, he'll only eat cake if he thinks it full of healthy ingredients. Apricot kernels taste like almonds. Substituted for some of the oats and sugar, they'll give the batter a rich texture and flavour. The appearance of health is key. Sean must not share the muffins with the wife and children she's seen online. Sean's family are blandly good-looking, their smooth faces unmarked by life or personality. Marilyn doesn't wish Sean's smiling wife or children any harm. Perhaps she'll use a little apricot brandy—that will ensure Sean won't share with kids and the brandy and syrup will mask the kernels' bitterness.

She smiles as she thinks of the kernels concealed in her suitcase. She's gathered them from several Portsmouth health stores, thinking it safer to buy from different retailers. Apricot kernels are a health food, but the B17 in them converts to cyanide when eaten. The body can handle a small amount but it's easy to overdose. When Sean eats her baking, he'll suffer headaches, nausea, insomnia, joint and muscle pain. His nervous system will inflame. Marilyn hopes he feels something of the fear he birthed in her.

She frowns as she stares at the iPad. Can she really make the muffins so tasty Sean will consume a lethal dose? A safe daily dose is two apricot kernels. A man in Montreal ate 40 and survived, but he'd been made aware of the danger and got himself to hospital.

Sean won't know.

The last time she'd made muffins was for the children at the Maine nursery school. Now, she feels a moment's aching sadness for those little ones she no longer sees. She walks to the kitchen window, looks down on the people waiting in the taxi line. A man senses her gaze and glances up, his eyes meeting hers. Alarmed and self-conscious, she darts away into the shelter of the living room.

English syrup might mask the bitterness of the kernels.

What was that thick, sweet kind Mum used to buy?

She paces. Treacle something?

I'll need nuts.

Chopped pecans will add sweetness and blend with the kernels. She can reduce the flour, add pecans instead. Will cherries work better than sultanas? No. She sighs. It's so difficult. How can she know exactly how much cyanide will kill Sean? And how can she get poisoned muffins into the hands and belly of a man who is powerful and protected?

She pauses, stares through the patio door to where Doug is tidying the small elevated garden. The koi fish lounge in their pool, unusually still. For a moment, Marilyn fears they're dead then wonders, with a spark of alarm, what the homeowners would say if they were. Finn is following Doug about the sun-dappled space. Winston rests in the shade.

The scene soothes Marilyn, and she thinks how stupid she would be to jeopardise the simple contentment she has found with Doug.

Stupid.

But her mind spins on and she wonders if, instead of apricot kernels, she should use English Yew. Google told her the seeds of a yew berry are poisonous. They act on the heart, causing rapid death. And it might be easier to hide a few seeds inside the muffins, it would take less of the yew to kill him.

Maybe I don't need to kill him. Maybe it's enough to sicken him, to put a dent in the shiny imposter.

She walks about the room, and feels once more, that close sensation of being watched, surveilled.

"Is it you, Ghost?" she says, glancing over her shoulder. "I don't believe in you. My haunting is in my own head."

She pivots to the window—*Don't let Doug see you striding about talking to yourself*— but her husband remains busy with the garbage.

"What do you think, Ghost?" she says as she resumes walking. "Should I disguise myself and take poisoned muffins to the church, tell Sean they're a gift, full of superfoods? I'll look him in the eye, flatter him." Once more, she stops at the kitchen window, stares at two elderly men chatting in the bus line.

"But can I act normal around Sean?"

Her mind turns to Laura's wig lying like a small bronze shield, a talisman, in her case upstairs. Dear, poor Laura. Marilyn had packed the wig with the idea that she might dress up sexy for Doug. She'd imagined herself a tempting auburn-haired siren. Doug would love it and Laura's wig would also be an effective disguise—the auburn so vivid, glowing. Marilyn knows that in Laura's wig, she acquires something of her dead friend's aura. At the edge of her consciousness, a question: what would Laura think of Marilyn wearing the wig she wore through all those months of chemotherapy for such a purpose? Marilyn stiffens, refuses the thought.

Laura can't be hurt by this.

But an uncomfortable notion does sneak through. She's noticed how Sean and David, although altered by time, still possess something of their original essence, some quality of the eyes, some way of carrying themselves, that's unchanged.

Will Sean see the girl I was?

She stands by the kitchen window. A man in the street feels her gaze and glances up. She twists away, into the room.

What is my essence?

She takes the duster from a drawer and passes it over the coffee table and the black glass around the TV. She must clean the kitchen again. She has not found the source of that mouldy smell she first noticed on entering the house and the odour has not gone away.

She moves the duster over the smooth round bellies of two Chinese vases that sit on either side of the sofa then pauses, distracted by the glorious golden hues of the birds and flowers detailed on the ceramic.

She puts down the duster, walks to the freezer, removes the ice cube maker, fills a large water jug with ice, returns to the patio window and packs the cubes around the delicate stems of the orchids growing on the window sills. Why do people have such fussy, creepy plants? What's wrong with tulips or cheerful daffodils? Her hands shake as she handles the ice.

What are you doing here? Why did you come?

Beyond the glass, Doug straightens, his hands full of weeds and garbage. She puts down the jug, pulls back the door.

"That wind last night sure made a mess," her husband says, turning to her with a smile. "It carried garbage up from the street."

Marilyn nods, looks at her man and the crisp packets and bits of newspaper in his hands. Her heart relaxes, opens, and she feels guilty that she ever thought of stealing Doug's painkillers. She could never poison Sean with her husband's drugs. Doug needs them to ease the pain of his bad back—the back he damaged lifting sick people like herself.

He steps toward her, holds out the dirty food and candy wrappings. "Get me a garbage bag, will you, hon?"

She nods. Doug is wonderful, kind and loving.

I will not risk him. I will forget Sean Adams.

Chapter 8

Paula watches the daycare owner. Maddie holds Paula's phone and studies the photo of Marion as a girl. She glances up. "It could be her," she says in her rolling Maine accent. "You said she's called Mar*ion*?"

Paula nods, smiles. She's already traipsed around three day-care centres in Bangor, Maine. She's tired, and disoriented by the strangeness of the small town, which is carved into a wilderness that lies all around. She's glimpsed the tree-filled emptiness pushing against Main Street, has watched the Penobscot River, too strong and wide to contemplate, surge by.

Paula needs this to be Marion. It's proving to be lonely, investigating without colleagues, without Jane to chew things over with at the end of the day. Paula has told Maddie that Marion's relatives have employed her to find the missing woman. Her hand caresses the police ID she's dropped into her pocket. She shouldn't use it, but ...

"Just a minute." Maddie gets up, walks to the far wall where a school picture hangs. She waves Paula over. Paula's heart surges happily.

Of course! A school photo!

"This is *Marilyn*." Maddie's finger indicates a thin woman, thirties. The woman has collar length dark blonde hair and is unremarkable in every way.

Paula studies the teacher standing among her colleagues and little ones. "Can I take a picture?"

"Go ahead." Paula takes out her phone and captures the image.

Maddie shakes her head as they return to their chairs. "Strange, she sounded as American as me. I wonder why she changed her name."

"Marion left England when she was young, after her father died. The family needed a new start."

"Oh." Maddie's mouth puckers into sympathy. She has a soft, round face and body that seem well-suited to her work. "Our *Marilyn* was a big woman at first. But she lost weight—too much, I thought. And then she kind of gained a bit, evened out, got healthier. It was good to see her happiness. I credited her new man. Marilyn loved walking the trail around the Penobscot. Later, she ran it too, with her husband." Maddie puts her hands on her desk, levers herself up. "It's probably her in the picture, but I'm not a hundred per cent."

"When did she leave Little Bear Daycare?" Paula stands too.

"Nearly a year ago, when she married the runner."

"Do you have her address?"

"Not anymore."

"Is there anyone who might know it?"

Maddie frowns, the expression looking odd on her smooth face. "She married in the Catholic church, the one on Main Street. They'd likely know."

"Thank you." Paula slips her phone into her pocket. "You've been so kind."

Maddie leads Paula back to the daycare entrance. Paula looks at the children playing in the rooms they pass. She smiles to see the children's clumsy toddling movements, their little faces and bodies. This is a good, happy place. She wonders if Marion Taylor misses it. "Thank you for your time," she tells Maddie as the woman unlocks the second of the school's security doors.

"Nice to meet you, dear." Maddie smiles. "I hope you find her."

The church is wooden, whitewashed. As Paula approaches, she admires the narrow steeple. It reaches skyward with a hopeful simplicity the older, grander steeples of home don't possess.

Inside the church's cool interior, she finds dark pews and stained-glass windows. A thin man clad in black is busy at the nave. The eyes he turns on Paula have seen too much life.

"How can I help you, my dear?" He sits down on the nearest pew, and she does the same.

"My name is Paula Moore." She smiles. Moore is an old Portsmouth name and she's proud of that heritage. It also sounds rather glamorous. Many times, Paula's been told she resembles Marilyn Monroe and she's admitted—although only to herself—that she does.

“I’m looking for a woman,” she says, “originally English but long settled in America. Her mother recently died.”

The engraved lines of caring on his face deepen. “I’m sorry.”

“Her name is Marilyn Taylor. She recently married one of your congregants.”

“Marilyn is British? Well...she married Doug Brooks, a great guy, a nurse.”

“I’m hoping you can give me their address?”

He pauses. “Well, if it’s for personal reasons ... Please accompany me to my office.” He leads her down the nave and into a small, untidy room they reach through a side door.

“The wedding was the Fourth of July,” he says as he unlocks a drawer and brings out a thick brown book. “Doug is a patriot.” He smiles. “You do know July Fourth is our national celebration of winning independence from the British?”

Paula nods. “I don’t take it personally.”

He chuckles and places the book on his untidy desk. “Ah, here ... They married and Marilyn changed her name to Brooks. They moved to San Francisco, where Doug was raised.”

Paula quells a grin. *I’m going to California!*

“Thank you.” She takes out her notebook and notes the address. It suggests they live in an apartment—29A. The street number is ridiculously long as American addresses seem to be. It’s in a place called Dogpatch. She wonders what Dogpatch is like. She will find out. “Thank you, it’s been nice meeting you.”

"You too, my dear." He holds her hand between his, smiles into her eyes. She smiles back, disconcerted by his weary yet gleaming kindness. "Safe travels," he tells her.

Paula leaves, grinning. Back at the Black Bear Hotel, she's happy to find an email from Sue, assuring her she's fine and that she went to the gym again. Paula's relief tells her she's still worried Sue won't make it, that the next suicide attempt might succeed. But Sue's got Alan, Paula reminds herself, she's got her parents, her son. And she's got me.

I tried that martial arts class you love, Sue has written. *Punching the air is surprisingly cathartic!*

Paula sends back a grinning emoji and a message: *I used to imagine I was punching that wanker John Hunt.* Hunt was a sergeant who made both their lives hell when they were starting out.

Paula sends Hugh a quick update and books her flight to San Francisco. She finds an apartment on Airbnb, just two streets from Marion's. Paula grins as she confirms the booking. It'll be interesting to see Marion Taylor. It will be tempting to approach her—she almost feels she knows this woman. But she won't. She will simply confirm Marion's identity and inform Hugh and David of her whereabouts.

She pauses as she closes her laptop. Why, really, did those two twitchy men in Portsmouth ask her to find Marion? Why did Marion change her name? Is Marilyn more American, did she long to fit in? Or did she choose a name similar, but different enough to allow a fresh start—a start that might have been psychologically vital?

Paula places her laptop on the bed, walks to the window and gazes at the Penobscot River. The river, its breadth and wildness, amaze her. What was it like for Marion to move here as a child? Did she like the wooden houses with their cozy porches and sun chairs? What about the Walmarts and the huntin' and fishin' stores, the McDonald's, and Dunkin' Donuts? Paula smiles as she recalls their slogan: "America runs on Dunkin".

She turns to her suitcase, yanks out her sweatpants and a hoody. Like Marilyn, she will run beside the Penobscot. It will clear her head.

She walks down the hotel's back stairs, emerging into an afternoon already sinking into nighttime cold. She strides to the river, and begins to run along the trail. There's no one around and the solitude feels both glorious and unsettling. She moves slowly at first—how long has it been since she ran? Her body and legs are heavy, but it feels great to move even though the trail is more a walking than a running trail. It edges the river, lifts and falls with the earth and hidden tree roots, meanders. The air and water are startlingly pure.

There's such space here. Where are all the people?

She pauses to watch a couple float by in a red canoe. She's amazed. There was a rim of snow on the grass this morning! Laughter reaches her—a girl's voice, high and light, a boy's, deeper, responding. The youngsters are alone out there.

She runs on, and her mind returns to the pair of awkward, sullen men in Portsmouth. I should have researched them, Paula thinks. I wanted—needed—this job too much. I wanted to get out of Portsmouth, and Hugh was nice about Husky.

Too late, she sees the tree root that lies, like a swollen, deformed finger across the trail. She falls, plunging onto her left arm that tries to protect her. She sits up, checks her hand. It's sore but she doubts she's broken anything. Through the trees, she glimpses another canoe, this one as green as the river. A young man rests inside, his head back, his legs extended, a can of something in his hand.

Paula watches the youth lift the drink to his mouth and smiles. She'll return to the hotel, ice her hand, then order a glass of red and some of that amazing American beef. In the morning, she'll fly to San Francisco. She gets to her feet and dusts off her clothes. She's going to California and it's not too late to look into Hugh and David.

Chapter 9

Marilyn stands and grins at her experimental muffins cooling on the rack. It's been difficult to get back in the kitchen but her concoction is sweet and enticing.

Revenge really does taste sweet!

Baking has awakened too many emotions from when she used her fluctuating weight and size as barriers to the alarming attention of men.

It was invisibility I craved, not sugar.

She's filled this creation with poison but still she longs to eat it, to gorge. Habit, she thinks—emotional and physical memory. It's depressing to know that eating still holds a darkness, a self-destructive beckoning.

She's tired. It's taken too long to create and test the batter. She's taste-tested tiny samples and gradually added pureed apricot and syrup to mask the bitterness of the apricot kernels. But now the muffins are risen and browned and filling the room with an enticing aroma.

"What do you think, Finn? Good enough to tempt a health-obsessed rapist?" She smiles down at her adorable, deep-eyed friend. "Yes, I know I should take you out, just let me go to the washroom and I'll be with you." She glances toward Winston who's lying on the rug by the sofa. He's dozing, his paws twitching with more energy than he shows when awake.

Good, I don't have to take him with us.

"I won't be long Finn." And she runs upstairs so she can use the spacious bathroom adjacent to the bedroom. She thinks how clever she was to persuade Doug to go to London for the day. He hadn't wanted to leave her but she'd insisted she had no interest in Churchill's War Rooms.

"You don't want me spoiling your fun," Marilyn said. "Take all the time you want."

"Well, if you're sure. That's good of you, Marilyn, thoughtful."

Now, she washes her hands and lets her wrists linger under the cold tap as she smiles at herself in the mirror. She feels triumphant, dangerous. She has the sense that she's crossed a line most people never dare approach, however deep their grievance. Her face is shiny with sweat, there is heat deep in her core. It could be the thrill of revenge or peri-menopause coming on early. After all she's put her body through, she wouldn't be surprised.

She dries her hands. Time to walk Finn. She sighs as she realises she must take Winston too—he'll need a pee. Striding across the bedroom, she runs down the stairs, keen to get outside and into the fresh air. As she enters the kitchen, Finn jumps back from something on the floor. He scampers away from her, his eyes wary, then cowers in the living room.

"Finn, what have you done?" Her eyes leap to the breakfast bar. The cooling rack has been toppled. Muffins are scattered across the counter and over the floor. There are bite marks, crumbs.

"Finn. Oh Finn!"

She rushes to him as he tries to hide in the corner by the patio. He hangs his head, glances at her with fearful eyes. He knows he shouldn't have stolen human food. He's been told off for it before, she sees.

What should she do? Take him to the vet? What will she say he's eaten? She could say he's lapped up household cleaners or maybe she could tell the truth? The vet won't know she's trying to overdose Sean. She daren't drive the owners' car. She's not used to English driving and has no insurance. A taxi, an uber?

We could walk to the vet, but what if Finn passes out in the street, has a seizure?

Winston wakes up, wanders toward the kitchen and the fallen muffins.

"Winston, no!" She runs at him, spreads her arms. "No!" She points to the living room. "Go!"

He studies her, backs away. If his face could express it, he'd look displeased at this transformation in her.

Can I make Finn sick? Yes. How?

She strides about, wrings her hands then grabs Finn's water bowl, puts it on the counter, picks up the salt cellar, unscrews the lid and tips salt into the bowl.

"How much, oh how much? Not too much, Marilyn. Don't give him kidney failure as well."

She stirs, returns the bowl to the floor. "Finn, come." She beckons. "Come, good boy, Finn, good boy."

Why did it have to be Finn? Winston is the greedy one.

"Come, good boy." She leans, strokes his back. "Good boy." She guides his snout to the water. "Drink Finn."

He stares at her, his eyes unblinking. He's puzzled by her tone and manner.

"Come, Finn. Come." She tips the bowl, swishes the water. "Come on, Finn, drink."

His head dips, and she stills the bowl. His tongue emerges. He laps.

"Good boy, Finn. Good Boy."

After four long laps, he looks up at her.

"Good Boy, Finn. More Finn." She shakes the bowl but he backs off. He's had enough. She's freaking him out.

She watches as he moves away and she breathes deep, tries to still her trembling limbs. "It's okay, Finn." She kneels, stretches her hand to him. "Come. Come."

He turns, moves slowly toward her. He stops, begins to retch. Marilyn scrabbles toward him, rejoicing in the harsh, rasping sounds. Tears fill her eyes as he vomits all over the tiles and her hands.

When he's done, she pulls him to her, wraps her arms around his dear, strong body and nuzzles his neck. "Oh Finn." She looks down at her reeking fingers, covered in watery cake mixture. A dense, nauseating sweetness rises around her. She sobs and hugs him tighter.

Chapter 10

Paula jolts awake. The bed is shaking, the picture of San Francisco Bay above her head is swinging like a metronome. Earthquake? She leaps up then wonders what the hell to do, where to go. Unsure, she stands on the shuddering floor, groggy yet tense, until the trembling stops.

Is it over? Please be over.

She listens for sirens, for chaos, but there's nothing. Encouraged, she walks to the living room, to the door of the balcony that leads off it, and steps out. The balcony sits on one side of a courtyard that contains a small water fountain. There are apartment blocks to the right, centre and left. No one else is outside. No one else is trembling on their balcony.

Maybe this wasn't a big deal.

Paula grins at her over-reaction, but is pleased to spot a robust looking hedge just below the balcony.

If the Big One comes in the next few days, I'll jump.

The Big One. It boggles her mind. How do San Franciscans live every day knowing that California could be hit by a truly decimating quake? Do commuters get in their cars and wonder if this is the day when they will plummet from a concrete overpass or drown in a tunnel?

They probably don't think about it.

Gazing at the block opposite, she wonders what is safest—a low-level apartment where you can jump from a window or a high-level one that might allow you to descend on top of everyone else as the block collapses? Does the threat make neighbours feel closer to each other, she wonders, like London in the Blitz? And they have summer wildfires too!

There's something to be said for boring old England.

She turns to the kitchen and the coffee maker. At least the tremor got her out of bed. The sun is already harsh in the sky. She makes her coffee and Googles the quake on her iPad. It was only a 3.5 on the scale. It occurred five miles underground, the epicentre was ten miles away.

She runs a shower, attempts to scrub away her exhaustion. Her jetlag is numbing and she slept badly. Uneasy sounds of her first night in San Francisco—sirens, rumblings, shouts—had fingered through her fatigue. She's now eight hours behind her normal schedule and feeling every second of it.

As she kneads her scalp, she notices how stiff and heavy her legs feel after running along the Penobscot. Luckily, the hand that broke her fall is moving normally although the knuckles are puffy. Back in the kitchen for more coffee, she pauses at the window and admires the courtyard that sits on this side of the building. The concrete space is filled with glorious stands of bamboo. It's a shame she can't linger, but she has to check out

Marion Taylor's address. Hopefully, Maddie's photo will allow Paula to confirm that the woman in Dogpatch is the woman from Portsmouth. She won't make the connection too quickly though. She has to spend some time online looking into Hugh and David, and she has reserved the rental for three nights. She's determined to see the Golden Gate Bridge, the Haight-Ashbury hippie district and Chinatown.

Right now, she'll confirm Marion's location, grab a bite to eat and return in the late afternoon to watch Marion's place. If Marion and Doug are working, and she has no reason to think they're retired, they're most likely to return at that time of day.

As she finishes her coffee, she reaches into her bag for a few almonds. Raw California almonds taste better—fresh and plump— in California. She swallows a handful and applies sunscreen to her weary face, then recalls she hasn't checked her emails. She finds a message from Jane. The sight of the much-loved name in her inbox makes Paula's heart lift with the habit of happiness before reality returns. She opens the email.

Some thugs attacked our house. Creeps in hoodies spray-painted Lesbo Cop Get Outa Town. I showed the police the security footage but they were no use. They said the kids couldn't be identified—hoodies. Neil is ok. This is your fault.

Paula stares at the words. *I'm sorry,* she writes then erases it. This isn't her fault.

Glad you called the police, she types, *let me know if anything else happens.*

She closes the iPad, grabs her bag and heads for the door. The apology is erased but she does feel guilty. Paula should not have whacked that scrote but she can't control the nutters that have retaliated in Portsmouth. Even she's been surprised by the vitriol. How long has it been since she dared go on social media? *It's not helping my business.*

She walks to the main entrance of the complex and finds a tall metal grill and gate. A security attendant, middle-aged, white, sits inside an office. Paula nods at the woman but she merely frowns. Perhaps she doesn't appreciate residents renting out their homes on Airbnb.

Outside, the air is warm and scented with flowers, construction dust and traffic. Paula smiles to see dogs being walked in the small patch of green adjacent to her block. She does a circuit of the tiny park. There's an orange tree, holding small vivid fruit. Paula stares, and trips over the legs of someone lying beneath a bush.

The legs belong to a young man. Slowly, his closed eyes open. They are dark, the whites yellowing. Around his head, his dreadlocks, chalked by dust and earth, spread like a sun. His eyes can't focus. He's drugged with sleep and narcotics and a despair that Paula has seen often and occasionally felt. The kid looks alone, unreachable, as if already lost to the possibility of help. Paula's heart swells, she fumbles in her bag and wedges a $10 note under his body so it won't get blown away or stolen. She recoils at touching him, fears he'll misinterpret touch—why would he not?

Moments later, she feels a pulse of excitement as she turns into Marion's street. The road is dotted with pretty wooden houses with curling eaves and pastel exteriors. Marion's apartment is in a new six-storey block, attractive, with windows suggesting light and space. Why don't they build higher, Paula wonders, maybe the earthquakes? Marion's block also has an attendant: a young man, thin, black. I'll chat to him if I don't see her, Paula thinks, say I'm an old friend.

She gazes at the sleek windows of the apartments, wonders if Marion and Doug also enjoy peaceful courtyards. What would it be like to emigrate? Exciting, maybe, liberating. But Paula doubts she could be happy anywhere but her home town, and there's Neil and her mother to consider.

She walks the whole road, both sides, and sees metal struts gleaming inside half-built apartments. Do they reinforce everything they build with steel? She passes numbered streets — 16th, 18th, 20th — how amazing to create a city from scratch, to organise. Some streets have place names, familiar yet exotic. She tests a word on her tongue. "Alabama."

She's looking for a café when she feels a tap on her shoulder.

"Money, ma'am? I need a drink. Five dollars will do."

Paula spins. A young man stands worryingly close. His sandy hair tumbles from his head and drops in tangles to his waist. She steps back as he moves close. "I don't want it for drugs," he says. "I'm thirsty, so thirsty. Please ma'am. Five dollars is good."

Paula fumbles in her bag. She tries to sort her money without pulling out her wallet—the kid might seize it and run. She tugs a note free, squints at it in the darkness of her bag—$20, another is a $50. Why do Americans make all their notes the same colour? She finds a ten, takes it out, shoves it in the thirsty lad's hand.

"Here you are." She hopes it's enough. She hopes he'll go away.

"Thank you, ma'am." And he turns and moves down the street with astonishing speed.

Sadness fills her. We're all fragile, she thinks, so fragile. Her heart is thudding. Why is she still alarmed? Because he was desperate, because she's in America where people carry guns. She strides away and calms only when she finds a cafe that looks clean and intriguingly American. She orders a cappuccino and a ginger scone then sees deep veins of delectable blue running through the blueberry scones and orders one of those too.

Hell, the Big One might come tomorrow.

Choosing a table in the window, she notices how American life seems to take up more space. Sirens shriek and howl, horns protest, vehicles gleam. Seeing a bus roll by, Paula consults the girl behind the counter and finds she can get to Haight-Ashbury and return before 4pm.

From the bus, the city is chocolate box pretty but many of the people on the pavements are as destitute as the boys in Dogpatch. There's a desperation that sits like a rash of boils on the city's lovely face. *Must be tough being a cop here.*

In Haight-Ashbury, Paula drifts past hippie-stores and lovely turreted homes and wonders what it would be like to live here, in a candy floss house, with the world walking past your window. She passes a green hill. A sign says Buena Vista, and she steps onto the path that winds up through trees. She grows weary but strides on. She was always fit and strong. *I will be fit and strong again.*

She glimpses a summit, an empty bench. Reaching it, she sees boats, far away, dotting the ocean with sails. A young man passes on the path, holding the lead of a small dog, a white poppet. Paula smiles, wonders how the young man got the dog so high.

"Afternoon, ma'am." The youngster nods.

Paula smiles. "Afternoon." How sweet the boy is, maybe a few years older than Neil. If only Neil was here, Husky too. How would California smell to Husky—exotic plants, different animals, everything new?

She doesn't notice her tears. She mistakes the moisture for sweat.

Those wankers better not hurt my son.

Rage heats her.

I'll kill them. I'll kill all the bigots and scrotes in Portsmouth.

She sobs, laughs at her impotent fury, then raises her head, remembering the boy, not wanting to alarm him, embarrass herself. But the boy and his dog are gone. She looks at the ocean and thinks that she must set this new grief on her back and carry on. The crazies will go away. The sadness over Jane will fade. Maybe she is simply getting older and this is what ageing is—the accumulation of sorrows, the bearing of griefs.

She finds a tissue, wipes her eyes and nose, checks her phone. It's 3.15pm. She must get back to Dogpatch and install herself outside Marion Taylor's block. When she returns to Portsmouth, she will pay her mother that long-overdue visit and see her son.

I'll spend all the time I can with Mom, and my precious boy.

She flexes her thighs, stands, finds the path, and walks.

Chapter 11

Marilyn keeps a close eye on Finn and he seems his normal self; no signs of poisoning. She washes her hands and the kitchen floor and walks and feeds both dogs. She samples a tiny piece of cooled muffin. It's good—moist and muskily sweet like the best brownies and ginger cake. The next batch of muffins, she will deliver to the mayor. Then she breaks the remaining muffins into pieces and flushes them down each of the house's three toilets.

She scrubs the entire kitchen and dusts the living room but finds she's still wound up, her nerves and limbs weak. Her mind turns to Doug's beers cooling in the fridge—one, just one, will help. She shouldn't drink while taking Xanax but she's managed to reduce her dose and she'll replace the beer before Doug notices. She strides to the fridge, pulls the tab on a can and downs the alcohol, relaxing as it swiftly warms and embraces her belly. She'd forgotten how quickly alcohol can soothe.

Alcohol is better than food or drugs.

She hides the can at the bottom of the recycling bag. Doug won't notice. He loves British beer and has stashed loads of cans in the fridge.

Doug returns and sniffs the air. "What's cooking, good-looking?"

Marilyn feels guilty. "I'm sorry, Doug. What would you like?"

"I thought you'd cooked, smells like ribs."

She wraps her arms around him. "What would you like?"

"Let's go to that Irish pub and have some fish and chips, Kilkenny beer?" Doug's face brightens.

"Okay, I'll just go to the loo."

Doug chuckles. "Marilyn, you said 'loo' just like a Brit. You said 'rubbish' instead of 'garbage' the other day too."

She shrugs. "You know what I'm like. I copy accents and mannerisms without meaning to."

He nods. "It's because you're such a sweetheart. You empathise with everyone."

It's true. She does empathise with people, more than she wants to. Her heart thumps as she runs upstairs.

At the pub, Doug gets animated over his Kilkenny. Marilyn stares at the golden liquid in his glass and wishes she could feel herself loosen further inside that alcoholic softness. But she cannot have a beer. Doug would be alarmed. He'd say it's too risky and go on about her previous addictions. He would not shut up so she is stuck with lime soda.

"The War Rooms were awesome, Marilyn," he says, grasping her hand over the wooden table. "They put you right there, under the city, in Churchill's war-time bunker. Next time, let's find a pet-sit in London. We've got enough good reviews to get the best jobs now. We're bound to get another five-star this time. We're just the right age. We're mature and reliable but not too decrepit to run after pets." He grins and glances toward the winter-darkened window. "Maybe we could get good jobs in the summer."

Marilyn nods. "People seem to like us." She feels a sense of disbelief. Doug is likeable, of course, loveable. But she struggles to believe people like her—that was never her experience.

Doug tightens his grip on her fingers. "The whole world is on that site," he says. "I took a look while I was on the train. Waddya think of six months in an eco-cabin in Argentina?" He grins. "Just kidding, we couldn't afford that long off work. We gotta be careful with my parents' money. How about Paris—sound romantic?"

Marilyn flushes. *He wants to be romantic in Paris with me!*

"I hear French people are too fussy about their pets," she says. "You know we always avoid the owners who sound difficult, who make unreasonable demands."

Doug chuckles. "Maybe, but we usually manage to avoid the nutjobs. We've had fun with pet-sits, haven't we? We've met amazing people and lovely animals. Do you remember the crazy cat lady in Montreal who said she had three cats but had five?" He shakes his head. "All those litter trays ..."

Marilyn chuckles. "You were so kind to insist on cleaning the litter trays. I did appreciate it. And there was that dog, Charlie, that wouldn't stop whining."

"The canine aromatherapy shut him though." Doug grins. "Yup. We've seen a lot ... It's a shame Charles Dickens' birthplace isn't open right now. We'll come back here one summer. There's so much to see along the coast. There's a famous crumbling cliff, Beachy Head. A popular spot for suicides."

"You want to go to a suicide spot, Doug?" Marilyn often went to Beachy Head with her family. The drama of the cliffs and the expansive views usually quieted her parents and quelled their rowing. She hadn't known it was a suicide spot.

"It's not *primarily* a suicide spot," Doug says. "It's a beauty spot."

"You're so good with animals." Marilyn doesn't want to think about suicide. She sees their two hands resting together on the table. His hand feels strong, like it could hold a drowning woman up. "You're so kind."

"You're good with animals too, Marilyn." His eyes are bright with love. *It's Doug's eyes that hold me.* "You're a good woman, Marilyn. You're the bravest woman I've ever met. And you're fun—my fellow adventurer."

Marilyn's eyes mist. *Dear Doug.* She glances around the dark pub beginning to fill with regulars. Fairy lights shine above the bar and in the windows. Pretty lights usually cheer her, but she feels weighted by the near tragedy with Finn. She longs to tell Doug about it. What would have happened if she'd killed

Finn? Would his owners have sued her? Do vets do autopsies on dead dogs? For about an hour, she'd felt so low she'd considered baking a whole new batch of poison muffins and eating them. She would leave a note for Doug, explaining everything, telling him she loved him but couldn't live with her pain, her past. Doug would forgive her. He'd go to the police. Her death might harm Sean and his political career, assist his victims. And she would escape. But protest had risen in her, a yearning.

Why should I lose Doug and the rest of my life? I've had so little life.

"I'm just tired," she says. "The drunks kept me awake again."

"You need your sleep." Doug's fingers massage hers. "I was selfish to go to London."

"No." Marilyn shakes her head. "You weren't."

They return to Warhol Way and make love. And Marilyn is so distressed, so in need of comfort, she forgets to be tense and inhibited. She nearly comes, might even have, if she hadn't realised what was happening and frozen in surprise.

"That was beautiful, Marilyn." Doug sinks onto the pillow, holds her tight against his chest. "We're getting better at this."

And Marilyn smiles. It is sweet, just like Doug, to say "we" and not "you".

She burrows in close to him, fits her cheek between the mounds of his chest, hears his heart pump, deep and low. He is real, a warm man.

He is my man.

He is life against her skin.

Chapter 12

Marilyn stares at the photos laid out on the bed. In one, she's a child, standing with her family on Southsea waterfront. In another, she's smiling beside Doug. It's their wedding day and she's wearing a lacey cream suit. Her eyes pass between the two pictures. Would someone looking at these shots recognise the young girl in the first as the bride in the second? What is the characteristic that could give her away, the essence that would reveal her to Sean? She imagines standing before the mayor with her baking, pretending to be an admirer. The detail that betrays a person can be anything—a wide smile, the tilt of a head, unusually large ears.

What will give me away?

She looks at the photo of her brother and sees the distinctive flatness in his eyes. Her mother's pretty mouth is smiling, but her face is already marked by the disappointment that sharpened her features and weaponised her spirit. Marilyn's eyes linger on her father's cherished image. Kindness shaped his face although he died young.

She studies herself as a child. In the shot, her face and body are solemn, closed up, her shoulders hunched. Her parents had one of their arguments that day, she recalls. There'd been tension before they left the house, she'd feared her mother continuing to lash out, verbally or physically, at herself and her father.

"You cretin! You, silly little bitch!" She recalls her mother's face—beautiful, even when distorted by temper. Her furies gave her skin a kind of glow, an intense spark, that lit her eyes, like joy.

Why was she like that? She must have been unhappy. Was she raised by violent parents?

I should know, Marilyn thinks. I should know her history. She must have been bored, lonely, being just a naval wife. She was smart and witty. She was jealous of Dad, maybe. She used to call him, "Your father, your bloody hero," long before his accident.

"You can't hurt me now, Mum," Marilyn tells her mother's frozen features. "You're dead, at last." Her words are vengeful, but grief rises, and a whimper escapes, then tears, sobs. She tries to stop this sadness, this buried, erupting hurt, but sorrow overflows in a howl that lifts her face, roughens her throat.

"Oh Mum, why didn't you love me?"

A warm nose prods her hand; a dense body pushes itself into hers. She opens her eyes as Finn licks her face. She shrieks, shocked and delighted, as his hot breath fills her nose and mouth.

"Oh Finn! I'm okay, I'm okay, hon." She clasps him, buries her face in his warm, soft neck. "So much better now you're here." She calms and wipes her face with her fingers. Finn lies tight beside her, and she rests her hand on his belly. "Thank you, Finn. You're a friend."

Her gaze returns to the photos, and she frowns as she recognises her mother's face in her own. They share a high forehead and delicate, blue-veined skin about the eyes. Those qualities won't give her away though, not under Laura's wig, and her own reading glasses will alter her eyes.

She returns to the picture of her wedding and is soothed by how different she appears in the two shots. Then she spots how, in the second photo, her shoulders rise toward her ears just as they do in the first. Her shoulders are defensive, like the battlements on a castle. They're still trying to protect the head her mother swiped, the ears she pulled and twisted. Marilyn's eyes mist. There's something so futile about those tense shoulders. She lifts her head and hears her neck bones click.

I must get back to yoga.

She puts her fingers to the back of her neck and flinches as they touch a tight, knotted area. She massages tense skin, rigid muscle.

Fear is my essence. My constant anticipation of harm. That's what will give me away.

She picks up the photos and carries them to the suitcase that sits in the corner of the room then puts the pictures back in their envelope and tucks them under the warm-weather clothes that remain in the case. Why did she bring the photos with her? She should have left them hidden at the bottom of her underwear drawer at home.

She walks to the mirror and pulls down her shoulders, straightens her neck, and lifts her head, then stands erect and breathes deep, from her belly.

"It's not surprising, Finn," she says to his watching image in the glass. "There was always Mum, her temper. And David—those eyes. Perhaps I always sensed something big, something worse, was coming."

She turns, walks again to the suitcase, lifts the lid and withdraws Laura's auburn wig then reaches into the slim flap tucked into the lid and draws out a small container.

Returning to the mirror, she places Laura's wig on her head, removes the brown contact lenses from their case, slips them into her eyes. She smiles at her new reflection, flips the glowing bangs. Now she is transformed, especially if she wears glasses too.

"Well hello, sexy lady." The door swings wide. "Did you colour your hair?"

Marilyn's temperature rises. She tries to meet Doug's eyes. "No, it's just a wig." For a moment she contemplates acting sexy, but panic is pacing her belly like a prisoner denied the exercise yard. "I'm...experimenting."

"Well, you look great." Doug moves past Finn who is wagging and circling, trying to say hello. Her husband grasps her waist, pulls her in. He stares into her face. “Your eyes are different too, brown. Wow. Were you planning to surprise me?”

Marilyn manages a smile. “Yes. And you’ve ruined it. I thought you were running further today, going for the 15k?”

“My calf hurt. I’m back, and not too sweaty.” Doug kisses her mouth. His lips are outdoor-cold. He moves her to the bed.

Marilyn returns his kiss, but her mind and pulse race on. Doug has seen her disguise. He’s closer to being involved, implicated.

They reach the bed, and he pushes her, lets her fall onto the smooth, white sheets. He begins to lower himself but stops, frowning. “Is that Laura’s wig?”

Marilyn nods. Shame fills her. “She said I could have it. She let me try it on, when I had that cancer scare. We joked about wearing the same colour wig if we had to undergo chemo together.”

Doug pulls away, rubs his hand around his chin. “You brought it with you?”

“Yes, a foreign trip seemed like a good opportunity for ... experimentation.” She tries to say the last word seductively, to thicken and deepen her voice. She reaches for his hand, draws him to her, but Doug keeps frowning.

“I feel a bit funny about the wig, to be honest.” He shifts back, away. “I need a shower.”

Marilyn watches him walk to the bathroom. Uncharacteristically, he shuts the door.

Her shoulders slump. Tears come. “Oh no,” she whispers, “Oh no.”

Chapter 13

Despite curtailing her visit to the Golden Gate Bridge and Golden Gate Park, despite almost wearing grooves in the sidewalk opposite Marion and Doug's block, Paula doesn't see Marion or Doug that evening. She doesn't see them the next day.

She's spotted an Amazon depot in Dogpatch, and considers delivering a fake package addressed to Marion but she doubts she could do a convincing impression of an American Amazon employee. She decides to speak to the building attendant. She'll lay on the English accent as she did in Maine. She approaches Marion's building, glances into the glassy cubicle, sees the young man she saw before, and presses the intercom.

"Yes."

"Hello, I wonder if you could help me. I'm looking for a resident, Marilyn Brooks. I believe she lives here with her husband Doug?"

"Can't you call her, email, text?"

Paula's pulse quickens. The kid's tone is patronizing. She's only forty-two, but he's acting as if she's senile. She wonders if she looks older. It's a troubling thought. She keeps smiling, maintains her polite demeanour. It's this lad's job to look after security, and in a city full of homeless people, addicts and guns.

She tells him about being sent by Marilyn's family to find her, implies that Marilyn is needed at a deathbed.

The young man's face relaxes, he shakes his head. "Can't help you, lady. She isn't here. In fact, weird thing, she's in England. She and Doug have gone to look after two dogs they found on a pet-sitting site. Doug was real excited, said he'd never been to England."

"Did Doug say where they were going?"

"Somewhere on the south coast."

Paula's heart beats fast. "Could it be Portsmouth?"

"Could be."

"When will they be back?"

"Not for a while. Doug said it was going to be a month, and they haven't been gone long."

"I see, thank you." Paula smiles at the intercom. Marion has been in Portsmouth all along? For a moment, she wonders if it's a trick, if Hugh and David have been testing her, seeing how fast she could track down Marion after they set her on the wrong trail. But why would they do that? This has cost money. There have been flights, meals, rooms.

"Thank you so much, do you know which pet-sitting site they use?" She smiles. "It might help me find the address."

He shrugs. "Sorry lady."

"Thank you." She walks away, heart thumping. Why is she excited? Marion has gone home, that's all. She didn't tell her brother, but why would she? The attendant said Doug told him about the trip, not Marion. Marion was probably too busy to chat. People, women especially, are always busy before a trip.

Paula returns to the intercom, presses it. "Sorry, one more thing. Was Marilyn with Doug when he told you about their trip?"

The attendant frowns; he thought he'd seen the back of her. "No, Marilyn's a quiet lady, doesn't talk much."

Paula mouths more thanks and scurries back to the Airbnb where she searches pet-sitting sites. There are quite a few, local and international. She focuses on the international, searching pet-sits in Portsmouth, UK.

Only one pops up, on a site called loyalpetsitters.com. A smiling young couple seek carers for two dogs so they can spend a month travelling with friends who've emigrated to Australia. The pets are a border collie and an English bulldog. Paula grins as she sees the dogs. What an odd pair they are. They can't be easy to manage together. She sees the photos of the couple's home and recognises the big windows and garish colours at the front of a modern townhouse.

Warhol Way. Marion is staying in Warhol Way.

Excited, she clicks to her own emails, pulls up Hugh's address. But her hands pause over the keys. She returns to Google, types in Hugh's name, his position and city, and finds him smiling above his bio. The deputy mayor grew up in Southsea, went to Cambridge to study economics. He worked in the City of London before returning to his home town to pursue public service.

It's the same information she read in Maine and she can find little beyond blurb about his family and charity work. David's information says he was a sportsman in his youth, playing on the county rugby team. He has his own communications company, works with Conservative interests in the city. He doesn't appear to have married or had children. Perhaps he's gay. Paula can't blame him for hiding the fact. There's no scandal attached to David either, no blaring headlines.

She returns to Hugh's email and hits reply.

> *Marion, now Marilyn Brooks, and her husband Doug Brooks are doing a pet-sit in Portsmouth. They're staying in Warhol Way with a bulldog and a collie. I don't know which house number—address not listed on the site. They'll be there for a few more weeks.*
>
> *Regards,*
>
> *Paula*

She goes to send the message but her hand hesitates. She should feel pleased. Her job is done, and so interestingly. But she gets up, paces the room, stares at the tumbling water in the fountain below. She's done what she was asked to but...

Why are Hugh and David lying?

She shivers, wraps her arms about her body. The air cools rapidly in San Francisco. Despite the cold, she walks to the balcony, looks down on the water feature, watches as the lights flick on to illuminate the water through the evening. If only she had someone with whom to discuss this: colleagues who respect the gut but know when to override it; Jane, calm, rational Jane—previously, calm, rational Jane...

She moves back into the room, strides to the kitchen and grabs a beer. She pulls the tab on the Miller Light, sips and paces the room. Hugh and David hired her to find Marion, although neither seem to want her found. They work for the mayor. The mayor is trying to move into national politics, and he's facing accusations of sexual assault.

Paula gulps the beer, frowns at the fountain. The mayor is turning out to be a scumbag. Her mouth twists as a distant memory of her father smeared in lipstick from an encounter with a girlfriend taps like a footfall at her mind.

Something is going on in Portsmouth. It wouldn't hurt to wait a day or two before letting Hugh and David know where Marion is staying. She strides to her laptop and deletes the message.

Chapter 14

"Shut up! I can't sleep!" Marilyn feels the cold night air on her bare arms, but she's not fully aware that she's standing on the balcony yelling at the drunks in the street until Doug pulls her back into the room.

"Marilyn, calm down. That's not the way to handle it." He rubs her arm, gazes into her eyes. She sees concern, love. Dear Doug. But her chest is tight, so tight.

"Go back to bed, you crazy bitch!" The drinker's tone is ugly, belligerent. Marilyn spins back to the balcony and the street. She is hot with fury. This kind of misogynistic English behaviour has always filled her with fear, just like the sharp, judgemental tones of many more refined English voices. Voices like her mother's. English voices, so many different ones, all redolent with threat.

Doug catches her arm and she almost falls. "Marilyn, no. It's noisy, love, but it's mostly just the weekends. We'll get you some sleeping pills for Fridays and Saturdays."

She nods, lets him shut and lock the door, take her to bed. "I'm tired," she says, "so tired." Tears come. She feels them wet her pillow. Doug strokes her hair. "Shh shh." And her breath comes easier.

The next morning, she's still groggy and confused. She must stop drinking. When Doug's out running, she goes to the fridge. She must be careful. She could open her mouth and tell Doug everything. She almost told him how the noise of drunks in the street has always upset her, how their noisy good cheer, their friendship that shifts to violence—there was a knifing in the news, a young man was stabbed outside a pub—reminds her of her mother. Mum's mood switched so fast, Marilyn longs to tell her husband. Mum would get incensed by a word, a facial expression. I never knew what would set her off. *I couldn't prepare, avoid.* But she zips her mouth tight, so tight her jaw aches.

Now, she sips a reassuring beer and sits at the table, Finn resting at her feet. Winston sleeps by the sofa. Marilyn breathes deep and begins to relax in the alcohol's warming numbness. "It's all right, Marilyn," she tells herself. "It'll be all right. Won't it, Finn?"

She glances down into his deep, reassuring eyes as he softly taps his tail on the floor. "Oh Finn, I do love you." She smiles. "And you love me."

She is starting to relax. The alcohol is so warm, the way it hugs and soothes. Her legs are heavy and still, her shoulders have dropped, her breathing slowed.

But Finn whines, and his gaze shifts to Marilyn's shoulder. A growl rustles through his throat.

"Finn, it's okay. It's only me here. Relax."

But Finn doesn't respond. He growls deeper, lower, his eyes wide as they stare into the space behind her left shoulder.

Marilyn spins, sees only the white wall, the wide window. She scans the kitchen, turns to Finn.

"Finn, chill. The people in the bus line can't see us here."

But Finn gets up, slinks away toward the patio window where he stands by the glass, his fur raised. He is staring at the space behind Marilyn's shoulder, still growling soft and deep.

"Is the ghost here?" Marilyn turns again and surveys the space. She lifts the nearly empty beer can and waves it at him. "Am I upsetting you, Finn? Am I projecting my distress into this house?"

She sighs, and gets up, unrolls her yoga mat and suspends herself in downward dog then she meditates on the orchids and the darting koi fish in the garden. Only then, when she has been meditating for at least five minutes, does Finn relax and return to her side. She smiles as she strokes him, feeling strangely, deeply happy. Life—Doug and Finn—are so sweet. Even these pet-sits have become precious. They've given her glimpses into what it means to have a full life—one with other hearths and tables to cluster around. It's a risk, every time she and Doug turn up on an unknown doorstep, yet they've never found a home filthy or an animal crazed. Simple warmth flows from the homeowners and their pets, although they meet so fleetingly. Perhaps it's *because* we meet fleetingly, she thinks. After all, I'm not good at any kind of intimacy. Whatever the reason, these connections feel real, and the pets are dear. They're dear little souls. She smiles—'dear little soul' is what her father called her.

Later, she and Doug take a water tour of the *HMS Queen Elizabeth* and Marilyn wishes she could tell her husband that her father died because he failed to land safely on a warship like this. She should have told him the truth at the beginning but with her history of self-harm and addiction, Doug already saw her as vulnerable. She smiles as she recalls the first time she glimpsed her husband. He'd walked onto the ward where she was being treated for bulimia, smiled at her, checked her chart. Did she begin to recover the moment she saw his bright, caring nurse's smile?

Perhaps, but the day of the church event is fast approaching, and she cannot be selfish and forget Sean's present and future victims. She owes it to them to annihilate Sean with poisoned food.

But I'm not ready, not ready at all.

"Okay Doug, I'm taking Finn out," she says later when they are home and the afternoon is waning. "Come on, Finn. Let's walk." She glances at Winston, and is pleased to see him snoring and twitching by the patio door. "Let's go, Finn."

Finn jumps up, follows her to the top of the stairs. "See you later, hon," she tells Doug, who's online, researching more fun things to do in Portsmouth. "Take care," he calls. "No wonder you don't want to run with me. You never stop walking."

Marilyn avoids the busy streets. She turns right and heads toward the Common and the Channel. The wind is sharp. Hopefully, it will discourage casual walkers and idlers. She wants to stride and think.

I don't want anyone in my way.

She and Finn pass the white-washed hotel at the end of the street: *The Victoria* it says in bright red letters across the facade. Doug wants to visit and try their cream tea. Marilyn crosses the street and thinks how the hotel looks like some kind of fancy confection itself, a meringue maybe.

They arrive at the green expanse of the Common and Marilyn avoids looking at the photo of Sean taped to a tree. Anxiety pulses in her neck, her belly. She glances at Finn. "What am I going to do, Finn? He can't get away with it. Men like him always do."

She strides across the path, toward the water, and sees an attractive blonde woman walking a big black and tan German shepherd. The woman and dog are approaching from the opposite direction. The path is narrow and Marilyn wonders if she should be walking on the left or the right side in England. She thinks it's the right, is walking on the right. But the woman keeps coming. She is tall. The dog has a slight limp. Marilyn moves to the extreme right to allow the woman and her dog to pass.

"Excuse me, don't I know you?"

The woman stops in front of Marilyn. She is curvy, sexy. *She must get a lot of hassle from men.*

"You seem vaguely familiar," the woman says. "Do I know you from school or somewhere?"

Marilyn's heart rate and temperature soar. She fears a panic attack. She hasn't had a full-blown attack in a while and the shock, the shame of it will make the symptoms worse. She won't be able to talk. She will sweat and gasp as the panic rushes up from her belly, as it spreads like fire, like disease, through her nerves and cells. Her face will turn red, her eyes blur and swell. This woman will think her crazy. I should have brought a Xanax, she thinks.

I should always have one in my pocket.

"No, I don't know you," she says in her best Californian drawl and tries to move on. The panic is growing in her belly. She breathes deep, distracts herself by shifting her attention to Finn, to the lead in her hand. If she can stop the fear before it reaches her chest, she'll be okay. But if the panic squeezes her lungs, her throat, she'll be lost.

The woman doesn't move. Marilyn nudges Finn onto the grass.

Okay, we'll walk around you.

"I'm sure I recognise you." The woman takes off her sunglasses and fixes Marilyn with bright brown eyes. Marilyn feels she should remove her own glasses. That would be polite, and she doesn't wish to be rude, but she needs their shield.

"What school did you go to?" The woman persists.

"Oakdean." Marilyn is surprised by her own truthful response but something about this woman's bright gaze elicits honesty. She has such an appealing face—lovely tidy features, a mouth so perfectly bow-shaped it looks like the work of a cartoonist. "But I left when I was 13," she says and she takes two steps forward. "I'm sorry, but I don't know you."

"Are you Marion Taylor?" The woman smiles wider. Her eyes really are very bright. There's something reassuring about her, something that reminds Marilyn of Doug. Marilyn feels she has, indeed, seen the woman before.

"You are Marion, aren't you? I was in the year below you." The woman's features soften into sympathy. "I am sorry about your father. I never got the chance to tell you."

Marilyn feels her fright ebb; her body begin to loosen. This woman does know her. This is terrifying, yet wonderful.

She knows about Daddy.

Marilyn removes her sunglasses. "I'm sorry but I don't remember you. What is your name?" she asks.

Chapter 15

It takes Paula a moment to respond. Marion's voice is startlingly high-pitched. Her tone is more typical of a girl of 11 or 12 than a middle-aged woman. But Marion's accent is impressive. Marion held her disguise, her aloofness, until Paula mentioned her father and then she trembled and removed her glasses. Paula almost feels guilty for misleading a woman who is clearly so vulnerable.

"I'm Karen." She sticks out her hand and smiles. She has no choice about the fake name. It is unethical to be talking to the woman she was hired to find. It's interesting to be face to face with Marion. Paula almost forgets the cold that has seeped into her body during the two hours she and Husky have been circling the Common. Paula has been hoping that Marion and one or both the dogs would appear on the route that leads from Warhol Way to the water. She's also been trying to ignore the abusive messages that rolled across her screen like a welcome banner the moment she took her phone off airplane mode.

Next time it'll be you, not your house, Lesbo Bitch.

Marion's blue eyes meet Paula's own. Marion looks tired. Her eyes are glassy, red-veined, the skin beneath them dark and puffy. Paula has seen that look in the mirror many times since all the crap with Husky and Jane erupted. Marion is pale, which is surprising as she lives in California. Paula herself caught the sun during her visit. Her face is lightly tanned, she likes it.

She glances at Husky who is sniffing around the dog Marion is walking. The dog is a handsome border collie, the same animal she saw on the website.

"Our dogs seem to have become friends," she says. "This is Husky."

"Finn," Marion says after a pause.

"Shall we walk and chat so the dogs don't get restless?" Paula turns her head to the inviting breadth of the Common and the distant shimmer of the Channel.

There's a lengthier pause. "Okay." Marion puts her sunglasses back on. "Come on, Finn love."

"Finn is a beautiful animal," Paula says as they begin to move along the path that leads to the water.

"Thank you." Marion doesn't divulge that he's not hers.

"It's funny," Paula says with a friendly sideways glance at the other woman. "You don't actually sound like you're from round here. You sound American."

"Really?" Marion doesn't miss a beat. "Well, I have spent a lot of time in America. But it's lovely to be home," she adds.

"It must be exciting to live in America. Are you back for good?"

Marion's mouth tightens. "No. What about you? Have you lived in Portsmouth all your life?"

Paula smiles. "Yup. I'm no adventurer. I doubt I'd have the guts to go far although I have thought of moving to London."

"It isn't always about guts," Marion says. "Sometimes change is...unavoidable."

Paula nods. "It must have been awful to lose your father so young."

Marion's lean jaw tightens. "Yes."

They reach the end of the Common and wait for the green light to allow them to cross. Then they turn left by Southsea Hoverport, skirting the yellow cranes and sea defence construction, and begin the walk along the waterfront.

"When did you get back?" Paula asks.

"About a week ago."

"Oh, not long. Tell me, what are your impressions of Portsmouth after so long away? It must be like seeing it for the first time." Paula waves her hand about to indicate the waterfront with its scattered cafes selling fish and chips, the deckchairs remaining despite the season, the monument to the dead of some war—the Crimean?

"At first, it did feel strange." Marion slows, gazes at Paula from behind her glasses. "I felt I was seeing it with fresh eyes, like an American." She smiles, taking the question seriously. "It all seemed so old, quirky. But then, after just a few days, that began to change." She surprises Paula by pausing, leaning back against the railing. She turns and glances at the sombre, lifting waves on the Channel. Paula moves closer, rests her hand on the smooth cold railing. She feels a pulse of excitement: Marion is opening up.

"I began to feel English again," Marion says. "My own early experiences came back—so strong." She smiles and her thin, drooping chin lifts. "Now I feel almost English again."

Paula nods, strangely touched that this stranger has confided in her. Is Marion lonely? Does she lack people to talk to?

"That's interesting," Paula says. "But not surprising. It's got to be the places we know first that mean home, that shape us."

Marion nods. She turns and takes a long look at the water then begins to walk again, briskly, her head down, as if she's walking alone.

"I can't imagine being able to see Portsmouth with fresh eyes," Paula says, as she catches up with Marion and Finn. She glances ahead, along the waterfront path, sees the crisp packets and sweet wrappers blowing in the gusty breeze. She breathes, fills her lungs; it's a struggle to keep pace with Marion. "I can't imagine seeing the old buildings, the litter, the Coke and beer cans, afresh." She feels as if she's scattering her breathless words into the wind.

Marion pauses to shoot a rueful smile. "It's true, the English do chuck stuff about." Above the sunglasses, she frowns. "It annoys me. It's...disrespectful."

Paula nods and takes another long breath, makes her legs move faster. It's amazing that Marion can maintain this pace, but she is as svelte as the border collie. Husky is loving it.

Despite the limp that scrote inflicted, Husky is keeping up with Finn. They are trotting along together, out front like two handsome horses in harness. The sight delights Paula although she's had to move Husky's lead into her right hand. His pulling has made the left hand, the one she hurt in Maine, throb.

Perhaps I should have seen a doctor.

"I was in America last week," she says. "San Francisco—awesome city."

"What were you doing there?" Marion doesn't slow.

"Just taking a break, a solitary break, actually. I'm getting a divorce."

"Oh, I'm sorry." Marion stops so abruptly Finn's neck jerks on his lead.

"Thank you." Paula is touched by Marion's concern. She sighs, with fatigue and residual jetlag, with the sadness that talking about Jane still evokes. "It's been rough but I'll be okay."

"Do you have children?" Marion asks, and Paula notes that her accent is now almost English in its precision.

"One son, 15."

"He must be a comfort."

"Yes. He's proof the relationship wasn't for nothing. Do you have children?" Paula asks. She senses Marion does not.

Marion shakes her head. "No."

Paula starts walking again at a slower pace, and Marion follows, slower too. Maybe she's realised she's moving so fast as to be rude.

"Do you know San Francisco?" Paula risks the question.

Marion shakes her head. "Not really." She stops again, very abruptly, makes a show of pulling out her phone.

"Wow, is that the time?" she says, and the California smoothness returns. "I gotta go. It's been nice meeting you, Karen, or meeting you again, I should say." She extends her hand and gives Paula's fingers a brief, limp shake.

"You too. Maybe we can walk again sometime?" Paula says as Marion turns back toward the Common. "It can be lonely walking with no one to chat to, and our dogs like each other."

"Yes, maybe see you around." Marion says, with a smile and a careless, casual wave, and she turns, hurries back the way they came.

I won't see her if she sees me first, Paula thinks as she watches Marion and Finn speed away. Marion is hiding things. Why not just be up front about the pet-sit? Why not admit she lives in San Francisco?

Because she doesn't want anyone to know who she is and that she's here. Why not?

Paula frowns. Marion is a nervy oddball, prickly. There's something strange—stilted and artificial—about her. Paula thinks of the old china doll her mother owned as a girl. The doll is now packed away in a cupboard at her mother's house. Its eyes are glassy, its hard features smudged and discoloured by the years. It's a disquieting face, the kind seen in horror movies. But the doll was part of her mum's childhood. She'd loved it, called it Eebord because she couldn't say Edith as a kid. Paula has considered getting Eebord done up, returned to her original condition, as a gift for her mum. But the doll creeps Paula out and she leaves it in the cupboard. There is something similarly malformed about Marion. She is not hideous but there is something ... missing, twisted maybe. But she'd been kind about the divorce.

Paula sighs. Her curiosity has not been satiated. Marion had been evasive, and there'd been no mention of the brother who's claiming to be looking for her. Still, Paula will have to let Hugh and David know where Marion is. She can't prevaricate any longer. She needs to get paid. She'll tell Hugh that a contact she made in America has given her new information about Marion's whereabouts. She pulls out her phone and texts Hugh: *Marion Taylor is in Portsmouth, she's pet-sitting two dogs in Warhol Way, don't know which number.* She presses send then reaches down and pats Husky's broad back. "You enjoyed that run with Finn, didn't you, boy?"

He lifts warm eyes to her, and she smiles. "Well, I'm sorry but we'll be going home at my pace."

Chapter 16

Marilyn's pulse pounds in her throat. It pushes the skin, fills her ears. She spins, studies the path. Someone is watching her.

Can Sean know I'm back?

The path looks empty. No one is spying on her from among the high-end yachts in the harbour.

"You're alone, Marilyn. You're just stressed." Still, she scans the elegant townhouses. It's a beautiful spot—such lovely modern homes, and the householders' yachts sit on the water like cars rest on driveways. Still, she studies every shadow, every corner. Nothing. Her heart takes note, begins to slow.

It was probably a bird or a cat.

But she can't lose the sense of being observed. The feeling is strong. A human stare feels different to that of an animal, an intent gaze is unlike one of passing interest. She'd felt that intensity, she had, on the back of her neck.

Is someone watching from behind net curtains?

She studies windows but sees nothing, just a few seagulls drifting among the masts and the sails that are wrapped tall and tight, still curled against winter. Gulls peck at the dockside. The Seasick Sailor is not far away and the gulls have carried trash from the pub's bins, dropped bread and chicken scraps beside the yachts.

"You shouldn't get so frantic, Marilyn." She lowers her shoulders, hears her jaw click. God, how she hates these feelings, hates, fears them, although she should be used to them by now, should have learned to see them as the drama queens, the empty tyrants, they are.

She sighs—she has soothed herself but her walk is ruined. She turns for home and regrets not bringing Finn with her. She'd intended to check out the charity stores, look for some bargains, but she can't do that now.

Back in the kitchen, she's thinking about supper when she glances into the street and sees her brother standing, gazing up into the window. Marilyn steps back, her pulse scratching her skin. She's thought about finding her brother. She has even imagined setting him up as Sean's murderer. Now, she puts out her shocked and trembling hand and rests it against the fridge. The coldness of the door anchors her and yet, when she looks again, David is still below, staring up. He waves, points to the front door.

She startles, reverses into the room, and stands by the stove, heart pumping. She edges forward, peeks. He waves again, again points to the door. She glances over her shoulder. Doug is sitting at the dining room table, his back to her, reading about bulldogs on his iPad. He's worried about Winston's wheezing. He's discovered that inbreeding has left bulldogs prey to an array of health problems.

"Poor guy, this really sucks, doesn't it?" Doug had got down on the floor beside Winston, stroked him with his nurse's kindness. Marilyn had pursed her lips and hoped Winston wouldn't die on their watch. She'd felt guilty that the prospect didn't distress her like nearly poisoning Finn had.

Doug looks absorbed in whatever he's reading, but she can't risk David ringing the doorbell. Doug might hear, jump up, run down the stairs, invite her brother in. Her husband would be polite, friendly, but later he would ask her why, oh why, she'd never told him she had a brother and an English home town, and...

"Doug, I'm going to Waitrose for yogurt. I'll get those pork pies you like."

"Okay, honey. Get the small ones." Doug pats his lean tummy, "Those pork pies are so fatty."

Marilyn walks over, kisses his forehead. "You're fine, you're perfect, Mr Slim." She snatches her bag from the door handle. "Won't be long."

She runs down the stairs, fearful that David may have tired of waiting, might now be standing outside, about to ring the bell. But when she opens the door, she sees him, on the other side of the street. He shoots her a cautious smile, and she snaps her fingers at him. *Come here.* She stands in the shadow of the house. If Doug crosses to the window, he will not see her.

David walks over. He's smiling, half smiling. He doesn't know how to greet her.

"Hello David." She looks up at him. It's hard to believe she's standing beside her older brother. His eyes are not as flat as she remembers. They hold a tentative light of friendliness and something darker—fear?

"Marion." He's almost as tall as their father. His smile widens. "I can't believe it's you. You look so... different."

"What do you want?" Her question is a snarl, harsher than she intended. He flinches.

He can't expect me to be glad to see him.

"I want to talk to you."

"What about?"

He frowns, colours slightly. "I want to discuss the past, Marion."

A pulse of rage heats her belly. She breathes, tells herself this might be her chance to disarm David, to begin the process of setting him up as Sean's murderer. That would be a beautiful symmetry. How satisfying to obtain justice against them both. But she can't keep her anger in. "As I said—what is there to talk about?"

"I want to explain myself."

"How did you know I was here?"

He sighs, glances at his feet. "Look Marion, can we go to a café? A pub? It would help to have a drink."

"I don't drink."

"...You could have a juice."

Marilyn hesitates. She needs to know how David found her. "All right, but I can't be long." She glances up at the building. "I'm married. He doesn't know ... anything."

David nods. "Good. I'm pleased for you."

"Come on." She turns and walks toward the Irish pub Doug likes. She averts her eyes from a picture of Sean plastered across the front page of the daily newspaper. *Mayor Leads in Polls.* When will these people reject this man? Haven't they heard the accusations? Do they think the victims are liars?

They reach the pub. David follows Marilyn inside and they find a table at the back in the shadows. The bar keeper waves to her. "Hello, Marilyn."

Damn. She should have chosen somewhere else. But David hasn't noticed the bar keeper call her the wrong name. Marilyn and Marion sound similar and David is keen to get a drink in his hands.

"What would you like?" He hovers as she sits.

"A soda water with a slice of lemon."

She watches him walk to the bar. He's still the same old David and yet, not. How does she look to him? Thin and tired, no doubt.

He returns and sits opposite then takes a long, slow slug of his pint—some dark beer. He liked the heavy stuff even as a teen. He puts it down.

"It's good to see you, Marion." His eyes rise to hers. "How have you been? Do you have kids?"

She shakes her head. "No, I'm recently married. ... My health ..."

I could never have had kids. What if I became a mother like our mother?

"David, how did you know I was here?"

His gaze falls to the smooth wooden tabletop. She notices, as she has before, that its surface is unmarked by years and spills. Doug likes this place; he can't be expected to know it's not a real old pub.

"Someone told me."

"Who?"

He shrugs. "Someone in the street said they'd seen you."

"Tell the truth, David."

"Seriously, I can't recall who it was."

"Was it Karen?"

He pauses, nods. "Yes, could have been." But Marilyn sees a moment's confusion or surprise in his eyes. What is Karen to David?

"Are you married?" she asks.

He shakes his head. "No. Actually Marion, that kind of leads into what I want to talk about. ..." His voice trails away, he flushes, takes another gulp of beer. Marilyn waits.

He clears his throat. "About what happened with Sean... I am...so...terribly sorry..." He looks up, and pain brightens his eyes. She is shocked to see such emotion.

"I shouldn't have done it." He shakes his head. "All these years, I've never reached out to you. I pretended it never happened. I was cold, like it was your fault, when I should have faced it, tried to make amends. ... Not that that would ever be possible."

She feels her eyes fog, her throat close with blended sadness and panic. She subdues the impulse to flee and takes a long, slow sip of her drink. "Why did you do it? Were you jealous that Dad paid me more attention? Or maybe Mum made you hate me, made you think hating me was okay?"

David's eyes cloud. The hand that holds the beer trembles. He puts the glass down, buries his hand beneath the table.

"No ..." He clears his throat, half-glances over his shoulder. "You see, Marion, I'm gay, and Sean found out. He caught me kissing another boy in the changing room—Toby Holmes, we always liked each other. Toby was a year younger, and Sean said that looked bad for me."

David shakes his head, gives a harsh laugh. "Sean threatened to expose me, said people would never allow a queer on the rugby team, said I was a pervert molesting younger players, said he would only keep quiet if ..."

"If you let him rape me?" Marilyn is surprised to hear her voice sounding calm.

He flinches, nods. "He didn't put it like that, obviously. I didn't realise what would happen. He said, 'I just want to get to know your sister.' Those were his words. I had no idea, I promise." He lifts his hands, lets them drop.

Marilyn's pulse patters. She feels her body falling, the smell of damp mud and grass, hard earth, Sean's hot breath, his hand across her face. *Relax Marion.* .... She gasps, breathes.

"Marion, are you okay? I'm sorry, I know how upsetting this must be."

"No, you don't know." She picks up her drink, distracts herself by focusing on the coolness of the glass, the condensation moistening her hand. She gazes at David's plump middle-aged face but in her mind, she watches her young athletic brother stand impassively behind her attacker, off to the side, like a servant, an equerry.

"It was like you were a statue, David, stone. The way you stood there, like you weren't real, weren't alive. And that's how I've felt about you all these years. I've wondered why you did what you did, but ... you've been dead to me." She's surprised she is composed. Perhaps she somehow knew this conversation would one day occur and she is prepared for it.

He flinches—even in the gloom she sees his face pale. He takes another gulp of beer then his glass hits the table.

"I have no excuse. ... But I was young, scared—remember how unacceptable it was to be gay back then? There were...violent incidents." He grimaces, sighs long and deep. Marilyn almost expects him to start stuttering as he had as a child. His voice always faltered. He was likely scared too, she thinks—of Mum, of the tension and violence in our house.

"And I was also raised by Mum..." he says, echoing her thoughts.

"You were her favourite. She rarely lost her temper with you." Marilyn blinks hard and fast as she tries to expel images of her mother's jeering face, her cruel hands and words. "I heard someone on the radio, talking about social media. 'We are all too contemptuous now,' the woman said. And I thought, contempt, that's the word. Mum was contemptuous of me."

David nods. "You used to fight her—goad her even. Then later, you grew quiet, nervous, and let her walk all over you."

Marilyn frowns. "Fighting back was futile. She always ... won."

David reaches out, tries to take her hands, but she darts them back.

He flinches again. "I was jealous, Marion, because Dad loved you so much."

"He did love me. Maybe he had to, because Mum hated me."

"No, he really loved you, Marion. He loved me too, although I wasn't the son he wanted. I felt his disappointment. He kept his distance with me."

Marilyn studies her brother's face. Was David really not the son their father wanted? She tries to remember, to see their relationship in retrospect. But she can barely recall her father and brother together.

"Dad knew you were gay?"

"I think he sensed it." David picks up his beer, drinks. "He was ... uneasy around me."

Marilyn dips her head, lifts her glass. The soda bubbles jump and fizz on her tongue. She focuses on the physical sensations—wills them to lessen the darkness of childhood in her mind, to bring her back to the pub, the fake table, her apparently repentant brother. She puts the glass down. "You were older, a boy. People weren't as physical or affectionate back then. And we were military, stiff upper lip."

She stares at him.

Did I really miss so much?

"I had no idea you were gay." She shakes her head. "I feel I should have sensed it at least. I feel I should have woken one day and understood." She takes a deep breath, looks her brother in the eye. "But the fact is you betrayed me, David. You sold me to Sean—for his silence and a place on the rugby team, you say."

He sighs, long and deep. "Yes, and if it's any consolation, Marion, it lives in my memory—your screams, the darkness, Sean's ... actions ... The feeling that I hated Sean, wanted to stop him, but also feeling that if you just let him do what he wanted, everything would ... end, and we would be okay."

"And now you're working for him, helping him become even more powerful. Sean shouldn't be powerful, David."

He nods. "I don't know how it happened. He had something on me, obviously, and our lives became entwined. And I do think he's different now. I saw him change, soften, when his kids were born. And he's a good politician, has done good things for the city. He's pro-business but also supports the arts and social spending, within reason."

She finishes her drink. "You just want—need—to think he's a good guy. I must go. I'm supposed to be in Waitrose."

"Why are you here, in Portsmouth?" He smiles. "Did you finally get homesick?"

She shakes her head. "David, please don't tell anyone you saw me. No one, especially not Sean. Please, it's important, not unless you want to ruin my life again."

Once more, he flinches. "Okay."

"Promise?"

"I promise."

"Thank you."

"Can I see you again, Marion?"

"I don't think so, David. I'm here with my American husband. He doesn't know ... anything."

He nods. "Well, I'm glad I had a chance to apologise to you, Marion. I'm glad you're married and happy."

"Thanks." She stands, looks down at her brother. "Are you happy, David?"

"Me? Oh, I'm fine." He flashes a grin, drains his beer.

"Good," she says, not believing him. "Do you have a partner?"

"No. You know me, always a crotchety sod."

She nods and is filled with unexpected sadness. She feels grief for her brother and almost puts out a hand to touch him. But this conversation has not brought any comfort or resolution. It cannot. "Goodbye, David," she says.

Chapter 17

"Thank you," Paula says as she pockets Hugh's cheque.

"Thank *you,* for a job well done."

Paula grins. "It's none of my business, but has David met up with Marion?"

He shrugs. "I've no idea."

Paula manufactures a twinkle in her eye. "How will he explain to Marion that he knew she was here, back in Portsmouth?"

Hugh glances at the doorway behind her. "I think that's between brother and sister."

"Right." Paula smiles, but inwardly she sighs. She doesn't want to be right about Hugh and David. She wants to get their money into her bank account and land more work. She needs to get out of debt—turns out splitting with your spouse is expensive.

"If you know anyone who needs a private investigator, please recommend me."

Hugh nods and leads her to the door. "Of course."

As Paula walks down the corridor, she hopes she won't be here again. She emerges onto the building's wide steps and pauses to breathe in the cool air. She's glad of the cold. She needs to cleanse away the discomfort of meeting with Hugh. It's the same sense of claustrophobia and unease she'd felt the last time she'd stood in his office. Her mind returns to the woman at the heart of their 'search'. It would be easy to set up another encounter while walking Husky. But she shouldn't see Marion. It's unethical and she has enough crap of her own going on.

She starts moving and her mind turns to money. She's pared back her expenses, stopped buying meat—she'll learn to like lentils and soy—and quit purchasing the expensive organic dog food. She's always been proud of Husky's gleaming good health, but other dogs survive just fine on supermarket food.

As long as Jane doesn't bring greedy lawyers into their mess, doesn't demand money for the big house she's now supporting alone. As long as none of that happens before Paula's got going in this new career. I'm lucky Mum has cancer, not dementia, Paula thinks as she passes the bronze statues honouring the emigrants who left for America. If Mum had dementia I might have to pay for her care, sell her house. She thinks of her mum's little bungalow near the seafront and wonders what it's worth. It's a bit dated but maybe she could live in it when her mum dies, or maybe she could sell?

Bloody hell, Paula, you greedy ghoul.

It feels good—clarifying—to walk beside the water although the wind is strengthening. A man walks by, ogles her breasts, winks.

"In your dreams," Paula says and strides on. When did she give up on men? She didn't decide never to sleep with men again. Maybe she was never fully bi? She was young back then, open to possibilities. Maybe she's just come to realise what pricks men are.

She steps aside to let a middle-aged woman run past. The woman is older than Paula and determinedly lean, her mature booty proudly displayed in leggings and a tight top.

Skinny cow, she must be freezing.

Paula sighs as the woman's leanness brings Marion to mind. What is it about Marion that has her so concerned? It's not just Hugh and David's evasiveness, or even Marion's own. It's her vulnerability, her darting eyes and quavering voice with its strangely alternating accents. She's like a kicked dog, Paula thinks, a whipped pup, and Paula recalls her friend Sue, who has struggled with PTSD so long and so unsuccessfully. But at least Sue's going to the gym, staying in touch, Paula reminds herself.

Maybe I can help Marion like I help Sue. Her dad's death stunted her maybe. What harm can a bit of dog-walking do?

The thought makes her smile, and she realises that she's always needed someone to look out for. Still ... she's not going to ambush Marion right now. She must visit her mother. She'll 'bump into' Marion and Finn in the afternoon. Dog-walkers usually take their pets out at the same time each day. That means

Marion and Finn will be heading across the Common at about 4 p.m.

Having made the decision, Paula strides on. She reaches her mum's care home and pauses to check her phone before going in. There's a message from Sue: *Yoga today. Liked it!*

Paula grins, and takes a deep, sustaining breath before walking into the home. There's no knowing what she'll find inside. Her mum's sadness she can be sure of, the vocal sufferings of the dementia patients vary. Paula hopes there'll be no howling or fighting today.

Her mother is sitting in the armchair beside her bed and smiles when she sees Paula.

"Hello, love," her mum says.

Paula feels her own lips lift. Her mum seems cheerful. Maybe she won't complain about the long time that's elapsed between visits.

"I'm sorry it's been a while, Mum," she says, sitting down on the nearby armchair. "I've been in America, working."

"America!" Her mum's still-pretty eyes brighten. "What was America like?"

"Big." Paula grins. "I went to a town in Maine—so much space—then to San Francisco. It was beautiful, but sad—homeless people, addicts."

Her mum nods. "You got the job done?"

"Of course."

"That's my girl." Her mother gazes at her with those blue eyes and Paula thinks how she'll be even more alone without her mother to love her.

"You have another job yet?" her mum asks.

"No, but I've re-posted my ad."

"The one with you as Sherlock Holmes? I like that."

"Me too." Paula grins. It had given her a buzz to re-post the ad in the print version of the local paper. Fuck the haters.

"And how are you doing?" her mum asks, "in yourself?"

"I'm fine." Paula's body stiffens. She hates that phrase, that tone. She doesn't want sympathy or questions about Jane.

"You've got to get back out there, you know."

"You mean dating?"

Her mum nods, her eyes mischievous.

What's got into her?

"There's that new gay nightclub, Paula. I read about it in the paper."

Paula's annoyed to feel herself flush. "Mum ... I'm not going to go after women in their twenties like some sad old dyke. ..."

Her mum's mouth purses. "You could never be undignified, Paula. And you're still gorgeous. There are websites too, you know."

"God, Mum, stop." Paula imagines herself in some bar waiting for an unknown potential to appear. Maybe the other woman would glimpse her overweight self and slink away before being seen. Paula can visualise the pitying eyes of the bartender, as portrayed in a million movies. Worse, the woman would show up and they'd make small talk, sizing each other up before deciding they weren't a good fit. Paula winces. Who would be a good fit? She can't imagine who she'd want, who'd want her. Does Jane have someone else? Maybe Jane has had someone else all along? Should she ask Neil? *No.*

"You can't pine away," her mum says. "I had fun after your dad left."

Paula feels her eyes widen.

"Oh, I know you see me as a tragic figure, and I was devastated, but life continued. I had boyfriends."

Paula gulps. "Well, great... I never knew."

"No. I didn't want you to. You were so upset about your dad. I didn't want you to have to deal with a parade of men."

"A parade?"

Her mum's delicate skin flushes. "Well, not a parade ..."

Paula studies her mum, still pretty despite being in her eighties and the cancer. She wishes she'd known about the boyfriends; she would have felt ... lighter. "You fox, you."

Her mum chuckles, leans in and fondles Paula's hand. "Get a life, love. Jane was always controlling, snobby, you know she was."

"Yes." Paula gazes at her mum's ropey, sun-darkened hand, and feels her throat constrict. Does her mum know she will soon die? Does she feel the darkness descending?

"Neil's coming around tomorrow," she tells her mum. "To the flat. It didn't go well last time. He walked Husky then made an excuse and left. The flat's so small. He's used to playing those online games and having a piano on hand. Jane's salary pays for ... extras." She doesn't tell her mother about the threats and the attack on the house. She hopes Neil isn't scared. He told her he was fine in a text but maybe he was acting tough. She'll know when she sees him, when she looks in his eyes.

"Neil does play the piano beautifully." There's a proud glow on her mum. "The way he makes those notes fall like dew drops, like in *Morning Has Broken* ... it sounds just like the Cat Stevens version."

"Yes, he's talented." Her mother is still holding her hand.

"But there's other things you can do together. You were always sporty, Paula. Get him running with you. Take him to that silly punching class at the gym."

"It's not silly," Paula says. Maybe she could afford the gym again if she cut back on something else. What? She sighs inwardly.

It must be hard for Mum, to see me like this—all alone, at the end of her life.

"I think you thought Jane was better than you."

Paula takes back her hand. "No. Jane just had more money. That gave her ... power."

Her mum nods, fondles the collar of the pink dressing gown that cradles her neck. Paula sees her mum's eyes are shiny with sympathy and sadness and, beyond her annoyance, she feels gratitude. She is lonely. The silence in the flat is so deep Paula sometimes feels as if she might dissolve, slip into it as if it were a horror movie fog. She forgets how it feels to be physical in the most ordinary of ways—to have words in her mouth, her voice in her throat, laughter in her lungs. Her skin is untouched, her tongue dormant. Husky is her only warmth. She dozes off with her hand on his body, comforted by the reliable rise and fall of his breath.

"Thanks for the pep talk, Mum. I just need time."

She turns, relieved to hear the tea trolley. Paula stays for a drink and a biscuit, and leaves wondering if her mum is imparting final words of wisdom or maybe she's just doing the maternal worrying thing? She looks fine, quite well really, all things considered.

Later, it feels good to fetch Husky and head down to Southsea and Marion Taylor. Husky pulls her along the seafront. Paula has to hold tight to the lead and lever her own weight to hold him back. She must take him out more. He's tormented by confinement in the tiny flat. "You're a good boy, Husky," she says. "I wouldn't blame you for chewing the furniture."

With the wind in her face, it seems a long way to the posh part of Southsea. Still, all this fast walking will surely slim her down. She pauses to admire the graceful grey rooflines of South Parade Pier. The lovely Victorian structure has been beautifully restored after being destroyed by fires and a huge storm. It's risen from the ashes. And you will too, she tells herself, and smiles at the corny thought that nonetheless makes her feel more hopeful.

As she nears the Common, she glances at the ferry heading toward France and thinks of all the Brits who've gone to make new lives in sunny Spain and France.

Lucky bastards, wonder if they are still pissed off about Brexit.

Maybe, if another job fails to come along soon, she could ask Jane for money, just a loan, until they sort out the house? Maybe she should see a lawyer? No. Not as long as she's got enough cash to send support payments for Neil.

I won't let Neil down. I'll get a job stacking shelves first.

She detours by the D-Day Museum because she feels compelled to pay her respects at the statue of the young soldier. Paula likes to read the inscription to A Soldier of World War Two:

Decades of easy peace may go their way
And tide, and time, may drift us far apart
But you who shared our savage yesterday
Will hold the highest places in our heart.

The words bring tears to Paula's eyes, as they always do. It is something to serve, she thinks. It is an honour.

Husky isn't pleased when she pushes open the door to Salty's Cafe. He hesitates, reluctant to step inside. Paula gives him a nudge—the wind is strengthening and Salty's is dog-friendly and directly opposite the turning into Marion's road. Paula can sit in the window and see when Marion and Finn set off. They're not likely to head down the street in the opposite direction as that route leads to the shopping centre.

"We don't need to freeze our balls off, Husky," Paula says as she manoeuvres him into a space near a corner table. "Don't worry, I'll make it worth your while."

"Hello Sharon." She smiles at the young server who approaches. "I'll have a large coffee with milk. And Husky will have one of those yummy oatmeal biscuits."

"Sure, Paula." Sharon smiles, and Paula tugs off her jacket and thinks how good it feels to be known.

Sharon brings the coffee and the biscuit, which Paula breaks into small segments and feeds to Husky in slow instalments. She smiles as his eyes follow the biscuit. He takes each morsel gently from her fingers.

"You're a dear old thing, Husky," she tells him. "Lucky you are food-motivated, as the vets say. Nothing wrong with that."

The biscuit and coffee are gone, and she's wondering whether to venture back into the cold—the café is filling and she doesn't want to hog a table—when she sees Marion emerge from the turning opposite and begin to walk towards the Common. Marion's head is down, her lean body bent into the wind like a curved exclamation mark. Finn strides ahead, his powerful neck straining at his lead.

Paula turns to Sharon, waves for the bill. She can't ignore the pulse of excitement the sight of Marion has sparked. An inner voice warns her to back off as she buttons her jacket. Curiosity killed the cat, Paula, she tells herself. "Come on, Husky lad," she says. "Time to get out there."

Chapter 18

Marilyn feels her mood bob up. It's good to open the door and sense the fresh air on her skin, although the day has turned chill. Never mind. She needs movement, to relax in the stride of her legs.

All day, she's been brooding. There was a fresh allegation against Sean on the morning news. Another young woman—the fifth—has accused him of assault. This woman, speaking in darkened silhouette like the others, said Sean grabbed her by the throat when she refused to have sex with him. Like the others, she feared for her life.

He is violent. He's gotten worse.

The news agitated Marilyn for hours. She re-considered David's news about Sean. Was David telling the truth about Sean's blackmail threat? Has Sean blighted her brother's life as well as her own? Or was David trying to disarm her?

But why would he lie? He can't know what I plan to do.

She doesn't want to forgive her brother, but she does feel differently. David seems a little less dark. She no longer wishes to implicate him in Sean's death but she refuses to recalibrate the past.

I am the injured one.

As usual, Finn is keen to get moving. He is pulling on the lead. He knows Marilyn is a fast walker, a kindred soul. She knows she should make him slow down and walk by her side. His owners won't be happy if he is unruly when they return. But she doesn't want to restrain him. Instead, she picks up her pace to match his as they reach the end of the street and turn the corner. As she enters the busier road, she glances about, hoping to see Karen. She plans to tell her not to let anyone else know she's in town.

'I'm in Portsmouth for a quiet visit with my husband,' she will say. 'We haven't been married long.' Karen will understand. It still amazes Marilyn that Karen knew David and that she'd recognised Marilyn and told her brother she was back. Marilyn can barely remember any of the kids from school, and she doesn't want to—little bitches, vile bullies.

She breathes better as she moves, anticipating the wide, open expanse of the Common. But something begins to nag at her mind and she slows. Something is wrong. She feels it, a niggling uncertainty in her brain.

I must have forgotten something. What?

She stops, causing a passing pedestrian to almost spill his coffee.

"Sorry." Marilyn smiles at the scowling young face.

What have I forgotten?

She checks her pockets. Does she have poop bags, dog treats, her phone, her coin purse? Yes. She can feel the purse's bulk and the keys' hard edges. The poop bags slip between her fingers. Does she have an appointment? No.

What is it?

She stands, gazes at the surrounding shops, at the Oxfam and Save the Children stores with their windows full of ancient mannequins modelling donated clothing. She looks back at Salty's, its windows foggy with warm breath. She sees the striped awnings and tempting displays of the old-fashioned bakery and butcher Doug loves.

Am I supposed to get something for dinner? No.

She turns, and begins to walk again toward the Common.

Finn is looking up, confused by her uncertainty. "Sorry Finn." She leans down, gives his back a firm pat. "If it's important, I'll remember."

Her mind begins to still again as she walks. It feels good to focus on nothing but the path ahead. Finn moves along, their legs in step, and she fantasises about taking him back to California. Would it be fun to walk him in San Francisco, or would he become a chore, too much of a responsibility? That might be the case. She's probably too selfish, too unstable, to be a full-time carer.

The wind is brisker as they approach the Common and it's rising. People scuttle past, hurrying toward the shelter of the narrow streets that slot together like a puzzle behind the fancy white Victorian hotel and the elegant homes now turned into apartments. I must remind Doug about having tea at the hotel, she thinks as she passes *The Victorian*. He'll be disappointed if he doesn't get a cream tea in England. The wind gusts still stronger as they cross the street and start to walk along the waterfront.

Two women pass. "They're stopping the hover ferry," one says, her words leaping in the wind.

"They should stop all the ferries," the other replies. "Such wild weather."

It is. Marilyn grins, enjoying the chaos, but maybe she should turn back. Litter, even small signs and other items, might get thrown about. Finn mustn't get hurt. "We'll just walk for a while, Finn. Just till it gets too much." But Finn isn't deterred. He's striding ahead. Marilyn watches his fur and ears toss and ripple and smiles.

They move on. They are now the only ones still walking the waterfront. Marilyn grins.

This is glorious. I'm not as cowardly as I think, feel.

The waves summit the little beach, curl along the sloping concrete barriers built to keep them out. It's hard to breathe. The wind, salty and heavy with spray, presses on her mouth, her throat and chest. Doug says she sometimes walks so fast she looks like a crazy woman. She must look crazy now, with her hair tossed and her face red and wet. When a triangular sign advertising fish 'n' chips bounces toward them, Marilyn concedes defeat. "Sorry Finn." She pulls him toward the crossing that will take them off the waterfront path. "We'd better walk inland."

It's surprising how much calmer it is on the road that runs parallel to the water. It's only a matter of metres but the trees and buildings provide protection. Marilyn slows, looks about at this monied part of town she's not visited in decades. She knows it though. Sean lives here. The TV cameras have captured him leaving his large, white Victorian house. The reporters shouted questions about the sexual assault victims as he moved toward his car.

I know where he lives.

"Come on, Finn." She turns, guides him across another road as doubt begins to pulse in her veins. She shouldn't do this. It's a risk, but she will. Maybe it's exhilaration, recklessness, caused by the violent weather, but she intends to see Sean's house for herself. Seeing his lair will give her resolve.

It doesn't take long. She knows Brighton Street, and Sean's house has a blood-red front door and is flanked by large planters filled with bushes sprouting crimson berries. The house is in the middle of a row of plush homes.

She stands on the sidewalk opposite his door and stares. She might have expected Sean's house to sit at one end of the street in an imposing corner lot. It doesn't, but it does seem to loom centre stage. It's the bright door perhaps, and the planters, the fact his front yard is tidier and prettier than others. Or maybe it's her own knowledge, her hatred that sets his house apart.

His house, all the houses, are huge and white. They resemble the city's Victorian hotels and apartment blocks, but they lack the spreading warmth of those buildings. They look stark, gleaming in their tall purity. They seem to have been built to keep people out. They're like white teeth, Marilyn thinks, fake Hollywood teeth—like Sean's.

Still, the sumptuous family homes provoke a circling envy in her gut. Doug is wonderful. He has saved her, but might she have found a good man and settled down sooner, built a fuller life, one with children, if not for Sean? Maybe she would never have had to struggle in a new country, maybe life could have been familiar, easier?

It's ironic that Sean's house looks so pure, but then his whole life is a whitewash.

Don't stand gazing at it!

The realization comes swift, speeding her pulse. She must move on. Someone will get suspicious. There's no one on the street, but there could be eyes watching from behind windows, net curtains. Everyone knows everyone else's business in England. She jerks into motion, yanking Finn who's settled at her feet.

"Sorry, Finn." She stoops to caress him.

He gazes at her and his eyes are so open, so trusting, her heart constricts. Tears fill her eyes. He loves her.

"You're a sweetheart, Finn, the dearest boy. Come on. Let's go."

Together, they walk down Sean's street. Marilyn feels compelled to turn and return to Sean's home, but she keeps moving. That's what dog-walkers do.

She's walked the whole street and is approaching his home again when the red door opens and his wife and children appear. Marilyn shrinks, ducks, as if she could disappear into the sidewalk, then straightens.

You're a dog-walker, just a dog-walker.

She stoops to stroke Finn, speaks gently against his soft, attentive head. "Good boy, Finn. Good boy."

He rubs his body against her legs, looks up at her with those wide eyes, but she looks away, toward the family—Sean's family. She knows their names. They look as they do online—wholesome, privileged, happy.

"Oh my gosh, it's windy," Sean's wife—Janet—calls over her shoulder as she walks down the wide, clean steps. "Put your coats on, kids."

Sean's wife is blonde, whether natural or coloured to hide grey like herself, Marilyn can't tell. She's slim, clad in tailored pants and blouse. Janet grew up on a farm. Marilyn read about Janet's early life and envied her growing up among peace and beauty, with happily married parents. Sean's wife looks like she spends much of her current life in the gym. Volunteering too, no doubt. Women with rich husbands always volunteer, it's something to do.

The daughter—Sarah—clamps her hand to her head as her baby blonde hair lifts and twirls in the wind. "It's crazy!" she yells. Sarah moves down the stairs. She's tall. Her body is one lovely, fluid line. Her head sits like a blossom on her delicate neck. Maybe she's a dancer. She resembles Sean in the confident way she carries herself. Lastly, Sean's son, Harry, is younger and plumper, maybe 13. He moves slowly, as if reluctant to leave home. In his hand, he carries a dark, rectangular case. It must contain a musical instrument, maybe a clarinet.

"Come on, Harry. We'll be late," Janet calls. Mother and daughter have reached the car parked at the sidewalk, a family-sized red VW. Marilyn startles as a large uniformed man emerges from the driver's seat, and she puts her head down, starts walking, as casually as she can, toward the end of the road.

Who is he?

"Afternoon, Ma'am." Marilyn hears the booming baritone of the man's voice as he greets Janet.

How long has he been sitting in that car? Has he been watching me?

The man opens the door on the passenger side. He stands, waiting for Sean's wife to get in. She approaches but turns to the house and her dawdling son. "Harry. You've got to go to your lesson. We agreed."

"You can't play games all day, Harry." His sister's voice is bright and scolding—a needling tone beneath good cheer.

"Shut up, Sarah." Harry lingers on the steps. "Mind your own business."

"Stop it, you two." Janet's tone is tired mum.

Marilyn stares at Sean's wife. What is it like to be married to Sean? Can he be a different person with his family? What does Janet think of the allegations? What would this happy woman say if Marilyn strode across the road and told her what her husband did to her when she was just a child, younger than her own daughter is now?

She watches them get in the car, hears the engine start. It drives off, and she keeps watching. Sean's family. So ordinary, yet so precious. Sean has a family and she does not. Grief and anger warm her blood and push tears into her eyes. She recalls her brother's sad face, his defeated shoulders.

Sean ruined our lives. And look at him. He lives here, in this palace, with a lovely family, rich and successful, with his own security guard.

Bastard.

She thinks of the TV show she and Doug watched the previous night. The American drama showed a woman murdering her husband by grinding cherry pits into his coffee. Would cherry pits be more poisonous and faster acting than apricot kernels? Maybe she should grind up her own Xanax? But her drugs were issued in America, the medication may be subtly different in the U.K., and an autopsy might reveal those differences. She sighs. Marilyn, what are you thinking? Watching a woman on TV murder her husband is not the same as murdering someone yourself.

"Come on, Finn." She strokes him, and he gets to his feet. They begin to head back between the tall white homes toward the waterfront. Marilyn's mind is still, Sean's success has emptied her.

It's not until she glimpses the triangular expanse of the Common that she identifies the thought that had been trying to surface when she left Warhol Way. She stops and unease crawls over her skin. She's been a fool, so shocked by David's sudden arrival and apology that she's overlooked the obvious. She never told Karen where she was staying. She did not. How then did David know? How had her brother come to be standing outside Warhol Way gazing up into the kitchen window? If Karen did not tell David where she was living, who did? And why did David lie about it?

Chapter 19

Paula stands inside Salty's doorway and watches Marion. She's surprised when Marion stops in the street and turns and stares back the way she's come.

Has she forgotten something? Paula waits for Marion to stride back to Warhol Way, but she does not. She stands still, oblivious to the people who have to walk around her—one young man nearly spills his coffee. Then she turns and hurries on her way.

"Come on, Husky." Paula opens the door and the cold swirls in. She pulls up her collar and steps out, begins to follow Marion and Finn. She keeps her distance, stays on her side of the street. Then, because the road widens and opens as it meets the Common, she crosses over so she is on the same side as Marion.

She glances in the shop windows she passes—if Marion should look back and see her, she can pretend she's just idling along. She doesn't want Husky to get close to Finn either. Husky will remember his new friend and pull on the lead, to catch him.

The wind is stronger than before, and it's still strengthening. Paula is startled to see Marion stride into it. She watches Marion head across the Common and toward the Channel. She must be mad, Paula thinks, knowing that it will be so wild by the waterfront it will be hard to progress against the wind. Instead of following Marion's route, Paula takes the road that runs parallel to the water. With luck, she'll be able to keep Marion in her sights and not risk getting swept into the Channel. "Good news, Husky," she says. "You don't have to be decapitated by a flying fish 'n' chip sign." And she manoeuvres Husky toward this new route that he is less familiar with and reluctant to take.

A short time later, Marion comes to the same conclusion for she takes the steps down from the waterfront path, and approaches the main road, pausing at the crossing. Paula ducks behind a tree, pulls Husky in. Marion mustn't see her, not yet.

Marion and Finn are now on Paula's path. She hangs back, slows Husky with gentle tugs on the lead. She walks and watches. Marion's pace picks up and she moves swiftly past the park with its new swing set and slide, past the aquarium, past the expensive fish restaurant. She crosses the street and walks beside the tightly knit shops and restaurants. Marion makes no allowances for the greater density of shops and pedestrians. She barely slows until she stops at the entrance to Brighton Road. Then she turns left into the street.

Paula reaches Brighton Road and turns cautiously into it, holding Husky back so he stands slightly behind her. Marion and Finn are about a hundred yards away. Marion is standing and staring at a house on the opposite side of the road.

Paula edges back up to the corner, rounds it, peers. She watches Marion from the shelter of the wall. Why is Marion staring at that house? Did she once live there? Paula is surprised to feel her eyes moisten. Is this the street where Marion lived as a child, when she lost her father? No, that's not likely. Hugh said the family lived on the military base. Her dad was a military pilot. And this street is expensive, always has been. Grandparents maybe? Wealthy grandparents or an elderly aunt and uncle?

She must be sad, Paula thinks, to stand there so long, so still. She must be freezing. Paula glances at Husky, silent at her feet, and smiles. "I did a great job of training you. Bet you wish I hadn't?"

Paula doesn't meet the eyes of the people passing by. They must think her behaviour odd. But Husky is here, sitting quietly. Dogs usually disarm people, well-behaved dogs anyway.

Paula looks back at Marion and something about the home's red door nudges a memory. She's seen that door, that house, recently. Where? On TV. Her pulse alerts, although she's not sure why. It's the mayor's house, Sean Adams. The media have been door-stepping him over the assault allegations. Things have been getting sticky for the mayor, although he's maintained his calm and charm, insisted on his innocence. He's charismatic, good-looking, but Paula never liked him, always found his politics too far right, although she approved of the funds he put into the city's police force. Why is Marion Taylor staring at his door?

What could there be between the city's handsome, charismatic mayor and this strange woman? It's not likely the mayor assaulted Marion—they would both have been so young. Could they have been childhood sweethearts? It doesn't seem likely, but time has not been kind to Marion. People age differently. Marion might have been more attractive in her youth—pretty, bubbly in that silly way men like.

Paula sees a movement in a large VW parked outside Sean's house. A man is sitting in the driver's seat. He's spotted Marion and is watching her in the wing mirror. He looks big, bulky—a private security detail. Sean might have received threats since the allegations broke. Marion is oblivious.

Hugh's awkward face and his dark, sombre office come to mind. Is Hugh acting for Sean? David too?

Is it actually Sean who wants Marion found?

Marion and Finn are walking away from the house toward the far end of the street. Paula considers following, but caution makes her wait. Just as well, for when Marion reaches the other end, she turns and walks back. She looks like she'll walk past the mayor's house. Paula pulls back behind the wall so only her eyes peep around.

The red door opens, and Marion pauses, as a woman, slim and smart, appears on the doorstep. Sean's wife. Paula has seen her on TV standing stoically beside her man, as wives in these situations seem to do. She's followed by a teenage girl. Even from a distance, Paula can see the girl has a delicate yet athletic beauty. Finally, a boy, 12 or 13, carrying a musical case. Paula hears voices but not what they're saying. The big man emerges from the VW. He walks around the car, says something to the woman, holds the door.

Marion watches until they're all in the vehicle. She waits until it does a three-point turn in the road and drives toward the far end of the street. Then she puts her head down and begins to stride back along the pavement. Paula shifts, pulls away from the wall. Her heart is thumping, which is ridiculous, but she's unsure what to do. She considers fleeing, but Marion is so fast she'll soon be upon her, might glimpse her running away. Should she duck into a shop? The nearest is a boutique, full of floaty dresses. They won't want Husky in there. No. She'd intended to bump into Marion and she will. She steps back a few paces, installs herself and Husky before the filmy gowns in the boutique window, and waits.

It takes seconds. Marion almost strides by, and Paula nearly lets her, but she pretends to startle, turns to Marion and Finn as they pass. "Oh hello, Marion. And Finn, isn't it?" Paula smiles at the dog, bends to pat him.

Marion stops, stares at Paula so intensely that Paula thinks she's not been remembered.

"Marion, hi. It's Karen. We met on the Common the other day?" Paula turns, waves a hand at the sumptuous creations in the shop. "Just doing some window shopping. Aren't these gorgeous?" She shivers, snuggles inside her jacket. "Isn't the weather insane?"

"Did you tell my brother I was back?" Paula is struck by how English Marion sounds, like an outraged toff.

Paula pretends to think. "Yes ... I told a few people. I bumped into several old friends from schooldays." She grins. "Not many of us were brave enough to go and live abroad, like you."

"I don't believe you." Marion's face and tone are so harsh Paula feels wary. Where is the nervous, evasive woman from the Common?

"No one would even remember me from school." Marion's face twists with pain. "I wasn't exactly popular. I was always a kid in the background, a shadow."

Paula feels her own face heat with stress. "You don't have to be popular to be remembered, Marion."

"So, you're saying I'm remembered because I was weird? Because I *was* weird, which you'd know if you really had any memories of me. My mum was a ... bully, and my dad died." Marion stares. "I was a weird kid, Karen. You'd know that."

Paula glances down. The dogs are exploring each other, snouts bumping, tails wagging. "Yes, your father died ..."

Marion cuts her off. "I don't believe you told my brother. He knew where I'm staying. I did not tell you that."

"I told him I'd bumped into you in that part of town," Paula says. "We met on the Common. You were coming from that part of Southsea."

"Yes, we met on the Common. But he was standing outside Warhol Way. He was staring up into the kitchen window. He was waiting for me, watching."

Paula hears the silence stretch out. "He must have guessed," she says. "It's a modern block—new people, homes rented on Airbnb."

"Karen, I am not an idiot." Marion glares. "And you were walking the wrong way when we met on the Common. You were coming from the water. We weren't walking in the same direction, so why were you so quick to turn around and come with me?"

Paula feels her mask slipping. "I wasn't in a rush and I was feeling a bit down, lonely, because of my divorce. I thought it might be nice to catch up with someone from school."

Marion frowns. "Karen, I'm quite sure I never knew you."

Paula's heart is jumping, she must look guilty as hell. "Well, I'm sorry to bother you, my mistake." And she turns and heads away. Husky pants to keep up. She's furious with herself, embarrassed and ashamed.

"Wait!" Marion calls. "Karen, wait. You have not answered my questions."

Paula keeps moving. She powers along.

Damn. Her face burns. You've upset that woman, Paula. You're ruining her visit home.

You've made everything worse. Leave that poor distressed woman alone.

Chapter 20

"Excuse me, ma'am." Marilyn feels a hand on her arm, and turns to see a frowning male face. The man is wearing the black uniform of a store security guard. "I believe you failed to pay for those items."

Marilyn glances at the shopping bag in her hand. It's her favourite cloth bag—black with an image of San Francisco's Golden Gate Bridge outlined in sunshine yellow. Inside the bag, she sees a six-pack of beer and the mini pork pies Doug likes. She has no recollection of walking out of the store. She barely remembers choosing the items.

"I'm so sorry." She speaks with her strongest Californian accent. "I am so sorry, Officer. I can't believe I did that." She smiles. "It must be jetlag, and ..." She shakes her head. "The drunks in the street yelling last night. I am so tired. They are ruining my vacation."

"Oh ... sorry to hear that, ma'am." The guard withdraws his hand. He frowns, and Marilyn sees he's pondering the difficulties of taking legal action against a sleep-deprived tourist. It isn't worth it, he's thinking. She'll soon have left the country, and she's right about the drunks. "Very well, ma'am, I won't pursue it this time, but please go back inside and pay for those items, and please be more careful in future or I will have to take action."

"Yes, of course, thank you so much." Marilyn nods and her eyes fill with tears of genuine gratitude. "Thank you, thank you, sir."

She goes inside, pays with cash, and leaves. As she strides away, she decides she will not return to Sainsbury's again. If the guard checks security footage he will realise she has not just arrived in the country. She will stick to shopping at Waitrose although it is more expensive.

"You're losing it, Marilyn, losing it," she tells herself as she hurries back to Warhol Way. "And there are still two weeks of the pet-sit left." She feels panic rise, a skin-burning tide. "Two weeks is too long. You're going to give yourself away." A sob catches her throat and it calms her, takes her out of her head, makes her realise she is talking aloud.

Marilyn, people will think you're crazy!

She glances about. A woman with a chocolate-smeared child, is staring at her. Marilyn zips her lips, tells herself two weeks is not so very long. She must act soon. She should never have let the chance to trap Sean at the church slip by.

It's because Finn got into the muffins, that threw me. It was so awful.

It was. The near-tragedy, and seeing Sean's children outside his house, made Marilyn realise her plan could harm an innocent.

Children should never suffer.

She will see Sean this afternoon. She'd learned from the TV that the mayor is scheduled to present a cheque to the Mary-Rose Museum at the Historic Dockyard. She'd instantly resolved to be there.

"The *Mary-Rose* is an important symbol of Portsmouth," the newscaster had said. "The ship was the glory of Henry VIII's navy, but sank off Portsmouth in 1545 during a battle against the French."

Marilyn had stared at the images of what remained of the ship's hull. The dark and gloomy remnants were raised in 1982 from the deep clay where they'd lain for centuries. The wreck is now displayed in the museum. "You'll want to see this ship, Doug," Marilyn had said as her husband entered the room. Doug had stared at the ancient timbers on the screen. "That looks fantastic," he'd said. "When are we going?"

"This afternoon. The mayor is presenting a cheque."

"That guy who's been accused of rape?" Doug had frowned, and she thought how kind her husband has been. When she was still his patient, she'd told him that a man raped her when she was a child, and he has never insisted on knowing the details. He has just supported her, faithfully, lovingly.

"Is that a good idea, Marilyn? Do you really want to go and listen to a rapist?" he'd asked.

"I'm curious to see if demonstrators turn up and heckle him. You know I always support victims."

"Well, okay then ..." Doug had said, doubtful.

Marilyn had nodded, recalling hearing about the *Mary Rose* as a child. Her father had found the ship and its mythology exciting. By the time the wreck was raised from its clay bed, Marilyn had left Portsmouth. Her father had died, and she was trying to start again as a brand new person, an American. But that can't really happen. She'd learned that. Wherever you are in the world, you wake up with yourself.

You must get through every day with and by yourself, she thinks now as she turns the key in the front door, closes it, and begins to carry her shopping up the first flight of stairs. As she walks, the dogs upstairs start barking manically.

"It's okay, Finn. It's okay, Winston," she shouts. The dogs pay no attention and she expects to soon see their angry faces at the top of the stairs.

What on earth has set them off? Has someone broken in?

"It's okay, guys," she calls again, but they do not calm, do not come to the top of the steps.

Has Sean sent someone to silence me?

She rounds the stairs and a stench, like the one that pervades the house but deeper, more disturbing, hits her. The dogs are standing below the second staircase barking at something higher up. Fear speeds Marilyn's pulse but she makes herself walk forward, glance up. There is a young woman, pale, dark-haired. The girl's hair is drawn back behind her neck. Her clothing is simple and drab—a long dress, brown, reaches to her ankles. The girl is gazing at the dogs who are vibrating with alarm. As Marilyn studies the young woman, the girl turns her head and stares into Marilyn's eyes.

At once, Marilyn feels a deep sadness grip her. In the girl's dark gaze, she sees grief, loneliness, combined with something dark and fierce—rage?

"Are you okay?" she asks. "Why are you here?"

The girl says nothing, and Marilyn is struck by an idea. "Are you one of Sean's victims? How do you know about me?"

Still, the girl says nothing. "Stop it, guys!" Marilyn spins to the dogs who have backed away but are still barking crazily. "That's enough!"

But the dogs don't stop. Their eyes are dilated with distress.

"Guys," Marilyn says. "Calm down, it's just a girl."

She turns again to the stairs, to the youngster, and the questions that are coursing through her. But the young woman has gone. Marilyn pivots and sees her standing by the huge kitchen window that overlooks the road. She is motionless, gazing out into the street.

Marilyn stares, struck by the girl's odd clothing. Her dress is made of some coarse material that Marilyn doesn't recognise. Despite her youth, the girl has chore-worn hands and rough elbows beneath the sleeves of her clothing.

"Who are you?" Marilyn says as unease sparks up her spine, as she glimpses the girl's belly, swelling, beneath her dress.

The young woman turns, fixes Marilyn with a tragic, burning stare. Then she steps forward, through the glass of the window, and disappears into the fume-filled air above the street.

Marilyn gasps, stares at the intact, unbroken window pane. Shakily, she walks to the sofa as the dogs run to her, finally silent. The young woman's eyes are burned in Marilyn's mind. So desolate, so alone.

Is she trying to communicate with me? Has my grief summoned her?

"Hey, hon." Doug stands at the top of the first flight of stairs, sweaty and glistening from his run. "You okay?" He stoops, picks up the shopping bag Marilyn has dropped on the floor.

"Darling, what is it?" He strides forward, drops the bag, and falls to his knees beside her. Doug puts out his hand, rests it on Marilyn's knee, gazes up into her face.

"It's nothing," she says. "I just felt a little dizzy. The dogs were agitated when I arrived. I wondered what had upset them ..."

"You're likely tired from all the walking, maybe not eating enough protein, maybe dehydrated." Doug gives his diagnosis swiftly. "Does this mean you're not up for the *Mary Rose*?"

"No, I'll go. I just needed to sit for a while."

"Good. I don't mean to be selfish but I really want to see that ship." He sits back on his heels. "Hey guys, what's up?" He turns to the dogs who have begun to recover, to nudge his hands with their snouts. He strokes Finn, strokes Winston. "Marilyn, if you're okay, I'd better get my shower so we can get going."

"Yes." Marilyn nods. "I'll get us some lunch."

"You rest. I'll do lunch. Be a minute." And he turns for the stairs.

"Doug," Marilyn says. He turns. "Can you smell anything ... unpleasant?"

He shakes his head. "All I smell is dog and that lavender soap you like. Please, do not start cleaning again."

Alone, Marilyn sits and breathes.

Don't tell Doug. He'll think you're crazy.

Her mind shifts to the upcoming event at the museum. Sean will attract a crowd. David might be there. She wants to see her brother with Sean, needs to see the two of them interact. She will hide in the crowd.

Doug returns from the shower, makes tuna and cheese sandwiches and Marilyn forces herself to eat. Then they walk to the museum, leaving time to tour the *Mary Rose* exhibition before Sean's event.

Marilyn's mood calms the moment she steps inside the first of the museum's dimly lit rooms. It's the atmosphere: sombre and respectful, like a funeral or cathedral. They study the exhibition that explains how the *Mary Rose* had been burdened with huge bronze cannon, making it top heavy and unwieldy as it faced off against the French. Pictures of the elaborate vessel show it as having many levels and extravagant turrets. It was like an American birthday cake, Marilyn thinks, the kind sold in stores: sickeningly lavish.

The ship was only just offshore, opposite the king's waterfront castle, when it was tossed by a gust of wind, and water rushed in through open portholes. Most of the 400 men on board ran to the upper deck to escape, but were trapped by nets of thick rope hung to prevent the French from boarding. Marilyn's mind spins as she imagines the doomed men standing on deck with the clean air in their lungs. They should have been able to jump, but the nets dragged them down. Of the 400, only 35 escaped. Some victims were just 11 years old.

"I've heard a lot of shipwreck stories but this is the most tragic." Doug's voice trembles as they look at thick coils of the ship's deadly rope. "Those men were so close to shore."

Marilyn nods, and grips his hand. The rope is well preserved, hay-coloured and glistening. It still smells of hemp and salt. Marilyn thinks of the cold, deadly water, and of her father, also trapped in the service of his country, also dragged to his death.

They move on, fingers entwined, and see reconstructions of the heads of drowned sailors modelled on their recovered skulls. Marilyn sees the skeleton of a puppy, found near a dead sailor. Her throat closes and her eyes fill.

What a dear, loyal dog—like Finn.

Finally, when Marilyn thinks she can take no more, they see the wreck of the *Mary Rose* herself, its timbers draped in a sombre blue light. Decks and struts reach like fingers into the emptiness where connecting links once were. The turrets are gone, destroyed by the Channel's scouring currents.

Marilyn shivers in the damp air which smells of old wood and chemicals. For a moment, she forgets why she's here. She forgets Sean. She's just a native of Portsmouth, mourning a tragic loss.

But as they turn from the wreck, she sees that at the far end of the room a crowd is gathering. She glances at her phone. It's nearly time for Sean to appear.

They approach the group and Marilyn finds a place behind a tall broad man. She resists Doug's efforts to edge her into a more open space. "I'm okay here," she murmurs. "I'm ... a bit shaken by the wreck."

Doug squeezes her fingers. "Me too."

They wait, and Marilyn almost flees, might have if not for the fear of breaking away from the crowd, of being seen. She can't risk bumping into Sean coming the other way. She breathes, unclenches her jaw.

He won't see you. Even if he does, he won't recognise you.

And then Sean is swooping through a lit space at the end of the walkway. He is striding, at the centre of a small group of supporters. Sean is here, in the same room as herself, after all these years. And David, David is behind him. A spotlight goes on, beams on to Sean. TV cameras swivel.

Oh no, there are cameras.

And Marilyn shrinks behind the big man.

Chapter 21

Paula's legs are heavy. She doubts she can manage one more jump, squat or kick. But it was worth forking out five pounds to join this class at the Community Y. She's pretending she's punching and kicking the creeps who are still texting her vile messages. She's imagining she's laying into the hoody-wearing toe-rags who spray-painted her son's home. The exercise is also lightening the physical tension, the loneliness, that's been building since her split with Jane. She misses physical intimacy—the softness, the closeness, sex. It feels like being a teen again, preparing to navigate this new world of dating and relationships, and this time she has even less idea how to go about it.

Her body isn't moving well, and the hand she hurt in Maine feels tender when she punches the air. It's probably too late to see a doctor. She's still sexy-curvy but out of shape. Her arms jiggle. She can feel the flesh swing, see it in the large mirror attached to the wall. It's hard to believe that, not long ago, she aced the police fitness tests. Never mind. She is loving feeling the sinews in her arms, the burning muscles in her thighs. Hello Body, she thinks. I'm back.

The woman teaching the class is enthusiastic bordering on overwhelming. A youngster, likely new at the job, she bellows her instructions: "Hold in your belly. Keep that arm up. Do you want a fist in your face?" The teacher is treating the class like a real self-defence session. The yelling is annoying, but the other, mostly very young women, seem energised. Their jaws are taut, their eyes focused. Maybe all the news stories about the mayor have highlighted awareness of self-defence.

Paula glances around and wonders how many of these women are victims of domestic violence. Domestics always account for the highest number of emergency calls and a third of all crimes involving assault with injury, and numbers keep rising. It's a troubling thought but with one fist tucked under her chin in a parody of self-defence and the other executing an upper cut, Paula begins to feel better. She's becoming her strong, true self again. Trouble is, the person she feels most like punching is herself. She shouldn't have lied to Marion. She's behaved unethically. She feels a moment's shame—I'm such a lonely sad-sack I ignored professional ethics—but she squat-steps across the room and the rhythmic thrum created by many feet moving together makes her feel less alone.

I'll be stiff as a board tomorrow.

She's in the changing room, towelling off after showering, when she sees the TV news about Sean's event at the *Mary Rose*. No, she tells herself. Do not go. She manoeuvres her breasts into her bra and frowns as she yanks the straps into place, acknowledging that she will indeed go to the *Mary Rose.* Marion's strange behaviour opposite Sean's house leads Paula to think there's a strong chance Marion will be there. Paula wants to observe her. And the museum is a cool place to visit. Paula hasn't been since she and Jane took Neil years ago. She won't have to pay the entrance fee if she attends Sean's event as it's free to the public. Attending will also be a break from her new job; a humdrum marital investigation that Paula knows she should be glad of—is glad of. She's been employed by a wife to check if her husband of 30 years is cheating. If he's still got it in him, he probably is, Paula had wanted to tell the woman. The main thing is, she has a job—her second as a private eye.

The large crowd Sean has attracted is already gathered by the time Paula slips in at the back of the hall. Sean is being introduced by one of the museum's directors. The woman describes the mayor as a great patron of arts and culture in the city. This latest donation will help the museum create a new display about the men of the *Mary Rose*. The director gives Sean a lingering look of gratitude, and he inclines his head graciously.

Christ, Paula thinks, don't we already have enough gruesome detail about those poor drowned bastards? She notes that the board of directors' representative is a little breathless in her dealings with the mayor. Well, the mayor is pretty hot, if you like that kind of thing, although his tanned face looks less healthy than usual. His skin seems pallid—maybe it's the blue glow cast by the lights in the museum, designed to protect the wreck's ancient wooden beams. There's also the spotlight and the shine of TV cameras. The security man Paula saw in the VW is standing off to one side. David, Marion's brother, accompanied the mayor into the room and has now disappeared.

Paula remembers she's here to look for Marion and glances cautiously about. She spots Marion standing at the back, beside a slim, grey-haired man Paula assumes to be her husband and who Paula immediately feels sure she has seen running along the waterfront. Marion is positioned directly behind a tall, bulky fellow. Deliberate, no doubt.

Sean thanks the breathless woman for her introduction and smiles at the gathering.

"Thank you all so much for coming." He swings a warm gaze across the crowd. "I really do appreciate it, although ..." And his eyes swivel to the brooding wreck that looms so close. "Who wouldn't seize the chance to stand in the presence of such an important piece of our city's history? And ..." He glances at the woman from the board of directors. "In such a splendid place—in this specially created and beautifully run museum. ..." His voice catches in his throat, he coughs. Paula thinks he's being paused by emotion, possibly feigned, but he coughs harder, puts his hand to his mouth. "I'm sorry, I seem to have picked up a germ. ..."

"You're working too hard," a male fan calls.

Sean smiles modestly. "Yes, probably."

"Mr Mayor, what about all these allegations?" A woman shouts.

"Yeah, what do you say, Mr Mayor?" Another female.

"Shut up, bitches!" A man bellows and the mood is instantly ugly. Everyone is shouting. Paula is not surprised but feels depressed.

When did we all get so loud and condemning, so fucking sure we're right?

"Do not accuse me of violence!" The mayor's face has coloured up. Despite the weird, blended hues of light he stands under, he's turned crimson. "Have any charges been laid against me? No. These allegations are being cooked up by my political enemies, aired by the left-wing media."

The mayor's breath rasps through his throat. Paula is sure his eyes are bulging. He stares at the crowd and his gaze rests on someone in the front row.

"My dear wife is here with me. ..." His voice sinks. "I'm a family man. ..." He coughs, hard into his hand, keeps coughing. He can't seem to stop.

Paula glances at Marion. Her body language is tense as she watches Sean, but then her body is always tense. She's put her head up. She's forgetting to hide. There's something fierce in her expression, Paula can see it even in the dim light. Marion is staring at Sean, unblinking, although at one point she glances away, toward the spot-lit ship.

Maybe she's fascinated by the conflict or embarrassed for him. Paula is. All that humiliating coughing, being heckled—it can't be easy. Sean is still coughing. The museum representative has gone to fetch him a glass of water.

"Shut up, you bitches! Can't you see the man's sick?" It's the big-voiced fan again.

"You shut up, asshole! What about the victims?" The original woman responds.

Paula grins approval and looks about. She can't see the woman, but she likes her. Normally, Paula's professionally trained mind disapproves of accusing people in public when no charges have been laid. But there have been a lot of very serious accusations against the mayor, and they keep coming. Voters deserve to hear his response.

"Yeah, shut up, asshole! Well, Mr Mayor?"

Paula freezes. She knows that voice, that accent that currently sounds Portsmouth born and bred. It's Marion Taylor. Marion looks defiant, although she's making sure to stay hidden behind the large man. Marion's husband is looking at his wife in astonishment.

The original heckler shouts again. "The women of this city, this country, deserve an answer Mr Mayor."

The mayor opens his mouth and the coughing resumes. He picks up the water the board rep brings him, takes long, slow sips, tests his voice in his hand. "I am ... so sorry." He smiles down at the front row. "I hope for your sakes I'm not still contagious." He grins. "Don't sue me if you get sick."

"You going to comment now, Mr Mayor?" The heckler.

The mayor pauses, stares into the throng as if he'd like to rush into it and silence his accuser. But he breathes deep, sighs. "I am not guilty of these ... terrible ... allegations," he says in a voice strained and roughened by coughing. "I am a family man." His eyes return to the front row, and Paula visualises his loyal wife, standing by her man, in the darkness.

"I am a husband and father. I have worked to improve the lot of working families in our city." Sean shakes his head as if being forced to state the obvious and defend himself is an insult.

"Family life is central to our way of life in Portsmouth." He turns, gazes up at the looming wreck of the *Mary Rose*. His hand lifts toward the dark timbers.

"More than five hundred years ago, our ancestors built this ship." His hand falls in dramatic emphasis, he turns to the crowd, "They built it here." He points downward, indicating the very earth, the soil, of Portsmouth. "They built it in our city, in our dockyard." He turns again, points up at the extraordinary spot-lit beams.

"Our ancestors manned that ship." His voice rises, strong and imbued with patriotism, love of place. Paula smiles. Despite herself, she feels a prickle of pride warm and tingle her skin. It's true; Portsmouth has a glorious, a nationally and internationally important history.

"Our ancestors died on that ship." The mayor's voice falls in sorrow. He lowers his pointing hand, sweeps it over the crowd. "And our ancestors found, they re-discovered, our ship." He raises a fist. "After years of work, of fundraising, of determination, our ancestors, together, raised that ship." He lets the fist fall, scans the hall. "And they built this museum to preserve and display our beautiful, our...precious relic." His voice chokes. "Our relic of Portsmouth's glory."

Paula feels her eyes fill. She shakes her head—don't be manipulated, you fool. But she feels warm, happy, moved by this blatant appeal to civic pride. The mayor is a fine politician. He has that quality—that shiny, smooth charisma that makes people believe.

People are always looking for a leader, always searching for The One.

There's nothing to say after such a performance, and Sean turns and leaves before the heckler can start up again. He walks out on a wave of whoops and cheers, flanked by the rep, his wife, his bodyguard, and Marion's brother David.

Paula turns and studies Marion as she hovers at the back with her husband. Marion looks unsure whether to leave, unsure, perhaps, how best to exit the cavernous hall. On an impulse, Paula strides toward her, feels her exercise-wearied legs already beginning to stiffen.

"Marion, hi."

Marion startles, she shrinks away then she straightens, pulls down her shoulders and glares. Keep your distance, her eyes say.

Her husband looks back and forth between them. "Well, this is nice," he says. "How do you two know each other?"

"We met walking the dogs," Marion says. "Karen has a lovely dog. Husky."

Paula nods. "Yes, it was great to meet Marion, and your dog. Finn, isn't it?"

"Yes, Finn, that's right." Marion nods. "Well, it was great to see you." And she turns into the line of people who are ebbing from the hall.

"But Finn's not our dog." Her husband gazes down at Paula, his eyes smiling, keen to chat. "We're pet-sitters, visiting from San Francisco. And you've got Marilyn's name wrong. It's Marilyn, not Marion." He shrugs. "Easy mistake to make." He glances at his wife, who's had to pause, return to his side. He pats her shoulder. "Marilyn's American accent must have confused you."

"Yes, must have." Paula nods, tries to meet Marion's eyes, but they slide.

"Goodbye." Marion gives Paula a brief smile. Her voice is Californian. Her lean jaw is a determined line as she takes her husband's hand and pulls him away.

"Maybe see you around," Paula calls.

Marion doesn't respond. She and her husband, move on, merge with the throng. Paula watches. She feels sorry for Marion, her husband too. He doesn't even know his wife is English, doesn't know he's visiting her home town. Paula sighs. What a lot of subterfuge and deception Marion is carrying around. The anger Marion has shown toward the mayor lingers in Paula's mind. She'd dismissed the idea, partly because Marion is not attractive and she's so stilted and strange, but it must be—Marion must be one of the mayor's early, maybe his first, victim.

Chapter 22

Marilyn finds it hard to sit at the dining table, hard to be in the kitchen, on the stairs, in the spaces where the ghostly girl was. Don't be silly, she tells herself. The dead girl is everywhere. Ghosts can go where they like.

She's likely been watching me since I arrived.

She shudders, and wishes again that she could tell Doug about the ghost. But that's impossible. He would think her unstable, influenced by the taxi driver. Maybe the taxi driver's words did influence her.

But the dogs, the dogs saw her, and that stench...so strong. A damp subterranean smell. The scent of despair.

She crosses to the kitchen window and sees a man standing in the street below, by the bus stop. He is young, lean, with short dark hair, and he's staring up, into the kitchen.

He's staring at me.

Marilyn stares back. She does not move. She's had enough of being studied from the street. He's not a big man, but his expression is ... hostile.

Marilyn tries to outstare him. She will not be intimidated anymore. But the man in the street does not flinch or blink. Surely, if he were just anyone, he would have looked away by now. He'd be embarrassed to be caught staring into someone's home.

Marilyn steps back, into the kitchen. She puts the dogs' bowls in the sink, and turns to the fridge. Opening it, she takes out one of Doug's beers. She pulls the tab, tips it, feels the cool liquid move into her mouth, down her throat.

She drinks the whole can in a few gulping swallows then turns again to the window. The man has gone. The bus stop is empty. There are just a few people in the taxi line. Marilyn shivers. "Get a grip, Marilyn. He was just a rude guy, waiting for a bus."

She moves to the recycling and buries the can at the bottom of the blue bag, piles other garbage on top. She takes a sugar-free mint from her purse and places it on her tongue. Then, she wraps her arms around her body and moves deeper into the room. Finn follows, and she snuggles with him on the couch. Winston waddles over, lies nearby.

"I should not have gone to the *Mary Rose*, should not have seen him," she tells Finn's sweet face. "It's made me feel worse, made me buy that cream cake." After the museum event, she had stood in the street and scoffed a fat, cream-filled bun. Doug had been baffled, worried.

"I'm starving," she'd told him. "It's all the walking. Don't worry, it's only one."

He'd smiled. "Next time a healthier option, an oatcake maybe?"

And she'd nodded and swallowed down her irritation along with the thick, sweet dough.

But it had been good to see Sean heckled at the museum. And it had felt great—powerful—to raise her voice with other women. Doug had quizzed her about it, of course. She'd said she empathised with the victims, wanted to support them and fit in, had altered her accent to do so—I am a good mimic, you know. And her husband had nodded, looked hopeful that she would finally share her own damaging past with him.

"One day, I'll be able to talk about it, Doug," she'd said. And he'd accepted that—wearily, patiently—as he always did.

Now, she sits up, swings her legs off the sofa. She will go to David and question him. She'd glimpsed her brother at the *Mary Rose* but he'd quickly vanished, so his presence had taught her little. Now maybe she can ambush him leaving the office for lunch. David doesn't look like a man who skips meals.

"Sorry Finn, love," she says, getting up. "I'm going out and you can't come." And she writes a note for Doug, who is taking another tour of the *Mary Rose*, then grabs her purse and leaves.

She strides along the waterfront toward the statues of the emigrants and the city centre. She sees her brother up ahead. She knows his ambling gait, the sideways roll that tells of a youth spent on the water and sports field. "David!" she shouts.

Her brother stops. He turns, smiles, walks toward her. "Marion! What a nice surprise. I hoped I'd see you before you left. How did you find me?"

"Online, of course." Why does everyone assume she's stupid?

He nods. "I was just going to grab some lunch. You want to join me?"

"Sure." Marilyn matches his step. Hopefully, lunch will give her information about David she didn't glean at the museum. She's studied the media images of the event but didn't see her brother after his arrival. She'd seen Doug, that woman—Karen—and her own sad self, standing small at the back of the crowd. Karen had been staring at Marilyn in one picture, a look of intense curiosity on her face.

What the hell does she want?

"It's good to see you." David grins, glances at her. "It sounds so American, the way you talk."

"I do live there."

"True."

They find a table in a tomato-and-oregano- scented Italian restaurant near the clustering statues of the emigrant family. Marilyn sees the beautiful figures and thinks of her husband, who she's deceiving—again—by sitting here with the brother he doesn't know exists.

She lets David buy her a slice of vegetarian pizza and a cup of tea although she longs for a beer. "David, when I saw you the other day, when you were standing in the street looking up at the house, how did you know where to find me?"

He pauses, a mouthful of pepperoni pizza wedged in his cheek. He puts down the slice, chews slowly. "I told you, that girl, what's her name ... Karen, told me."

"Karen isn't a girl. She's in her forties. She claims to know me from school."

"I meant girl as in female," David says. "These days I never know whether to say woman or lady. Lady is old-fashioned, but woman just sounds rude to me." He shrugs. "Girl is wrong too, I guess. Sorry."

Marilyn ignores this attempt at distraction. "Tell the truth, David. Karen didn't know where I was staying, so how did you?"

His brows rise. "It's busy there, opposite Warhol Way. There's the taxi line, the bus stop. I stood there and looked about, looked up." His eyes risk hers. "Those houses have such huge windows. They're an invitation to peeping toms. I'd get net curtains if I lived there."

She doesn't believe him. But she longs to. It is plausible—almost. How many times has she caught eyes staring up from the street below? How many times has she stepped away from the glass into the shelter of the room? Maybe she should just stand in the window and stare back at everyone, stare and stare until they look away.

But you tried that, and that guy outstared you.

"You didn't hear it from someone else—Sean, for instance?"

"No." His gaze is steady.

Marilyn looks about the little restaurant, at the pictures of sunlit Italian countryside, of pretty hills and villas, all covered in a mellow glow that reminds her of California. Maybe they could get a pet-sit in Italy? She sighs, longing to be elsewhere. She wants to believe her brother. She is so tired, and the alternative is unthinkable. But she shouldn't trust him, she won't.

"David, why did you tell me all that the other day?" She frowns. "You know—about being gay and Sean blackmailing you. Why would I even care about your problems? I can believe Sean blackmailed you, but why think I'd care?"

He blanches. "Marion ... I feared seeing you. ... But when I realised you were actually here, in Portsmouth, I felt a ... kind of hope, a need to explain. It felt like ... something I must do."

Marilyn studies her brother. She has no idea whether to believe him.

His eyes slip away, return to his lunch. He picks up the pizza, bites, chews. He still sits with his arms around his plate, as if fearing someone will snatch his food. Their mother always scolded him for it.

"Did you ever try to find me, David, over all these years?"

His eyes bob up, sink. "No. I wasn't brave enough."

He chews and swallows. Marilyn is beginning to think he will not speak again until his second slice of pizza has gone when he clears his throat. "The other day I heard military planes. A couple of jets shot across the Channel. The roar of the engines reminded me of Dad. Do you remember him coming home in that flying suit? What was it called—a jumpsuit?"

"He had different suits, one that smelled of rubber and sweat, and a second green cloth one," Marilyn says. "There was a see-through plastic patch on the knee with writing on. I don't know what it said."

"It was probably his name and number, the squadron number, in case ..."

Marilyn stills. Of course—it was a message in case a pilot could no longer speak for himself. She sighs. "Daddy had friends who died in flying accidents—before he did. I always knew when someone had died because Daddy was ... subdued."

David nods. "Yes. I counted four men from his squadrons. I used to look at the squadron plaques he had on the living room wall—the ones with the coats of arms and mottos—and study the dead. It puzzled me, the way they looked as young and carefree as all the other pilots standing, grinning beside their planes. I felt there should have been some darkness, a shadow, that set them apart and marked them for early deaths."

Marilyn shivers. "Don't say that, David..."

"There were probably more than four who died," he says. "Each plane had a pilot and a navigator too. They had those ejector seats but sometimes it was too late ..."

"Sometimes they didn't have enough height and time to bail out." Marilyn pauses, surprised. It's been decades since she's thought of that military phrase. Bail out. Jumpsuit. So many years since she's heard those words, but now they feel natural on her tongue. If only Daddy had been able to bail out. "You can't bail out from the deck of an aircraft carrier," she says.

"They could have bailed out underwater," David tells her, the pizza suspended in his hand. "But they would have had to wait till the cockpit was full of water. And the cold of the sea—they were in the North Atlantic—would have incapacitated them, killed them first."

"Oh, David!" Marilyn pushes her chair back, fresh horror churning her gut.

"I'm sorry." David leans forward, reaches for her hand. "Dad's accident preoccupies me, and there's no one else I can talk to. I wonder how he came to misjudge it. The pilots had lines on deck that helped them get aligned. Maybe he miscounted them."

Marilyn lets her brother hold her hand, lets their fingers rest together for a moment, before taking hers back. She picks up her tea and drinks. The memory of her father in his flying gear is powerful. She can smell the rancid rubber and sweat as he leans down to kiss her. She sees the imprint of the tight-fitting goggles still circling his eyes, the flying helmet dangling in his hand. Her lip trembles. *Daddy, why weren't you more careful?*

David shakes his head. "Those military people are brave. ... I wonder if Dad was often scared, if he missed us when he was away onboard ship for months on end."

"He must have missed us," Marilyn says. He missed me; she thinks. "He always looked so happy, so smiley and tanned when he finally walked in the door."

David nods. "I hope it's safer now."

Marilyn smiles as a memory comes to mind. "You know, when I was a girl, I thought I'd never marry a civilian. I thought only men in uniform were real men."

David grins. "What does your husband do?"

"He's a nurse. I guess he wears a uniform!" They both chuckle. David doesn't ask how she met her husband. Perhaps he's scared to know.

David finishes his pizza, eyes Marilyn's uneaten slice. "I had another memory pop up," he says, "Mum and Dad dancing together in the living room."

Marilyn shakes her head. She can't believe this. Their parents' marriage was unhappy. Why is David pretending otherwise?

"It was some years before Dad died," David says. "They put a record on and danced in front of the fire. Mum was wearing a long red nightgown. It floated around her legs. She giggled, threw her head back. Dad smiled down at her." David's face clouds. "They looked happy. I'm glad I have that memory."

Marilyn frowns. "Are you sure, David? Where was I?"

"Probably in bed. They did love each other, Marion. I saw it. There were many bad times. Mum was a bitch. Dad should have protected you. Dad risked his life every day, but he didn't protect his own daughter."

Marilyn feels her face flush. Her shoulders and neck tighten as her head snaps to attention. "It wasn't Daddy's fault. He was busy training, going to sea"

David shakes his head. "He didn't ... rein Mum in. I think he was more interested in his career."

Marilyn's eyes mist. She looks away, her eyes fall on a painting of the Colosseum in Rome. She stares at the picture—what a beautiful ruin. She would love to visit, maybe she will. Panic is moving into her chest. David mustn't criticise their father. She breathes deep, pulls down her shoulders.

I will not have a panic attack in front of David.

"David, you're wrong. Daddy was a wonderful father. He was young. He had to think of his career. Neither of us have kids. It's easy to criticise."

David leans forward, stares deep into her eyes. His eyes are bright with pain and memory. She wonders if his gaze was ever as consistently flat as she remembers. "And why do you think we have no children, Marilyn?"

She swallows, takes a slow sip of tea.

"Are you going to eat that pizza?" David asks.

"No." She pushes it toward him.

She watches her brother eat—so solemnly, with such focus and attention—and she ponders his memory of their parents dancing. Would she have felt differently if she had such a beautiful image locked in her mind? Would she have loved her mother better, forgiven her even? After all, if Daddy loved her, Mummy could not have been all bad.

"I used to make myself small," she says, as an image of her mother's eyes, gleaming and suffused with her spiteful energy, appears in her mind. "Around Mum, I was small, so I didn't provoke her. I used to wet myself when I was alone in my room, you know, waiting for her to come punish me. I was ... so scared

I peed my knickers. I think she was worse—angrier—when Daddy was away."

"Yes." David's eyes soften to sympathy and he reaches across the table to where her hand rests by her cup. She snatches it back and tucks it in her lap. I still do that, she thinks, make myself small. I'm not a real adult, an individual, like other people are.

She forces a smile. "In fact, David, I assumed they married because Mum got pregnant with you. Back then, that's what people did. Mum and Dad were always vague about their anniversary date, there were no wedding pictures in our house."

David chuckles. "Probably true."

"What about Sean and all these sexual assault allegations?" she asks.

David stills. "What about them?"

"He hasn't changed. Why are you supporting the career of a violent rapist?"

David runs a hand through his sparse hair. "I don't know if the allegations are true, Marion."

"I can't believe that." Marilyn gets up. She hadn't known she was going to leave; her legs are being moved by anger. "Thanks for lunch." She grabs her purse and jacket, turns away.

"Marion ..." David protests, spreads his hands. "Marion, let's talk about this."

She spins to him. "It's all you, isn't it, David? As long as you're all right, as long as Sean helps your career ...Why don't you speak up, David, do the right thing? Are you ashamed?"

"Marion, hush." He glances about, embarrassed, into the stilled faces of a middle-aged couple of diners, who are looking displeased.

Marilyn glares at the couple. She's filled with an unstoppable, furious energy. "Eat your pizza," she tells them. She turns, stares at another, younger, couple who are watching her with interest. "And you two—eat up."

"Marion!" David is horrified.

"Why David?" She hears her voice, high and outraged. She interrogates the room. "Why won't you speak?"

"Marion ..." He sighs, long and deep. His eyes are dull, yet bright, both sad and angry. "Why won't you?"

Chapter 23

Marion is on the move again. From the shelter of Salty's, Paula watches her stride from Warhol Way and turn right, in the direction of the Common. Marion is wearing an auburn wig, but it doesn't disguise her. No one walks like Marion. As usual, her lean body is a curved, forward-leaning exclamation mark, her gait implying energy and desperation.

Paula sighs as she leaves the café and crosses the road. She can't quit now. If, as Paula expects, Marion walks to Sean's house, Paula plans to confront her and give Marion an approximate version of the truth about her own involvement in her life. That won't be pleasant, but Paula can say she was employed to find Marion. She won't say who by, although Marion might guess.

Over the two days since the *Mary Rose* event, Paula has pondered Marion's situation. She's decided to ask Marion outright about Sean Adams. If Marion confirms he assaulted her, Paula will try to persuade her to go to the police. So far, no charges have been laid against the mayor, although journalists report that police are investigating the complaints. They better hurry up, Paula thinks, or Sean Adams will be elected to an even bigger, national office where he'll do even more damage.

"Come on, Husky," she says. And they set off at a safe distance behind Marion and Finn.

Paula has made her plans, but she hopes to be thwarted. She'd like Marion to slow down and stroll along the waterfront. She'd like her to stop for fish and chips or ice cream. It's an unusually bright warm day, the kind that invites relaxation amid the season's chill. Paula hopes to see Marion sit on a bench and gaze at the Channel with lovely Finn. If that happens, Paula will turn for home and never see Marion Taylor again.

Paula wishes this, but doesn't expect it. And she knows as soon as Marion turns left at the Common and takes the road that leads to Sean's street that it won't happen. When Marion reaches Brighton Road, she turns left. Paula installs herself with Husky in the same spot as last time, at the far end of the road. She watches Marion stride up and down Brighton Road. Marion is pretending to be walking her dog in the quiet, attractive street. She doesn't stop or stare at Sean's home, but she can't prevent her pace from slowing as she passes, her eyes from straying to his vivid front door.

Paula sighs when she sees Sean's security detail. The big man is sitting in a different vehicle—a pale blue VW this time, parked further from Sean's, but he's watching Marion in his wing mirror. Marion is clueless—that silly, ill-fitting wig. Doesn't she realise that Finn alone gives her away? Leave, Marion, she thinks. Go back to Warhol Way or take all the courage you have and go to the police. Better still, return to San Francisco.

As if overhearing her thoughts, Marion turns and begins to stride toward Paula's end of the street. Paula steps back so she will encounter Marion more naturally. *Okay, here goes*. She steps into Marion's path.

"You!" Marion's face turns crimson.

"Marion." Paula steps toward her. "I need to talk to you, about something important." She puts up her hand as Marion opens her mouth. "Hear me out, please. I want to discuss Sean Adams."

Marion's features close up and her face assumes its mask. "I have nothing to say about Sean Adams."

"Then why are you standing in his street gazing at his house—again? Why did you attend his event at the *Mary Rose* and shout at him?" Paula softens her tone. "You should know, Marion, that I'm a private investigator. I was employed to find you. I tracked you to America, to San Francisco, and here, to your home town."

Marion stares. Paula can see a thin blue vein at the side of her mouth. It's bulging, pulsing like a subterranean river.

"I knew you were lying." Marion spits the words.

Paula nods. "I was trying to protect you, am trying to protect you."

"Who from—Sean?"

"I hope to find out." Paula hears her own voice sounding steady, reassuring. It feels good, familiar to hear her authoritative self. Once a cop, always a cop. But the security guard might follow Marion, might even be watching them. She glances about. The security man has not appeared, not on foot or in the VW, but she turns, indicates the darkened window of the restaurant adjacent to the boutique

"Please Marion, give me a few minutes. I'll buy you lunch, it's the least I can do." She indicates the restaurant's open door, which is spilling a deep spicy aroma. "Please, the dogs will be okay. I've taken Husky here. He loves their naan bread."

Marion glances about and seems to catch Paula's caution. "All right." And she leads Finn inside.

They settle themselves about halfway down the restaurant, far enough from the window not to be seen by passers-by. The dogs allow a young female server to pet and fuss them, then they settle on the floor, their snouts gently touching. Paula smiles. At least this drama is bringing Husky some exercise and companionship.

They order chai tea from the young woman, then Marilyn changes her mind and requests a beer. They order samosas, onion bhaji, and some plain naan bread for the dogs then settle back and look at each other. Marion removes her sunglasses and takes a long drink of beer. Paula is about to come right out and ask if Sean ever attacked her, when Marion lifts her eyes to Paula's and says, "He raped me. Sean Adams raped me."

Paula feels horror prickle, cold as ice, across her skin. She'd not fully expected rape. She'd imagined assault, harassment.

They were so young. ... On the other hand—look at the allegations. We've been deceived, she thinks. Jane voted for him.

Marion looks and sounds different now—slowed, her hysteria dissolved into plain statement of fact. This explains Marilyn, Paula thinks: her childish voice; the doll-like face and body; her passive eyes that leap to violence. Paula's seen it before, how victims become stuck at the time of an attack, how they cannot move on and become normal mature individuals. Marilyn is one of the frozen ones.

"When did it happen?"

"Years ago. I was 13, Sean 17. He and my brother David were friends. They were on the football and rugby teams together."

Paula thinks of Marion's evasive brother, his shifting eyes, the body that speaks of former athleticism. "Where did it happen?" she asks gently.

"Southsea Wood. The boys played football near there, on the green." Marion doesn't blink. "Sean raped me, and I've never spoken of it—only to therapists, and they haven't helped, or not as much as I thought ..."

"And what do you want now?"

Marion stares into Paula's face. She seems to be wearing brown contact lenses. "He should be punished," she says. "He's still abusing women. You've seen the news. The latest woman says he grabbed her by the throat." She shakes her head. "I feel ..." Her hand drifts to her heart and her face folds into grief. "I feel so much for those girls, feel I must protect them."

Paula nods. "Will you go to the police?"

Marion's eyes dip. She picks up her beer glass, wraps her hands around it.

"The police?" Paula prompts.

"I can't." Marion's eyes bob up. "My husband doesn't know. I can't tell him. He'll be ... he'll think I've deceived him, that he doesn't know me."

"Does he even know you're English?"

Marion flushes, takes a sip of beer. "No."

There's a silence, and Paula thinks how English Marion sounds when they are just two women sitting in a restaurant in their home town. She drinks her tea. She sips the rich, fragrant liquid and wonders what this small, vulnerable woman has in mind for the charismatic mayor.

"Thank you," she says as a middle-aged man—the server's father, maybe—brings their food.

Marion drinks and puts down her glass. She's silent as the plates are set down. Then she starts speaking, a sneering note in her tone. "And who are you—really? Is your name really Karen?"

Paula flinches. "You're right. My name's Paula Moore. I'm a former police officer, now a private investigator."

"Who asked you to find me?"

Paula shakes her head. "I can't say."

Marion smirks. "The mayor or someone working for him. Tell me one thing: Did you tell anyone I was staying at Warhol Way?"

Paula hesitates, shakes her head. "No." She wishes she were a better liar; she can't admit she told Hugh and David where Marion was staying without revealing they hired her.

Marion's eyes dip again. Paula picks up her fork, lifts an onion bhaji and a samosa onto her plate. She is hungry, maybe it's all the walking, maybe it's all the tension. As she adds sauces, she glances at Marion. The other woman does not move. She just stares at her empty plate.

Paula eats and says nothing. She watches the man and the girl move around their restaurant. The girl's voice reveals she was raised in Portsmouth. The man speaks with a foreign accent—Indian, Pakistani? Paula wonders how life has been for him, opening this restaurant, building a clientele in this cold, grey country. Was it hard to gauge how 'authentic' his food should be for English palates? Did he want to give up, flee back to the warm climate that birthed him?

"The food is delicious," Paula says.

Marion picks up her fork, messes with a samosa.

Paula chews and looks about. She admires the large bronze buddha that sits on the floor by the bar, a trickling stream of water flowing across its outspread hands. She eats and waits for Marion to tell her what she intends to do.

But Paula has finished her share of the food, and Marion remains mute. "Okay boys." Paula breaks the naan bread into pieces. "One piece for Husky, one piece for Finn, one piece for Husky, one piece for Finn. ... Good boys. Delicious, isn't it?"

The dogs eat and gaze at her with deep affection. She wonders about asking for some water. They could share a bowl; the staff wouldn't mind. Marion has eaten nothing, although her beer is gone.

Paula's phone pings, and she glances down: *Lesbo cop, you better watch your fat, juicy ass.*

The abuse is so repetitive, tedious. Still, the message sparks a small, skipping fear. When will this hell stop?

"It wasn't your fault, Marion," she says. "The rape, all that was done to you when you were a child, none of it was your fault. I hope you know that."

Marion says nothing, just stares at the table top.

Paula sighs, impatience beginning to tighten the tension in her head. "Marion, what do you intend to do about Sean Adams?"

Marion looks up, straight into Paula's eyes. "Someone must stop him," she says. "And I feel it must be me."

Chapter 24

It feels good to hear herself say the words, although they don't include the key words 'poison' or 'kill'. Marilyn expects Paula will know what she means, but she's glad she hasn't said it out loud. She would sound crazed and ridiculous—a skinny, weak woman pitting herself against a man with physical and political power. Anyone would laugh or summon a psychiatrist. "He's got away with it so long," she says.

Paula's face is solemn. "Marion, if you're harbouring thoughts of revenge, you must abandon them. If you have a complaint, go to the police. I can help with that—come with you, offer guidance, support."

Marilyn shakes her head. "I told you, my husband doesn't know and I will not risk him finding out. It's too late for the police." She feels rage rise in her, the hot, furious anger she's felt watching other women on the news—women who've had their allegations ignored or mocked, who've been scoffed at, diminished, condemned.

"People wouldn't believe me." She breathes, tries to keep her voice calm. "You know how defence lawyers torture victims in court. I can't even remember the exact date it happened, what I did after the rape, how I got home. My factual memories are blurred. Only Sean's actions, only the attack, are clear in my mind." She pulls down her shoulders, blinks. "Sorry ... but I get upset, I hate talking about it. It was terrible to be in the same room as him at the *Mary Rose*. I thought I was going to throw up."

Paula reaches out, pats her arm. "Marion, I said—none of this was your fault."

Marilyn flinches away. She doesn't want this trickster's sympathy. She resents the blend of personal and professional concern in Paula's voice. She has seen many broken people like me, Marion thinks.

I am not just a number.

Paula takes back her hand and reaches into her jacket. She pulls out a wad of cards confined in an elastic band and works one free then pushes it across the table. "Here's my card. You can call me anytime, day or night."

Marilyn frowns at the stiff piece of paper and considers rejecting it. But she picks it up and slips it in her jacket. She might need it. "Thanks."

"I want to help you, Marion, but if anything happens to Sean Adams, I'll be compelled to go to the police. The U.K. has an extradition treaty with the U.S."

"Of course." Marilyn sighs. *Everyone treats me like an idiot.*

"You know you've been seen," Paula says. "By Sean's security guard."

Marilyn feels her heart still. "How do you know?"

"I saw him notice you—twice. He was sitting in different cars outside the house. He was at the *Mary Rose* too. There were cameras—overhead shots of the space. If they'd been looking for you ..."

Marilyn's pulse re-animates. Is Sean watching her? Maybe she wasn't imagining being followed? "I think Sean's worried about how the women he's attacked might damage him. His staff are trying to find out who all the victims are, whether they'll go to the media, the police. The young ones are speaking out and there might be older victims like me—women who could show his lifelong pattern."

"Exactly," Paula says with a nod. "If you step forward, you'll sound more plausible because of the recent allegations. You'll do more good that way, Marion. You can help those girls without risking yourself."

"Without risking myself!" Marilyn hears her own harsh laugh. "You haven't been listening. I won't be interrogated, humiliated. I will not risk my marriage."

"Marion, I could go to the police myself, tell them what Sean did to you."

"I'll deny it!" Marilyn shouts.

"I could go to your husband—now. He'd help you."

"You bloody dare!" Marilyn feels her face burn. "You bloody ... trickster." Tears threaten, and she blinks hard. "You don't understand how lonely I've been, how I've worked ... so ... hard ... to become half normal, to have a relationship ... And I'm not there yet." She shakes her head. "I hope I live a long time so that, by the time I die, I am finally normal. I want to know what it feels like to be a regular person. I'm only this good because Doug is so kind. ... He was my nurse, that's how we met; no other man would want me ..." She stops, breathes. "I refuse to go backwards. Don't betray me."

Paula says nothing. Her eyes glow with sympathy, which Marilyn hates but at least she's got through to the other woman.

Paula nods. "I understand. But if anything happens to Sean Adams ..."

"Yes, you've said. You've said, you've said."

Paula looks away, stares at her hands.

Marilyn breathes, pulls down her shoulders, hears her jaw click. One beer wasn't enough. It's terrible to discuss all this with a stranger who's pursued and lied to her. She glances at the door, at Finn at her feet, and considers fleeing. But she doesn't. She feels unsafe, yet she stays. Why? Does she actually want, need to talk?

"There was a smell on Sean's breath," she says. "Alcohol, maybe something else." She recalls his arm across her face and alarm uncurls in her belly, rises, heats and slicks her skin. Sweat crawls under her hair, *Breathe, Marilyn, breathe.* "And he's kept ..." She shakes her head. "Those girls, they're just kids, like I was ..."

"Maybe you were his first victim," Paula says. "Maybe he ... got a taste for it. Do you have any reason to be ... concerned?"

Marilyn feels herself flinch. "You mean violence—more violence? I did feel someone was following me as I walked by the water. But there was no one there. I am very ... jumpy. I likely imagined it."

Paula nods. "It's unlikely anything will happen. Don't worry."

"I don't feel safe in that house," Marilyn says. "It's so big, lots of hiding places, and yet the main rooms, the important ones, have no privacy. ... Everyone stares up from the street, so many eyes ... What does the security guard look like?"

"He's big, tall and white. Have you seen him?"

"No."

"Keep an eye out, but as I said, nothing's likely to happen."

Marilyn says nothing. She doesn't feel comforted although the security guard doesn't sound like the skinny man who stared up from the street.

I'm on Sean's radar.

"When do you leave for America?"

"In ten days. I can't wait to go. Being here has been too much, much harder than I expected. I actually hoped for a meeting with Sean, an apology. I'd hoped for ... peace, a renewed sense of home."

"It must feel strange, staying in a stranger's home, with their pets?"

Marilyn nods. "A pet-sit always feels weird at first. ... For the first day or two, I feel disoriented, grouchy. But then I get used to the house and routine and it becomes fun—all the different neighbourhoods, the pets. It feels like we get to ... live more, sample different lives."

"Do you feel American now?"

Marilyn shrugs. "I guess. ... I go from day to day."

"Are people in San Francisco afraid of earthquakes, The Big One? I wondered about that when I was there. And there's all the wildfires now, climate change."

"Sure, but you make plans. Doug and I have emergency bags packed and we've arranged where to meet, assuming we both escape the earthquake. We keep a supply of things we'll need if the apartment survives—toilet paper, soap. And one-dollar bills, because no one will have power, be able to make change, use credit cards."

Paula nods. "I can't imagine living with that threat. But you all do, every day."

"There are things that scare me more. And a big city can be a refuge, a distraction, from ..." Marilyn touches her chest, her head. "What's inside ..." She sighs. "You tricked me, Paula."

Paula frowns. "You can't blame me for finding you, Marion. It's my job. And it wasn't smart of you to hang around outside the mayor's house."

Marilyn glares. "They wouldn't have known who I was if not for you. I'd just be a woman walking a dog ..."

Paula says nothing. Marilyn is pleased that at least she's not denying she was employed by the mayor's office.

"Why did you go to his house?" Paula asks.

Marilyn shrugs. "Fascination, fury, trying to get my courage up. I don't want to be a victim anymore. I don't want to be a woman who's pitied and bullied. I've had enough of feeling weak ..."

Paula leans forward, reaches her hands toward Marilyn. She tries not to recoil.

"Marion, you are a brave woman. You've built a life, overcome many difficult things, not just the rape. Use your courage to keep moving on, to live, with your husband."

"I don't need a lecture." Marilyn feels her body stiffen.

"I still hope you'll go to the police, Marion." Paula sits back, withdraws her fingers. "We, the police, are supportive of victims. There are specially trained female officers, counsellors, nurses."

"No." Marilyn shakes her head.

Did you hear a word I said?

Paula sighs. "Well, I must get going." She glances at Husky, who stretches his limbs and stands as if responding to her words. Paula waves at the young woman standing by the till. "Bill, please. I'm off to visit my mother in the care home," she tells Marilyn. "With my son. I'm looking forward to seeing them together." She shrugs. "But you never know how teens will be, they are so moody. And Neil's been ... frosty since his mum—his other mum—and I split."

Marilyn wonders why Paula has shared this personal information.

Probably trying to win me over.

"Yes, loss is difficult for kids." Marilyn gets up. "Come, Finn. Thank you for lunch."

Paula nods. "Take care of yourself, Marion."

"Yes. And it's Marilyn."

"Sorry, Marilyn. Remember, you can call me, anytime."

Marilyn walks back to Warhol Way. Several times, she checks her shoulder. Is she being followed by Sean's security guard? She's glad she has Finn with her and glad when she sees the looming glass bulk of Warhol Way. It's good to hear the front door close behind her, and good not to hear the dogs barking manically.

As she walks up to the first floor, she realises it had been a relief, a lightening, to tell Paula about the rape. She'd left out her brother's role in the attack. The omission hadn't been deliberate exactly, the words just hadn't come out of her mouth. Perhaps I don't hate him anymore, she thinks, maybe it's true what they say—that blood is thick.

Before the mirror at the top of the stairs, she pauses to remove Laura's auburn wig. Then she tips her head forward and takes out the brown contact lenses. She looks at herself in the glass. *Hello again Plain Jane.* In truth, she'd felt like herself all along. The disguise hadn't made her feel any braver. Paula had recognised her.

As she reaches the kitchen, Winston heaves himself up from his bed and wheezes over to say hello. Marilyn thinks of Sean's kids. If anything happens to Sean, they'll be left without a father, as she was, as David was. But losing Sean wouldn't hurt like losing their father had. It wouldn't be the same thing at all.

While she waits for the kettle to boil, she googles Portsmouth private detective, Paula Moore. Reports of Paula's exit from the police force appear and Marilyn reads with interest. She learns how Paula admitted to bludgeoning a suspect who kicked her dog. Good for you, Marilyn thinks. Poor Husky. She smiles to see Paula's Sherlock Holmes-themed ad.

Paula had threatened to go to the police if anything happened to Sean. But realistically, what could Paula do? She's a disgraced officer, a new detective who's lied to a subject. She's not going to want any of this to come out. She'd better not speak to Doug. But again, would she, really? She doesn't know how Doug would react. Neither do I, Marilyn thinks. She smiles—she'd liked Paula better when she'd finally admitted who she was and stopped pretending.

She walks to the kitchen. It's time to get Winston's raw meat out of the freezer. She'll let it thaw while she walks the dogs. Then it will be time to give them dinner and Doug will be back from the Historic Dockyard. He's visiting an exhibition on military training that Marilyn hadn't wanted to attend. She's growing warier of the dockyard. It's feeling like a trap, as if, when she walks into it, she falls back into the sadness—her own, her family's, her city's.

She walks upstairs, strides to her suitcase and packs away Laura's wig and the brown contacts. She takes out her photos and kneels on the soft white carpet and gazes at a picture of her father. It's the one with him standing alone and proud in his full uniform. The bars of his rank, lieutenant commander, gleam gold at his wrists. One hand rests atop the handle of the sword that sweeps to the floor in a smooth, gleaming line from his hip. Marilyn stares at her father's proud face. He looks so young. "Oh Daddy," she murmurs and she smiles. "Why couldn't you have been a banker?"

She tucks the picture away with the others in her case. What would it feel like to show this photo to Doug? To tell him about her hero father? It would be good to create a connection between the two men she loves. Would Doug smile and say, "Marilyn, I see the resemblance—I see your father in you."

Downstairs, Winston's meat is thawing. "Not long boy," she tells his round, fleshy face as it appears at her knees. "It'll soon be dinnertime." She should clean their bowls. Yesterday's food is still crusted on the silver chrome. She's getting lax.

She picks up the dirty bowls and looks from the kitchen window. The young man is there again, the thin one with the short dark hair. He's staring up, he is staring at her. He smiles, a thin, knowing grimace.

He knows who I am!

She backs into the room then darts to the fridge and grabs a beer. She pulls the tab, fingers trembling. *Who the hell is he?*

Chapter 25

"Paula, how you doin'?"

Paula smiles. The sound of Rob's voice takes her back to the street where she grew up, back to the years when Rob and her older cousin Andy ruled the neighbourhood. They'd been bad lads, not vicious, but they'd pushed their luck. Rob had spent time inside for handling stolen goods. Fortunately, Andy sorted himself out before he got a record.

"I'm okay, you?" She hears the smile in her voice. It feels great to speak to him. She can almost feel the sand and dirt under her nails, the ice cream on her tongue.

"Can't complain." Rob's tone holds the deep good cheer of a radio host. "What can I do for you?"

Paula feels bad she's not calling just to say hello—next time she will. "Do you know anyone who can trace phone numbers? I've been getting abusive texts. I need to know who's behind it." She hears her voice wobble and swallows hard. "I need to do more on social media, for my business, but I can't get going till I know who the crazies are. I need it to stop."

"Sorry to hear that, Paula. Is this since the ... incident with the scrote and your dog?"

"Yes."

"That was bad luck. Sorry to hear about you and Jane splitting too."

"Thanks. I'm okay."

"I do know someone with those skills," Rob says. "But why don't you just go to the police, the telecom company?"

"Not yet." Paula isn't going to tell Rob that she's trying to avoid her former colleagues. None of them have reached out to her, asked how she's doing. She might as well be dead. Fuck 'em.

"It will cost a few hundred at least, Paula. That okay?"

"Yep, no problem." She'll find the money somehow.

She hangs up and walks toward her mum's care home. She thinks about Rob and Andy and wonders if Andy escaped jail because he had a stable home. Paula's seen it often—financial instability, losing a parent, can cause kids to lose their way, make them embittered and explosive, like directionless little missiles. I've gotta remember that Neil needs me, even if Jane makes it hard to see him, even if he doesn't want to see me. She winces at the thought of Neil rejecting her but she won't be proud and keep her distance.

Neil needs me whether he knows it or not.

Her heart lurches as her phone pings. It's a text from Sue: *Zumba today, rocked my skinny hips.* Paula returns a winking emoji. Neil's not the only one who needs her.

Her son is sitting with her mum when Paula arrives at the care home. It's a joy to see them together, her boy perched on her mother's bed, his long legs wound beneath him so as not to rest his weight on his grandmother's frail body. There's a bright happiness in her mum's eyes. Neil is telling his grandmother about a musical performance at school.

"It'll be awesome," he says. "A few of us are going to play heavy metal, I mean heavy. It'll be the finale." He grins. "The parents will hate it; some might even walk out."

Paula and her mother chuckle. The thought of people striding out, running away, makes Paula think again of Marion. Paula's seen fantasies of revenge before in victims of violent crime. It's a form of self-defence, a way of trying to take back agency and dignity. Victims don't understand why prosecutors struggle to secure convictions. Defence lawyers are tricky, always finding some loophole, some slipup in procedure, to get their scumbag clients off. Most sentences are a joke, an insult to victims and hard-working officers and prosecutors.

But victims rarely strike back, however much the system lets them down. The reason is simple—they're not violent people. Poor Marion. But she'll soon be gone. She'll spend another few days striding about Portsmouth and then she'll fly back to America. And Paula's new case is going smoothly. The wife suspects her husband of having an affair with a woman in Eastbourne. All Paula has to do is trail the spouse along the coast and get some incriminating photos. That'll cost money for the hire car and petrol, but she'll get it back in expenses and it's a nice drive along the shore.

"Paula, what are you thinking about?" her mum says. "Your face is like the changing weather—first a frown then a smile."

"Just work. Sorry."

"At least you're not walking a beat anymore," Lorraine says. "That makes you a bit safer. And since Brexit we don't get all those foreign criminals coming over."

"There's always criminals, Mum."

"But now they are our own, English, criminals."

Paula grins. "Homegrown scrotes are all right, are they?" She thinks of tonight's lentil supper. Maybe if she spices them up with paprika? She's always loved a good curry, a hot chilli.

"What's your new case, Mum?" Neil asks.

Paula grins, delighted her son is interested and that he calls her 'Mum'. "It's a marital dispute, wife suspects husband of an affair. Don't tell anyone. It's confidential."

"Well, you haven't told us their names," her mother says.

Paula nods. "True."

"Will you come to the performance, Mum? It's Friday night," Neil says. "I know you don't like metal but, you know, you always come to my shows."

Paula feels her face redden with happiness. It's short notice, maybe he hadn't planned to invite her, but who cares? She wonders if Jane will be there. How will she handle it if Jane turns up with another woman? *You'll handle it fine.*

"Mama is coming too, of course." Uncertainty flickers in Neil's eyes. "But you two can sit in the same room together now, right?"

"Of course." Paula nods. 'Mama'—how pretentious. Jane isn't French. She could have been Mummy to Paula's Mum. But again, who cares? Neil is forgiving her. He's forgiving her for embarrassing him, for being thrown out of the police force, for splitting up their home—well, she didn't do that alone.

"I wish I could go," Lorraine says.

"I wish you could, Gran." Neil slips his fingers through his grandmother's. Paula smiles. He's a good lad, loving, empathetic.

Family is the only thing that really matters.

"Never mind, Mum," she says. "I'll record the performance on my phone." She grins. "When you hear the metal, you'll be glad you couldn't go."

Neil laughs. "Yes!"

They stay with Lorraine for a cup of tea and a biscuit then Paula walks her son home along the waterfront. He's working hard he tells her. He wants to study business at university, maybe go into tech. Good God, Paula thinks, have we raised someone with financial acumen? That must be Jane.

"I'll see you at school," Neil says, as they reach the house.

"Sounds great." Paula gives her son a long, tight hug. Over his shoulder, she stares at the beautiful, well-kept Southsea home where she lived for so long. She feels a detachment. Those bricks are Jane's now, maybe they always were.

"There haven't been any more … incidents, have there?" she asks. "No more spray-painting, abuse?" The house is clean, with no sign of the earlier drama.

Neil shakes his head. "No, Mama put in extra security lights and cameras. It's so bright at night it's hard to sleep."

Paula grins. "Good to know. Do kids at school … say anything about me leaving the force, being gay?"

"Nah, it's all good."

Paula doesn't believe him, but is grateful for the lie. He does seem okay. If it was bad, she'd see it in his face. "Don't put up with any shit," she says. "Go to the principal, let me know."

"I'm okay, Mum." And he hugs her so tight she blinks tears.

"Later, Mum," he says and he turns and walks up the front path and into the house that used to be home to all three of them. Paula feels a small pang seeing him go, but it's a pang, not a stab.

She turns and begins to walk back to her flat and Husky, who will be desperate for a walk. She sees a slim woman, fifties, striding along the waterfront—what's with all these warrior older women these days—and again thinks of Marion. The way she'd stared at the mayor with that furtive, furious intensity, her shouting, her stalking, her stubborn, impassive face when questioned.

Can I really be one hundred percent sure Marion won't attempt something stupid?

Paula frowns, pauses. Could there be a genuine, dangerous bloodlust behind Marion's doll-like stare?

She pulls out her phone and calls Rob.

"Twice in one day!"

Paula grins. "Hi Rob, this is about something different. There's a woman. She's pissed with the mayor. I fear she might do something ... silly."

"There's a lot of women upset with the mayor."

"Yep, but I'm concerned about this one. Can you let me know if you hear of her looking for any kind of weapon? Her name's Marilyn Brooks, nee Taylor, could also go by Marion. She might try and acquire a weapon under an entirely false name but I doubt she'd think of it. She lives in America, sounds American—sometimes. She's thin, nervy, early forties, blondish. Let me know if she tries to get a gun or something."

"A gun?"

"She lives in America, Rob. They sell guns in Walmart. You know Walmart?"

"I do. Okay Paula."

"Thanks, Rob."

She ends the call and wonders what he's up to and how he lives. She visualises his stocky body standing by the water at Eastney, hands deep in his pockets, his face and manner still open and friendly despite a life that should have taught him to be guarded. She sighs—no doubt Rob's been hearing a lot of scrotes rejoicing in her downfall. She must call him more often, keep in touch. She lost touch with him when she married Jane. Rob was never Jane's cup of tea. She sighs, feeling bad about letting Rob down, about losing herself.

Her phone pings—Sue. *Ran 5k, am Superwoman.*

Paula grins. *Let's get together soon.*

Sue responds at once. *When? Salty's?*

Yes. Will be in touch.

Paula walks and wonders why she didn't state a time—she's not exactly busy. She's still avoiding people, even Sue. But she's enjoying her walk. It's a warm day, suggesting spring. She darts to the edge of the pavement as a man walking the other way almost collides with her because he's staring at his phone.

"Watch where you're going," Paula says. The man—not even young—looks at her blankly.

"You nearly walked into me." Paula nods at the phone in his hand. "Be careful. You could be hit by a car."

"Thanks for the warning, Mum, or is it Grandma?" His eyes scan her breasts, assess her hips in their tight jeans. "Sexy Grandma. Anyone ever say you look like Marilyn Monroe?"

"In your dreams." Paula gives her standard response and strides away. *Grandma?* She frowns then grins as she feels the sun emerge from a cloud and slant warmth onto her face. She feels something loosening, freeing in her mind and chest. Tears swim in her eyes as she realises she is returning to herself.

Chapter 26

"Look what Winston can do." Doug leans down and takes Winston's collar. He leads him away from the kitchen and into the middle of the living room. Marilyn watches.

"Okay boy. Let's go." And Doug picks up his pace, begins to run Winston, in a slow trot, toward the low-slung sofa, his hand tucked inside Winston's collar.

"Doug, you'll hurt him!" Marilyn yells as Winston lifts into the air and thuds onto the sofa beside Finn who is resting after a long walk, his snout on a cushion decorated with an image of a stout English bulldog.

"Well done. Winston!" Doug whoops and claps. He turns to Marilyn. "Yesterday, he was standing and staring at the sofa, grunting. I realised he wanted to get up, to lie with Finn, so I taught him to take a running jump."

Winston is settling in beside Finn. He's heaving his big body around to find just the right spot on the sofa. Finally, he puts his head down near Finn's, rests on another bulldog-themed cushion.

"They do look cute with their heads together," Marilyn says. "I'll take a photo, send it to the owners." She takes the photo, checks it. "Perfect." She types: *Two happy pooches enjoying each other's company* and presses send. She glances at the resting dogs. "This house needs some cushions with border collies on. Maybe I'll find one in that store opposite—John Lewis—and leave it as a gift. Don't let Winston injure himself. He could hurt his legs if he lands wrong."

"He'll be okay," Doug says. "Don't worry."

He walks over, leans in to kiss her cheek. He gazes out of the kitchen window to where tired lines of bus and taxi passengers huddle against the grey day. Marilyn shudders and turns away. She doesn't want to see the street, that intense young man. She's been avoiding the window, then succumbing to it, all morning.

"Weather's getting wild again," Doug says. "It's been a good time here, hasn't it? But I'm looking forward to getting home, seeing real sunshine. People here must get depressed, living in this climate."

Marilyn nearly tells her husband that Portsmouth can be glorious—that warm spring and summer days can be golden, softer, and just as uplifting as sunny days in California, that they feel even more precious because they're rarer. It's a shame Doug won't experience a full English spring, but he has praised the daffodils and pansies already sprouting on every patch of grass.

She nods. "It is gloomy here."

"Okay then," he says. "I'm off to the dockyard, thanks for not minding. I'm going to tour that ship that was in the Second

World War. Did you know that some of the Allied forces sailed from here on D-Day?"

Marilyn shakes her head, feigning ignorance, and wonders how Doug can not see how the history of this place runs through her.

His brow furrows. "You feel all right? You look pale."

"I'm just tired, couldn't sleep again last night—the wind and the drunks."

"You've been doing too much—all the dog-walking, sight-seeing too."

He leans in, pulls her close, and Marilyn rests her head on his shoulder. His arms tighten and he lifts her face, drops light kisses on her lips, her neck. "I could go see that mouldy old ship later," he murmurs.

Marilyn softens and breathes in the familiar soap and masculine scent of Doug's skin. Her shoulders fall, her jaw and neck loosen. Doug makes everything better.

"How about we make out right here?" he whispers against her hair.

"On the sofa, with the dogs?"

"No here, on the kitchen floor." He pulls back, gazes at her, his eyes bright and cheeky.

She twists her head toward the kitchen window. "So, all the people in the street can see us?"

"They won't see—we'll be on the floor. Okay then, on the other sofa, the loveseat. We'll cozy up."

And he takes her hand, leads her toward the sofa that faces the patio and the tiny elevated garden.

Marilyn feels a pulse of daring warm her body. "The dogs might wake up," she says. "You know Finn always sticks his snout in when we hug."

"I can handle Finn." Doug lifts her T-shirt and undoes her bra. He pulls down her jeans, her panties. His hands and eyes are warm, focused. Marilyn glances at the patio door as if someone might suddenly appear. Not possible. The patio is raised above the street. It's got walls around it. Maybe the owners will come back early? No. They're in Australia. Maybe the ghost is watching.

Stop being uptight.

Doug has thrown off his clothes. He tips her back onto the love seat and lowers himself onto her. "I love you, Marilyn," he murmurs. "I love you."

Tears fill her eyes. "I love you too." She doesn't say it often, not enough. *I'll say it more.* Doug deserves more love, more affection and attention. *More than I give him.*

His mouth moves down her neck, slips over her breasts. She trembles, both from the room's cold air and from something she can't at first identify—desire.

"Honey." She wraps her arms around his neck, seeks his mouth. "Doug."

"Oh Marilyn." His breath is hot in her face. He's speeding up, but she slows, kisses him. "Don't rush," she murmurs. "That old ship isn't going anywhere."

"I want to look at you." He pulls back. There is glowing love in his eyes, a half-smile on his lips. For a moment she's alarmed. This is too much, this nakedness. She longs to shut her eyes, to hide from his gaze, but she won't hide from Doug, not anymore. She wants it too—real love and connection. She smiles, returns his gaze, although her eyes still want to blink, to shut him out, just for a moment. "I love you, Doug."

"I love you, my fellow adventurer." And she sees gleaming tears in his eyes, and she comes so fast and unexpected that for a moment her mind rushes to absorb what's happening. She is coming with Doug, with the man she loves, like a normal woman.

They lie together, and Marilyn holds him, feels his hair tickle her chin, his sweat cool and prickle her skin. She's cold and uncomfortable but she doesn't move.

Doug grins. He looks happy and proud as he pulls back and smiles down at her. "You know, the other day I ran past a sex store called *Pleasurable Gifts for Sexy Couples.*" His grin grows. "How about I buy us a memento of our time in Portsmouth?"

She blushes, giggles with a deep happiness.

"Come on," he says. "How about a pleasurable gift?"

She shakes her head. "We can't take sex toys through customs. Imagine the border guards going through our bags. ... There's plenty of stores like that in San Francisco." She smiles. "Let's get something when we get home."

Doug's fingers find hers. He lifts her hand to his mouth, kisses it. "Okay, sexy lady."

He pulls back, peels his body from hers. "Well, if I'm going to see that ship ... or do you want me to stay?" He glances over at the dogs, snoozing on the sofa. "We could walk the boys together, watch some TV. We haven't got many more chances to watch the British quiz shows you like."

"No, you go," Marilyn sits up. She reaches for her T-shirt that lies on the floor. She's tired and exhilarated.

"Okay, if you're sure." Doug dresses quickly. He leans in, softly kisses her. "I'll see you later, my love."

And Marilyn marvels at how quickly he's ready to face the world. She's glad he doesn't feel the need to shower, to wash her from his skin. "Yes, see you later."

"Leave the dogs till I get back."

"No, I'll do it." And she will. She will not let herself cower inside because there was a rude, menacing man in the street.

Even if Sean sent him to scare me, I will not be intimidated.

It takes her a while to wash and dress, to smooth her hair. Both dogs are awake and anxious to get outside by the time she's ready.

"Come on fellas." She takes Winston's meat from the freezer—she should have done it before, it'll need microwaving—and walks downstairs, closely shadowed by both dogs. She tucks poop bags into her pocket and clips the pets' leashes around their necks. I'm going to miss them, she thinks as she opens the front door, even Winston.

She studies the people in the bus and taxi lines as she turns left. The menacing youth is not there. Still, she moves the dogs swiftly past the lines and up the road. Pedestrians chuckle when they see the dogs together, and Marilyn thinks how she will miss this too.

She walks the dogs then turns for home. As they near Warhol Way the sky begins to darken. *Poor Doug will get wet.*

"Come on, Winston, hurry up." She tugs his lead. "You can walk quicker than this. I just watched you jump on a sofa."

Winston grumbles deep in his throat. Finn trots ahead, snout and ears up, sprightly on his young paws. Dear Finn. She will take more photos of him. Maybe Doug can take one of her and Finn together, a special picture for her to keep, to print and place by her bedside in a pretty frame.

Back inside the house, the dogs cluster around her feet as she puts the kettle on, and she decides to feed them early. What harm can it do? The sky is so dark, they probably think it's dinner time.

"Okay, lads." She prepares their food, defrosting Winston's meat. She puts Finn's bowl on the floor first. As Finn eats, she keeps Winston back, blocking his attempts to get to Finn's bowl.

"Look Winston, look at this." She shakes a tin of treats. He gazes at it, enraptured. Feeling mean for teasing him, she unscrews the lid and shakes a couple into her hand. "Look Winston, yummy."

She drops the little nuggets of liver protein by his feet, one at a time, very slowly, and she thinks of Paula feeding naan bread to

Finn and Husky. She makes Winston wait for each one. "Hurry up, Finn, eat up."

"Okay, Winston, your turn." She spins to the counter and lifts his bowl to the floor. "There you go, good boy. Good boy, Winston."

He lunges at the bowl, his breath fast and rasping. He races through the food, snorting, grunting. Marilyn feels her face twist in distaste. "Don't be unkind," she tells herself. "He can't help the way he is. It's inbreeding by humans."

Finn lingers over his bowl, gives the chrome several long licks, then turns away. Marilyn bends to stroke him. "Was that good, Finn? Was it?"

He rubs his body against her legs. "Good boy. I suppose I should think about our dinner now. Doug will be hungry. He's always hungry."

The thought of dinner exhausts her but she wants to treat Doug, to surprise him. She will go to Waitrose and find something good. Maybe she can get one of those ready-meals that only need to be heated. Some of those meals are pretty healthy. "See you in a bit, boys." And she shuts the living room door so they won't follow her. If they think she's going out, Finn, at least, will want to come along.

Her bag isn't hanging on the living room door handle where she usually leaves it. It must be upstairs. Oh well, fetching it won't take a minute. She can draw the curtains while she's there, shut out the nasty afternoon. She runs up the two flights of stairs and smiles. It feels good to move. She will take up running again in San Francisco.

She walks swiftly into the bedroom, strides toward her bag where she sees it beside the bed on the floor. But as she moves across the carpet, she hears a sound. She pivots. The man from the bus line stands there. He is blocking the stairs.

His mouth twists into a thin, ugly smile.

“Hello, Marion,” he says. “You should have stayed in San Francisco.”

Chapter 27

"There's one phone number that keeps coming up," Rob says, and he states the digits slowly and clearly. "Mean anything?"

"No," Paula says although the number does seem familiar.

"We got the location it's coming from," Rob continues. "Fifty-three Hampshire Close?"

Paula's skin crawls. "Fifty-three Hampshire?"

"Yup."

"You sure?"

"Yes."

"Thank you, Rob. I'll get back to you."

She ends the call and sits down, reaching for Husky, but his warm bulk doesn't bring the usual comfort. It can't be. Daniel is the sweetest kid, one of Neil's best buddies. She frowns. Shit.

She reaches for her phone again: *Got time for a chat?*

The response comes fast. *Salty's at two?*

Sounds good.

Paula wraps her arms around Husky's broad back. "Oh Husky," she whispers. "Oh hell."

When the time comes, she leaves Husky at home—"Sorry, old boy, I don't want distractions, not even you." She arrives early at the café and chooses a table in the window. She wants to see Sue walk down the street, wants to see her enter. Don't look angry or accusing, she tells herself, be normal.

"Paula, hi." Sue strides into the café and across the room, pulls out and slips into the chair opposite. She smiles and her eyes gleam with affection. "It's so good to see you. You've been travelling. Was it fun?"

"It was okay." Sue's put on a bit of weight and it's good. She looks healthy, attractive in jeans and blue winter jacket, her dark hair curling on her collar.

"I ordered us both a coffee," Paula says as Sharon brings their drinks.

Sue raises a brow. "You drink coffee now?"

"I do."

"So, how's it going as a private eye?" Sue pours milk.

"All right, bit slow. ... What's been difficult is all the abusive texts I've been getting, the ugly comments online. You know, bigots, crazies."

"Sorry to hear that." Sue's gaze is genuine.

She doesn't know.

"I expected it to stop, after the fuss over me whacking that scrote died down. But ..." Paula shrugs, "I was wrong, so I hired someone to look into it. And ..." She pauses, "One number came up more than others. We traced it to an address. Sue, it was your address."

Sue's mouth opens, her lips move in silence.

"Sue, it was Daniel's number. I think Daniel has been sending me hateful texts, abusing me on social media."

Sue shakes her head. "Paula, I can't believe that. The boys are friends."

Sue's eyes are huge, hurt. Paula ploughs on. "But it is Daniel's number and it's coming from your house."

Sue sighs and looks from the window. "I don't believe it's him but if it is, he's young ..."

"Not that young." Paula shakes her head. "You should see what he writes."

Sue colours up. "If it is him, Paula, and I'm not saying it is, you can't entirely blame him."

"What?"

"Well, I've never had a problem with you being gay, but you know, it's a bit weird, all the attention you got when you whacked that scrote. Some people held you up as some kind of hero. The press going on about you being gay and married, and a mother, about the good work you'd done as a cop ... acting like you were all kinds of role model. I mean, I love you, Paula, but I don't believe it's natural for people like you to be married, have kids. It's not ... good for society."

Paula feels her temperature rise. "Have you met my son? How is my son not good for society?"

"You know what I mean. The news made it seem that being gay and having children is ... normal. Young people shouldn't think that."

"I see, well if this is the kind of shit your son hears around your dinner table that explains it." Tears threaten. Paula drops her gaze, swallows.

"It's nothing personal, Paula. I love you. You're my friend." Sue reaches for her hand. "We've been through so much together. I even liked Jane."

"No." Paula shakes her head, tucks her own hand. "No, we're not friends." She leans across the table, stares into Sue's pale face. "We're not." She picks up her coffee, tries to swallow and clear her throat, but her hand is shaking and she puts it down. The cup rattles, wobbles. "I never want to see your face again. I never want to hear from you." Tears blur her eyes as she gets up and walks, still shaking, to the door.

She longs to return to her flat and hide with Husky but it's Friday, she's got to go to Neil's school and sit with Jane and listen to heavy metal. She walks and cries behind her sunglasses. If only she could sit with Husky for a while, but if she gets home, she won't leave and she can't let Neil down. She makes for the school.

She takes the long route in order to calm down but it's still early when she arrives. The hall is empty and she finds a table near the door where she can see Jane enter. Neil texted to say Jane will be happy to sit with Paula and that's good news. They need to be civilised for Neil's sake. Should she tell Jane about Sue? No, there's no point.

She sits alone and thinks how she and Jane have often sat in this room for Neil's performances. The circular tables are small and intimate, and the organisers turn the lights low to give the young performers the illusion of performing in an adult venue. Often, Paula and Jane have slipped their hands under the table and linked fingers. This evening will be very different, but Paula will be polite, she'll ask about Jane's work, whether her mum has got over her hip fracture. It would be easier if the school still served alcohol. They used to have a cash bar—that was one of the good things about Neil being at a private school—but some prig complained it set a poor example for the kids. Paula thought it set a realistic example. Never mind, she'll make do with a cup of coffee and cake—one slice.

The room begins to fill, someone dims the lights. Paula's pleased. She doesn't want to talk to anyone. She wonders how many people in this room actually loathe people like her, find them unnatural, disgusting.

Fuck it, Paula, she tells herself, don't let Sue get inside your head.

The young musicians move on and off stage. Neil walks out from behind the curtain and places his score on the piano. He looks smart in black shirt and tie. A teary mist fills Paula's eyes, and she blinks hard. She recalls his birth—her amazement that something so male had been birthed by her female body. It wasn't just his stubby, comically assertive penis, it was his whole being—the masculinity inherent in his thick limbs, his solid head.

And now the alien is grown, almost a man. He's standing in the middle of the stage and he sees her, and waves. She waves back. *He's glad I'm here.*

Jane appears in the doorway. Paula raises her hand and Jane starts to walk over. She's talking to a woman, and Paula assumes it's a mother, someone she can't yet place. She fixes a smile. Jane and the woman stop at Paula's table. Jane turns to the new arrival, puts her hand on her arm. "Paula, good to see you. This is Amanda. She loves Neil's music so I invited her along. I hope you don't mind."

Paula rises, extends her hand. "Of course not. Pleased to meet you, Amanda."

"You too." Amanda is young, max 30. She has shoulder length blonde hair, thick and shiny. Her face is attractive, subtly made up, her tailored skirt and jacket expensive. She looks like success. She looks like Jane. Maybe she's also a lawyer.

They sit—Jane next to Paula, Amanda on Jane's other side.

"I love these events," Jane tells Amanda. "It's a treat, seeing the kids perform." She taps Amanda's hand lightly, lets her fingers linger. "Neil is always the best performer, isn't he, Paula?"

"He is." Paula nods and takes her eyes from Jane's playful fingers. Jane has brought a girlfriend to Neil's event, with no warning, not even a text.

"Excuse me," Paula says. "I need coffee—long day." And she joins the queue that's forming before the table of refreshments. She swallows hard. There's only one word to describe the feeling heating her face and churning her gut—humiliation. You're here for Neil, she reminds herself as she chooses the biggest slice of carrot cake on the stand.

Paula returns to the table. The queue for food and drinks has grown. Good. She hopes Jane and Amanda will stand in line and leave her in peace. She's glad she didn't offer to get their bloody refreshments.

They do get up to join the queue as Paula returns. Paula sits down, stirs her coffee, moves the cup very deliberately to her mouth, places it back in the saucer. Thank goodness the room is dark. Shame burns her cheeks. She can't reason it away, can't ignore it.

She eats her cake, slowly. She takes out her phone, studies it as if she's a busy professional. There's nothing on the phone except a message from the wife who suspects her husband of cheating. Paula agrees to meet her the following day. She studies her phone as Jane and Amanda return, each carrying a cup of tea—not a slice of cake or biscuit between them. Not for the first time, Paula wonders what Jane saw in her. There'd been a lot of heat between them but it was more than sex. Their disagreements made them feel alive.

Maybe I was Jane's bit of rough. Jane married her rebellion. Maybe I did too.

The kids are emerging from behind the stage curtains with a blended shyness and pride that brings more tears to Paula's eyes. The gathered parents and grandparents, the younger and older siblings bullied and threatened into attending, all clap. There's the odd whoop. Paula smiles. *Fuck Jane. Fuck Sue.*

Neil strides out. His eyes swivel in their direction. Jane raises her hand but Neil doesn't respond. He's upset, embarrassed for Paula. She grins, gives him a cheerful wave.

Don't be upset for me. I'm having a great time.

The music teacher appears and launches them into Bohemian Rhapsody. Too ambitious, Paula thinks. Hopefully, they'll warm up and improve. Paula fixes her smile and wishes she hadn't eaten all her cake. She's tempted to get another slice, maybe a biscuit. What would Jane and Amanda think?

The kids do warm up. They pass smoothly through hits by the Beatles and the Stones. Singers come and go. Is it time for the heavy metal? Paula feels like screaming herself.

A pale young woman appears—short dark hair, massive kohled eyes. The girl grips the microphone and, as the band begins to play, she opens her mouth and howls. It's a shocking sound, especially in the earnestly supportive auditorium. Paula feels her lips twitch and rise as surprise travels like a wave through the audience. She glances at Jane and Amanda. Their eyes and mouths are open. Good. Neil didn't tell Jane this was coming, but he did tell her.

Amanda giggles and Jane's fingers reach for Amanda's, dance with them on the table. Paula looks away and studies her son who is hammering on the piano, his entire body rocking to the shocking sound he's creating. She tries not to see Jane's hand. *We are here for Neil.* Paula wants to lean across the table and remind Jane of the fact. But she can't speak. If she does, she will start a fight. She will shout, accuse. She will embarrass herself and her son.

People are shifting in their seats, muttering, and then a few parents—women—actually get up and walk out. One even has her hands over her ears.

"Well." Jane turns to Paula as the performers take a bow. "That was interesting. How are you getting home?" Jane asks as the kids begin to exit the stage and the lights rise.

"I'm walking." Paula can barely meet Jane's eyes. How did she ever love this person? How was she relaxed and intimate with her?

"Would you like a lift?" Jane raises her brows. "It's no trouble."

"No, thanks." Does Jane have to highlight that Paula has no car? "I'll call a taxi." She raises her butt from her seat. "Excuse me, I must say goodbye to Neil." And she moves away, doesn't bother saying goodbye to Amanda. She walks toward her son, who is striding toward her, flushed with the thrill of rebellion.

"Well done, love." She holds him in a hug.

"Thanks Mum." He leans down and into her because of his greater height, and hugs her longer than usual. He pities her, and she doesn't want that. "Really well done on the metal," she tells him as they separate.

He chuckles. "Thanks."

She hurries out, past the chattering groups of parents and children, away from the elegant exterior columns that flank the wide front door. Outside, it's cold and a soft rain is beginning to fall. But it's more mist than rain, it will be good to walk, to stride away. When she gets back to the flat, she'll take Husky for a spin around the block. She'll fall asleep with her hand resting on Husky's warm shaggy back.

Another day tomorrow.

Chapter 28

Marilyn stares at the man from the bus line. She sees black hair, neatly combed as if for an important event. She sees dark eyes coolly watching her, almost the same colour as his shirt and pants. His body is nearly invisible against the wall that is shadowing into evening. His face is set, steady, not as hard and hostile as it was when he stared up from the street. His expression is clear and focused. He's come here with a purpose.

He moves toward her, and she steps back. It's instinctive. She's in a dance with a predator and her actions feel choreographed. She's moved like this before, with her mother.

The youth takes another step. He knows the dance. There's a light like pleasure in his eyes. She thinks of her mum, of her mother's gleaming, violent energy. Her mother taught her to be small and silent. Her mum taught her to duck and run.

Following his lead, Marilyn makes another move—one step that maintains the distance between them. Can she reach the bathroom before he lunges? She doubts it. He may draw this out for his own pleasure, but he won't be careless.

He smiles. His voice when it comes is soft and calm. "You should have stayed in San Francisco, Marion."

She doesn't respond. Can she dart inside the bathroom and lock it, lean on the door, throw wide the window, scream over the rooftops? Oh, she would scream so loud. But she will not reach the bathroom in time. He is small and lithe, like her. He'll be on her long before she can slam and secure the bathroom door. How long would the lock hold anyway?

The balcony? Can she leap over the wide, white bed? Can she reach the glass door and yank it back, hurl herself onto the concrete deck? Is the balcony door locked? Is that how he got in? No, can't be. It's too high for him to climb, and too public. Can she scream at the people in the street below? There must be someone—there's always someone. Or will he reach her, drag her back into the room before the breath leaves her throat?

He moves again and she sees that he's wearing transparent gloves, the thin, rubbery kind she uses for cleaning. His cloaked fingers are curled around something. A knife? She sees a glint and imagines her blood, spilled and reddening the white carpet. She will not let that happen.

She leaps back, feels her body hit the bedside table. Behind her, the table rattles, a lampshade shakes. The table and lamp tell her she is further from the bathroom than she thought. She must not take her eyes from his.

He moves again. She moves at the same time, leaping around him in a wide arc and flinging herself at the staircase. He lunges, his arm darting toward her. She sees his reaching fingers and the knife drops to the floor. He'll have to pause to retrieve it. She leaps down the stairs, feels herself crash onto each step, her arm wrenching as she clings to the banister. She hears him behind her—thumping feet, hard breath. Her eyes graze the window. If only she'd turned the hall light on when she ran upstairs, then people outside might glimpse her fleeing for her life, might call for help. For a mad moment, she considers leaping at the pane of glass, flinging herself through it. She would rather die from falling, from crashing to the ground, than give Sean the satisfaction.

But hope, self-preservation win, and she runs. She reaches the bottom of the staircase and sprints down the hallway. She will grip the top of the next banister and fling, propel, herself down the stairs. If she reaches the bottom, she will stand a chance. If she can keep ahead of him, she might reach the front door, might yank it open before he's on her.

But she feels him closing the gap. She hears his breath, nearer. She feels herself caught as he snags the hem of her long cardigan. He jerks her back, she resists, but almost falls. With everything in her, she resists harder, hurls herself toward the living room door. If she can get in there, if she can get the door open, the dogs might scare him off. There are two of them, they will bark, maybe attack. She will shout. Kill him, Finn, Kill. Her tone will tell them what to do.

The door handle is in her hand, cold and smooth. She turns it, as the attacker again yanks her backwards. She pulls against him, flings herself forward, and spins, tumbling into the living room. She screams and hears her voice, high and other-worldly.

"Finn!" She yells his name and he's there in a moment. He passes in a blur. She hears his growl, low and dangerous. She falls, sliding across the floor as her cardigan is released. She hits the end of the love seat and rotates, leaps up.

Finn is attacking the man from the bus line. His jaws are around his arm. Finn is hanging on, refusing to be shaken off. The attacker's eyes remain calm, and that terrifies Marilyn. He should be scared. He should be turning, running down the stairs and from the house. But he is not. She watches him watch Finn. She watches him reach up his free hand and transfer the knife.

"No!" She screams as the knife comes down. "No!"

There's a terrible sound, a gurgling, and a swift, appalling wash of blood. Finn falls, and Winston rushes up and stands trembling, barking at the attacker.

Heated, propelled by fury, Marilyn grabs the nearby Chinese lamp and lifts it high. She leaps forward and brings the thick round base down on the attacker's head. There's a crack as ceramic hits bone. The man stumbles. He leans forward, puts his head down, steadies himself against the banister. Marilyn stares. Is he going to fall to the floor?

Have I killed him?

No. He breathes deep, looks up, directly at her. Marilyn's instinct is to flee but she sees Finn, lying at the thug's feet, his throat a gaping horror. She sees blood pulse from Finn's neck and slip across the smooth wooden boards. Winston is circling the attacker, barking, and making quick forays at his legs.

Don't abandon Winston.

The intruder ignores Winston. The man is dazed from the blow to the head, Marilyn sees it in his eyes. She sees anger, but his gaze has lost its focused malevolence. She watches his eyes move past her to the patio door. His mind has turned to escape.

She turns to flee herself. Her instinct is to get ahead of him in case his fury heightens as he passes her. But she sees the knife, still protruding from Finn's neck. The attacker has either forgotten the blade or decided he doesn't have the strength to retrieve it. He does not dare bend down before her, perhaps.

She feels a small surge of triumph.

Should I attack? Can I kill him?

She's enraged, lit with violent energy. She feels her limbs clench in anticipation but doubts buzz at her brain. She stares at the blade. She must grab and hide it. Doug will call the police later. If the police see the knife, they will know this was likely no ordinary burglary. The knife may lead the police to the attacker and his motives in breaking into Warhol Way. The knife may lead to Marilyn and her secrets.

She darts to the other end of the sofa and yanks the second Chinese lamp from the wall, raising it to defend herself. But the attacker still thinks only of escape. He staggers past her, toward the door to the garden. She watches him step through and out into the small, elevated green space. Will he fall? Will he slip from the high, encircling wall or is he strong enough to get safely over it and away?

Will he recover and return to attack me?

She studies the door then realises she must move, must lock him out. She dares to glance away, toward dear Finn. Her breath catches at the sight of his poor, ruined body. Winston is beside Finn. Winston is lying in Finn's blood. Scattered pieces of golden ceramic surround them, the shards are staining, deepening to red. Winston's snout is resting against Finn's, just as it did when they lay together on the sofa.

Tears rush Marilyn's eyes and she looks away, back to the door. Taking energy from grief, she strides forward, turns the key that sits in the lock. She stares out into the dark garden, fearful of glimpsing the attacker's crouching figure, his sinister face. Nothing. Dare she believe he's gone?

She moves toward the kitchen, where she kneels and removes a pair of transparent cleaning gloves from the space beneath the sink. She pulls the gloves onto shaking hands and grabs kitchen towel from the counter. She walks toward Finn and Winston. She must do it now, while still enraged, while still alight. She reaches the dogs. "It's okay, Winston," she says. "It's okay boy."

Winston doesn't move. His round eyes watch her as she bends over Finn and pulls the blade from his throat. It comes more easily than she expected. There's just a faint click and a rustle of torn bone and cartilage, a fresh crimson seep.

She stares at the blade. Through Finn's blood, she sees the gleam of metal. For a moment, she feels dizzy. This knife would have finished her as quickly as it finished Finn. She sees a dark button on the handle and realises it's a switch-blade. She should clean the blood away and tuck the blade back inside the handle. But she can't face Finn's blood. She will hide the knife. As she wraps the blade in the towel, she wonders where she can conceal it where neither Doug nor the police will find it.

Her mind spins, and she breathes deep. She is not a suspect. The police will have no reason to go through her things. Still, she dares not bury it in her suitcase. Under the sink in the master en-suite? At the back, wrapped up? Doug won't look there. Doug doesn't clean houses. There's a space at the back, behind the curve of the pipe. If the police find it, she'll deny all knowledge, let them think the attacker hid it. They can't prove otherwise. Let them assume the attacker didn't want to risk being caught with it on the street. Let them think he intended to return to finish off the home-owners. They must, after all, be his real targets. She is just a pet-sitter, from America.

Why would anyone want to harm me?

She picks up the knife and carries it upstairs where she tucks it behind the pipe under the sink in the en-suite. Then she returns to the dogs and removes the plastic gloves, resting them on Finn's flank. She must dispose of the gloves and her top, which is spattered with blood. She must hide them where no one will find them. And she must seek help. Her actions must seem plausible to the police.

What should I do? What would an ordinary victim do?

Stay in the house and call Doug or the police. That would arouse the least suspicion, but she has to get rid of the gloves and her top. They cannot remain in the house. Her mind turns to the garbage cans that sit in the building's communal basement near the homeowners' green Volvo. She could dump the gloves and clothing in the bins, but no ... it's not likely but the police could search the bins. Doug will now be walking back from the city, through the darkness. She must find him. She'll dump the gloves and top on the way, wrap them up and bury them deep in a public bin. She'll tell the police she left the house because she feared the attacker would break in again.

I am American. I don't know England. I don't know what to do.

She looks at the stairs, the front door, but pauses. What if the attacker is out there, waiting? What if he's recovered? What if he's standing, disguised, among the weary commuters and shoppers in the bus and taxi lines? What if he sees her leave and slips away from the queue and follows her?

Marilyn looks toward the patio and the garden. He won't be there now—that is one place he won't linger. But she can't go out there, into the darkness. She can't go out the front door either. That is surely more dangerous. Perhaps he's injured. Maybe he's lying crippled at the bottom of the garden wall, in the dark alley between the rows of houses? She will look over the top of the wall before she jumps. She will scan the street. If he's jumped safely, he will not be there.

"Good boy, Winston." She bends to him, strokes his back, feels the warm comfort of his body, the trust and affection in his deep gaze. "You're a good friend, Winston." She cannot look at Finn.

She runs upstairs, snatches a dark sweater from her suitcase, pulls off her top, making sure no cloth catches her skin, then rolls it up and holds it between her knees as she pulls the sweater over her head.

Then she runs downstairs and wraps the gloves in her top, making sure not to touch them. She grabs a plastic bag from the kitchen and strides to the patio door. Swiftly, before she can change her mind, she unlocks it and yanks it back. This is how he got in, obviously. While she was walking the dogs. Doug must have left the door unlocked. She feels the cold evening air in her face and she passes through the door, shuts it. As she strides toward the wall, she scans the garden. Could he be hiding behind that miniature bonsai tree? No, it's too small. Behind the deck chairs that have been tossed about by the wind? She makes herself look. No. He's not there.

She reaches the wall, peers over. Nothing, just the dark empty alleyway.

He's not here. He's not.

Trusting herself, she puts her hands atop the wall and pulls herself up. She rests at the top, looks at the drop. It's deep, maybe six feet. She could break an ankle, even a sprain would slow her. But she crouches, recalls the balance long practiced in yoga. Muscle memory. She's decided on this. She breathes, lets herself be light and falls.

She lands in the alley between the houses. Her feet and legs buckle, waver, but she's not hurt. No one is on the street. Tears of relief rush her eyes. But she darts up.

Run Marilyn. Run.

And, instead of moving left, toward the end of the street and the bus stop and the taxi rank, she moves right, into the deeper darkness between the homes. He will not expect this.

She sprints, pounds up the alley. When she reaches the end, she turns. Nothing. Still not daring to believe he's gone, she runs on. It's almost dark, and cold. Doug loves the route along the waterfront, but at this time of day he will take the inland route, past the private school and the military college and the bar that screens American sports.

She reaches the Common and pauses to toss the blood-stained gloves and clothing into a bin. She leans forward, tumbles garbage—fast food wrappers, coffee cups—over them. Then she turns right, taking the inland route.

Doug, where are you?

And she glimpses his shadowy figure, his loping, bouncing gait.

"Doug!" She runs to him.

"Marilyn, what's wrong?" He puts out his hands to catch her, although she's not tired or unsteady. She could run all night.

"Doug!" She falls into his arms, and they close around her.

She weakens. “Doug”. She shudders and feels the tears. “Doug, oh my God. Something terrible has happened.”

Chapter 29

It's a fine day to drive to Eastbourne, although Paula doesn't relish having to spy on the cheating husband so his wife can punish him. She recalls the acrimony and silences of her own parents' divorce. After seeing Jane at the school, she knows she wants a divorce but the process terrifies her.

She cheers up when she collects the rental car. It's a fun green fiat and she always enjoys the coastal drive. It feels good to sit—her body is sore after a weights class at the YMCA—and she admires the views of the Channel and the characters of the communities she passes through. She used to come along here with her parents, long ago.

She passes signs for Brighton. She always liked Brighton, although she can't stop today. As a kid, she'd adored the city's noisy arcades and slot machines, the fair ground's glittering rides. She won a big purple dinosaur in a shooting booth. The ludicrous toy is packed away in a box in the flat. She'd taken Jane to Brighton with Neil—once.

"Brighton's a vulgar place," Jane had said, looking about at the shops with their seaside trinkets, silly hats and trashy me-

mentos. She'd frowned at the crowds feasting on fish and chips, soft vanilla ice cream and Brighton Rock candy. "Brighton is full of litter and drunks," she'd said as she gazed at the pier stretching into the water, at the thin, rocky strip of beach. "This is not a proper beach." She'd turned to Paula. "Why did you bring us here?"

Paula had frowned, upset and embarrassed. "It's the British seaside. Of course it's vulgar. That's the point."

"You don't like nature like I do," Jane said. "Real nature."

"I do," Paula said. "But I like people too."

Paula had recalled that her father hadn't liked Brighton either, that he'd walked its promenades with his arms and mouth tight, as if fearing contamination. Mum probably made him come for me, Paula thinks.

God, I married my father.

Eastbourne is entirely different. Genteel. Its tall, white-washed Victorian character remains sedate and respectable, probably because it's home to many retirees. What was it her mother used to say? "People go to Eastbourne to die then live another 20 years. It's all that fresh sea air." Her mum's eyes softened with memory. "I loved walking on the South Downs, loved those cliffs. You can see all the way to France."

Paula wishes she could stride across those white cliffs today, take in the thrill of crumbling Beachy Head, the troubling drop. But there's not time.

Arriving in Eastbourne, she motors along its strangely quiet waterfront and parks opposite the hotel where the husband is thought to be conducting his affair. The wife's information is precise. She'd found a receipt in his wallet. Paula was surprised he was so unguarded. Did he want his wife to find out? Perhaps, if only subconsciously. People don't always understand themselves. Jane may not have realised she was waiting for an excuse to end their marriage until Paula whacked a criminal and handed it to her.

Paula feeds the parking meter then gets back in the car and reclines her seat so she can stretch her gym-weary legs. She turns the music down low—it's a mellow Aretha Franklin kind of day. She unwraps the large sausage roll she bought en route. Mm, that bakery is as good as ever. The Chelsea bun and cup of coffee are equally tasty. The bun is rich and doughy, sweet like childhood. She'll keep the packet of salt and vinegar crisps for later. As a kid, she'd loved the crisps' surprising sharp flavour—a taste she later came to associate with beer in darkened pubs. Okay, Paula, she tells herself as she wipes the cake from her mouth, that's enough. Lucky there's a combat class at the Y in the morning.

It's about another half hour—Paula's thinking she'll have to exit the car to find a loo—when she sees the husband strolling along the waterfront with a blonde. The couple are coming from the city centre, and Paula wonders if they've enjoyed lunch in some expensive restaurant. She thinks of the wife at home. Poor cow. Paula takes out her phone, snaps a few pictures. As the couple move closer, she sees that the woman isn't the young blonde she'd expected, she's more the age of the silver-haired husband. Maybe it's his sister or an old friend, but then the man laughs and leans in, tilts the woman's head for a kiss.

Okay, maybe not. Paula takes more pictures. She feels bad about spying on the couple, but it's her job and he really should keep it in his pants. She takes another photo of them on the steps, and smiles. Now she can get out of the car and have a pee. It will be good to stroll along the waterfront. It would be a shame to leave without checking out the water and the pier.

And she does enjoy the pier, just as she always did. As she walks out on the old wooden boards, she thinks of the people who built this long, tongue-like structure over the Channel—the Victorians or Edwardians, she's not sure—but she imagines women in long skirts carrying parasols, men, handsome, in striped jackets and boater hats. As a kid, she'd walked out on to the pier and stared down, watched the swirling grey water between gaps in the wood. There'd been a sense of danger, of disbelief that she was literally walking on water. She'd always found some excuse to hold her father's hand.

The drive back to Portsmouth is pleasingly uncomplicated by traffic—she could start missing driving if it was always this easy. She drops off the fiat and walks home. As she nears her flat, dusk is erasing the warmth of the day and she feels the night-time damp moving off the water. She huddles inside her jacket, the sudden shift in temperature and atmosphere reminding her of San Francisco.

As she walks down her street, she sees a man standing by the gate that leads to her block of flats. She thinks nothing of it—there are ten flats in the block—and is startled when he steps forward and obstructs her way. "Paula?" he says, "Ms Moore?"

He's an unremarkable looking guy—bulky in dark clothes, thinning dark hair. As he steps forward and puts out his hand, she remembers. This is David, Marion's brother.

"Hello Paula, David Taylor," he says. "Could you spare a few minutes?"

Paula craves a warming cup of coffee and a biscuit and she should walk Husky. It must be hours since the dog-walker was in. But David looks worried. He's almost pleading. It's such a contrast to his evasive manner when she met him in Hugh's office that she's intrigued.

"I know I couldn't have made a good impression when we met," he says, unaware she's already decided to hear him out. "I've been under a lot of stress. But I'd be grateful for a few minutes of your time. It's getting late. Could I buy you a beer, a glass of wine?" He nods toward the pub, The Jolly Sailor, that stands on the corner of Paula's street.

She smiles. "A beer and a packet of crisps. But I must be quick. I need to take my dog out."

He nods. "Fine."

They walk to the pub and find a booth. The pub is dark inside and quiet—not many about so early in the evening. Football is playing on a screen above the bar, and a gaming machine blinks in a corner. Paula notes that David chooses a booth far from the door and that he glances around the pub before going to the bar for their drinks. She wonders what he fears and what he wants. Is he trying to find out how much she knows of the mayor's attack on his sister? She'd better be careful.

He returns with two glasses, a packet of crisps, and sits down. "Cheers." He lifts his glass, and she does the same. He's got a dark ale—Guinness or a bitter. She requested a pint of the local red. Her beer smells good, the glass is nice and cold. It's been difficult, cutting back on beer—much harder than substituting meat for lentils. Paula smiles and reaches for the salt and vinegar crisps. This is better than a coffee and a biscuit.

"How can I help you?" she asks when he doesn't speak, after he's taken a long, slow drink of beer.

"You're a private investigator?" She nods. He knows this. "You were asked to find Marion," he says. "Hugh asked you."

"And you did. Although I never believed either of you wanted her found."

He flushes. "We didn't. It was Sean, the mayor, who did."

Paula tries to keep the interest from her eyes. "Why?"

David studies his beer. "Well, that's the thing. I want to employ you, Paula. I need someone to investigate, watch, the mayor. I'm worried he might ... do something."

"What?"

He glances over his shoulder. "Can I tell you something in absolute confidence?"

"Yes."

"Years ago, when we were all little more than children, Sean ... attacked my sister, Marion."

Paula studies his face. "What did he do?"

David's eyes dip. Paula hears him gulp. "He ... raped her."

"How do you know?"

Again, he glances over his shoulder at the still largely empty bar. "Because I was there. It was ... partly my fault. Sean was blackmailing me. I was gay, am gay. Sean found out, said he would 'out' me, get me kicked off the sports teams, out of school." He glances at the table, looks up with murky eyes. "Sean said he wanted to get to know my sister, told me to take her to the wood near where we trained. If I did, he would keep quiet."

Paula feels her pulse beat, fast and fascinated in her neck. "And you did?"

He nods. "I didn't think it would go that far." David picks up his beer, swallows.

"Why didn't you intervene? David, she was your sister—your little sister."

"I know." His eyes are so pained she almost feels sorry for him. "I feared the consequences of standing up to Sean. Physically, he was stronger than me, mentally too. It was like I was frozen. I ... waited for it to be over."

Paula lifts her beer to her mouth. She drinks and drinks again. She's furious, although she sees that David too has been living with a terrible burden.

He shakes his head. "I was terrified of people knowing I was gay. It was a big deal back then. There were some horrible ... incidents ... I thought at the very least I'd be ostracised if it came out. And—this is no excuse—our father had recently died. I don't know what was going through my head."

"I'm gay too," Paula says, although he must know that. "I've recently split from my wife."

"Yes." David nods. "Can I ask how old you are?"

"Almost forty-five," Paula says. "I never tried to hide being gay, my mother was supportive. I didn't feel the need to hide although I agree it was scary. The prejudice was strong ..." She sighs, "Is still strong ... Are you open about it now?"

He shakes his head. "I've lived my life as a gay man, but quietly. I wouldn't want it to come out, it would look ... deceitful. People would wonder why I hid it."

Paula nods. "So, why did you go along with this fake hunt for your sister? Wasn't leaving her alone the least you could do?"

"It should have been. But Sean is ... you don't defy Sean, and I wanted to see her. She was ... is, my sister." His eyes dip. "I'm pathetic ... My whole life has been about doing what Sean wants. Sean's running for national office. He can't have the story of the rape, committed when he was about 17 and Marion just 13, come out. Hugh and me, we've been trying to get a grip on the accusations against Sean, get a sense of the damage they might do." David shakes his head. "I feel bad for Hugh. He's devastated by all this. He's an honest, an honourable, guy. He had no idea what Sean's like. ... But he's in it now, like me, his fortunes tied to Sean's."

He reaches for his beer, gulps. "I hoped Sean just wanted to know that Marion was safely in America, living her life, not paying attention to him. This ... search started off ... quietly."

"So, what changed?"

"She's here! In Portsmouth." His voice is a hissing whisper. "You know that. I've seen her, and she's still angry about the rape, eaten up. She's furious about the new victims, seems to feel some mother complex over them. She is ... obsessed with Sean." He shakes his head. "I don't expect her to come out and accuse him, she wants me to do that, but ... Sean is worried about her. And this latest accusation against him, they keep getting worse."

David stares at Paula, and she sees genuine fright in his gaze. "I'm concerned he might get someone to go after Marion, to harm her." He shrugs. "After all, no one knows who she is. She's in her home town but she's alone. We're the only people who know who she is."

Paula nods. Marion Taylor has been alone most of her life. "Marion does have a husband," she says.

"Yes. I haven't met him. It's good obviously. But she said he doesn't know about ... any of this, doesn't even know she's British. How can he protect her if he doesn't know?"

"Even if he did know, he probably couldn't protect her against Sean. Have you seen evidence of Sean's temper yourself?" Paula recalls the mayor's fury when he was heckled at the *Mary Rose*. "I mean, recently?"

"Oh, Sean's temper ..." David shakes his head. "I thought he'd curbed it, I did ..." He frowns. "Sean has a lot to lose, and my sister is ... vulnerable."

Paula studies him. His confession in the darkened pub, the warming and tongue-loosening beer, tempt her to tell him she also knows Marion fantasises about revenge. But she can't trust David. What if he's here at Sean's instigation, to find out what she knows?

He reaches for his beer, finishes it. "Can you watch Sean and Marion? Keep an eye on them? I'll pay you well."

Paula picks up the packet of crisps and chews and swallows. The salt and vinegar are indeed the same as when she was a kid—the same deep, sharp delight, although perhaps the packet is smaller. She wants to take David's job. She doesn't trust the mayor, and she understands Marion's rage even if she doesn't believe Marion will act on it. But Sean first employed her to find Marion. This would be a conflict of interest, and she can't believe Sean would harm Marion again. It seems as unlikely as Marion harming Sean. They both have too much to lose.

She puts the packet down, pushes it across the table. "David," she says. "I'm sorry for Marion, sorry for you ... but I can't help. I'm busy, too busy with other work."

He sighs. "Can you suggest another investigator?"

Paula meets his gaze. "You should go to the police. If you think Marion might harm Sean or vice versa."

He nods and toys with the crisp packet. "I feared you'd say that."

"And?"

He takes a crisp, chews and swallows. "I'm scared ... that everything will come out."

"You're scared for your reputation?"

"Of course. My whole life has been spent in this town, Ms Moore."

She nods. "Mine too."

"Yes. And you know what it's like to be ... publicly disgraced ..."

She nods again. "I survived."

His eyes fall to his empty glass. "It would be harder for me ... because of what I did. It would be ... the end ..."

"You'd find out who your friends are." Paula turns and picks up her jacket. "David, if you believe there's the potential for violence ... why are we here, wasting time?" She frowns at him. "You know what you must do."

Chapter 30

Doug calls the police, calls them right there in the street. He ignores Marilyn's protests that they don't want trouble, that they'll soon be leaving for California, that the attack was likely a burglary gone wrong, that if the house was deliberately targeted then the homeowners were the targets.

"Marilyn, stop!" Doug raises his hand. "The police must be told. This was extreme violence. Someone nearly killed you, someone has ... killed Finn." Doug's voice breaks, and Marilyn holds him. They stand together, sobbing in the dark street. Dear Finn. Deep tremors pass through her even though Doug has already removed his jacket and wrapped it around her shoulders.

"You're shaking, Marilyn. It's shock. We must get you in the warm, get you a hot drink."

He leads her to the nearby sports bar, installs her in a booth then goes to the counter and orders them both a hot chocolate. He returns, calls the police again, tells them they'll soon be back at Warhol Way, that he's getting his wife a drink because she's in shock and he's worried about her.

They sit together in the dark, secluded booth. Marilyn keeps an eye on the door. What if the attacker walks in? She knows he won't—*I injured him*—but she fears it. She tries to distract herself by watching the basketball on the big screen—the Golden State Warriors are playing Toronto's Raptors. She keeps her eyes on the game and tells herself she's safe, everything will be okay, they'll soon be back in San Francisco.

"Oh darling, you're so pale." Doug gets up, comes and sits beside her, tucks his body tight against hers. "You're still trembling. It's okay, the drinks will be here soon."

It's a relief when the hot chocolate is delivered by a smiling young woman. The deep, sugary aroma comforts Marilyn although she struggles to swallow. Her stomach clenches and she gags. Doug soothes her. "It's okay. We won't leave until you're ready."

She nods, grips his warm, safe hand. Her eyes fill. "I'm trying not to think about, Finn, Doug, but all I can see is his poor body. He saved me. ... And dear Winston, he tried to help too, and he tried to comfort Finn. He was lying next to Finn, in Finn's blood."

"Oh Babe." Doug's grip on her hand tightens. "It will be awful going back. But we have to. It will be better with the police there. You see that I had to call them? That's not our house. Finn wasn't our dog. You understand?"

Marilyn shrugs. "You know me, Doug, I can't handle stress. I want all this to go away."

"I know, darling." He sighs. "Oh God, we'll have to tell the homeowners. Don't worry, I'll do it. Ironic, isn't it? We live in San Francisco, but it's here in quiet Portsmouth we encounter real violence."

They finish their drinks and walk back to the house. A police car is outside, its white lines sleek in the darkness. They pause and a middle-aged man in plain clothes gets out of the driver's side, a young woman in uniform emerges from the passenger seat.

"Mr and Mrs Brooks?"

Doug nods. "Yes Sir."

Marilyn breathes deep. She's going to have to be strong, she's going to have to lie.

The senior officer extends his hand. "DC—detective—Charles Wallace, CID," he says in a slow, deep voice that matches his heavy face and body. "And this," he says indicating the young woman at his side, "Is Officer Kate Hussain."

Marion glances at the woman, standing straight and proud in her uniform, and thinks of Paula. She must have started out like this youngster. Does Paula miss the police force, miss being part of a team?

"Can I make a request, please sir?" Doug says. "Can you go ahead of my wife and cover the body of the pet who died?" He glances at Marilyn, squeezes her hand. "There are blankets on the sofa you can use. My wife has had a terrible fright and seeing Finn will re-traumatise her."

"Of course." The officer turns to Marilyn. "Where is the body, Mrs. Brooks?"

"At the top of the stairs, the first flight." Marilyn's throat tightens.

"Mrs. Brooks, would you prefer to be interviewed at the police station?" The detective's voice is kind yet authoritative. "We have a very comfortable victim suite. It makes talking easier?"

Marilyn shakes her head. Going to the police station would make her feel like the criminal. "It's okay. I'm okay, thank you."

The detective nods, and he and the young woman turn to the front door. Doug takes his key from his pocket and inserts it in the lock. Marilyn hears the key turn and her heart jumps, sweat dampens her skin.

"It's all right, Marilyn." Doug takes her hand. "We'll just stand back and wait."

They stand aside and the officers move into the house. Marilyn glances over her shoulder. What if the attacker should appear, seize her in the darkness?

Stop it. The police are here.

She and Doug stand for what seems an age in the dark, cold street. The damp air seeps inside Marilyn's clothes. She breathes deep, grasps Doug's hand tighter.

"Let's go inside now," Doug says. "We'll wait at the bottom of the stairs. You're freezing."

They step inside as the young officer appears at the top of the first flight. "Come up," she says. "We're ready."

They move up the staircase. It's too narrow to walk side by side, so Doug goes ahead. "I'll make sure it's okay, Marilyn. Don't worry."

She ascends and sees the mound of Finn's body through the banister. It's covered by the dark blue blanket from the sofa. A sob catches in her throat. Just yesterday, Finn was lying on that blanket, resting after a walk. She reaches the top step. The young officer reaches out, takes Marilyn's hand and leads her past Finn's body before even Doug can help her.

As Marilyn enters the living room, Winston gets up from his bed by the patio and waddles toward her at surprising speed. His short coat is tinged with Finn's blood, but Marilyn can see the officers have cleaned him up, maybe they used the blanket with which they've covered Finn's body. "Winston." She kneels and embraces him. "Poor boy, poor boy ..."

"Sit here, ma'am." The young woman indicates the sofa by which Marilyn is kneeling. The officer's eyes are kind, and Marilyn smiles, grateful. "I've put the kettle on," the young woman says.

Marilyn sits on the sofa that faces into the room, so she doesn't have to face the awful dark mound that is Finn. Winston settles at her feet, and Doug slips onto the sofa and grasps her hand. Marilyn wraps her fingers around his. She breathes and waits.

"Tea?" The young officer is looking in the cupboard that holds the homeowner's numerous varieties of tea. "There's camomile. That's calming. Would you like camomile?"

They nod and thank her—even Doug, who rarely drinks tea. Marilyn wonders where the detective has gone. Is he upstairs? Checking the house is secure?

What is he doing?

He appears. She sees him walking down the hall and knows she was correct. Maybe he was making sure there was no one in the house. He does not have the knife in his hand. His heavy face is sombre. This is a serious matter. His questions will be tough. He sits on the sofa opposite, waits for the young officer to bring the tea, then when she's settled mugs before each of them, he turns to Doug. "So, this is not your house, Mr Brooks?"

"No, sir." Doug shakes his head. "We're here while the owners are on vacation. We live in San Francisco and travel as pet-sitters."

The detective smiles, raises his brows. "Pet-sitting? That's a thing, is it?"

"Yes sir, it's a great way to see the world and spend time with some awesome pets." Doug grins. "We were so glad when the pandemic was done and we could get back to it. We don't tell immigration officials what we're doing because, you know, they might not like it. We told the officials at Heathrow we were just taking a regular trip."

"I see." DC Wallace nods.

Marilyn's chest tightens. Doug should shut up. He's too honest for his own good.

Too honest for my good.

"And when do you leave for home?" DC Wallace asks Doug.

"In one week."

The detective frowns. "Very soon." He turns to Marilyn. "We'll have to make this a very thorough interview. Often, we wait 24 hours in a case of aggravated burglary, such as this. It gives the victim a chance to ... compose themselves. But you're leaving so soon and we need to get the facts."

Marilyn nods. "I understand."

DC Wallace turns to his colleague. "You may begin recording, Officer Hussain."

The woman nods, and touches a rectangular device attached to her chest. A red light comes on. Marilyn freezes. She must keep her story consistent.

Make good eye contact.

The detective turns to her, fixes his deep, evaluating gaze on her face. "Mrs. Brooks, had you ever seen the attacker before this afternoon?"

"No."

"And have either of you ever been in Portsmouth before?"

Doug shakes his head. "No, sir. I told you, we're pet-sitters. This is how we see the world."

The detective returns his unblinking gaze to Marilyn. "And you, Mrs. Brooks—have you ever been to Portsmouth before?"

"No, I have not." Her voice is surprisingly steady.

Just seven days to get through.

"Have either of you been in the United Kingdom before?"

Doug shakes his head. "This is our first U.K. pet-sit. Although we hope for many more—had hoped for more."

"And you, Mrs. Brooks?"

"No." She meets his eyes without difficulty. She's watching her accent, making sure she sounds Californian. She's been slipping recently—the past has been sneaking out through her mouth. She hopes the detective doesn't ask to see their passports, that would suggest suspicion on his part. But it won't matter if he does. Hers states she was born in Bangor, Maine. She bought a fake birth certificate from a contact she met in the hospital. It cost three months' salary.

"Have you argued with someone in a shop?" The detective asks. "Encountered road rage? Been followed home? Tempers are shorter, behaviour more volatile, since the pandemic."

"No. We don't even drive here," Doug says. "Have you figured out how the intruder got in?"

DC Wallace glances toward the patio door. "Yes. We see it a lot—intrusions from back alleys. They are such quiet spots, these old lanes between rows of houses or gardens. They are little used, these days."

"But this garden is so high," Doug marvels. "There are walls."

"If you're fit and light you can leap, get purchase on top of the wall." The detective smiles, glances down at the bulky belly that overspills his waistband. "I can't imagine doing it myself." He turns to Marilyn. "But you, Mrs. Brooks, on the phone your husband said you scaled the wall and fell safely on the other side?"

Marilyn nods. "I've done yoga for decades. My balance is good."

He turns to his colleague. "You hear that, Kate? I hope you do yoga—might help you escape the thugs and criminals."

She nods. "I do, Charles."

"Why did you risk the fall?" The detective asks Marilyn. "Why not use the front door, or telephone?"

She'd known he'd ask this. "I was terrified. Maybe I didn't act rationally. My mother was ... a violent woman. ... Violence frightens me even more than the average person. I go into a ... haze ... of fear, a panic."

Both officers nod, with what looks like sympathy. She'd been right to share. Doug's hand tightens on hers. She knows his eyes are full of tears.

There's a pause. Doug breaks it. "But why?" he asks. "Why? It was so ... savage. Why not just turn and flee when Marilyn disturbed him in the bedroom?"

"Why indeed?" The detective again turns his eyes—so tired he looks as if he could doze off but also worryingly astute—on Marilyn. "Can you tell us exactly what happened, Mrs. Brooks?"

Despite thinking herself prepared, Marilyn feels her face flush. She glances down, recalls making love with Doug on this very sofa. A horrible thought arises—could the attacker have seen them? Could he have been hiding there, waiting, in the rooftop garden?

She glances at Doug and he squeezes her hand. "Doug went out," she says, "To the Historic Dockyard. He wanted to see the World War II ship. I stayed with the dogs. I gave them their dinner then I was going to walk them ..."

The detective frowns. "Thank you, Mrs. Brooks, I understand this is very difficult to talk about. This appears to be aggravated burglary, but ..." And he gazes around the living room. "Nothing appears to have been taken. Upstairs, in the master bedroom, there are several diamond rings sitting under a glass dome. I lifted the dome. The intruder could have pocketed the rings, even as he heard you coming up the stairs, yet he did not."

"Thank God for that at least," Doug says. He glances at the remnants of the shattered Chinese lamp. "Just the lamp was broken."

DC Wallace studies Marilyn. "What happened next, Mrs. Brooks?"

"I walked up to get my bag. I was near the bathroom when I saw him. He must have been standing in the shadows. There are long curtains by the balcony. He must have emerged from them as I walked in. He cornered me. He was at the top of the stairs."

"Did he say anything?"

"No."

"What happened next?"

"He came at me. He moved slowly, maybe he thought I had a phone on me, could call the police. He moved closer. I wondered about darting into the bathroom and slamming the door but I didn't think there was time. I wondered about leaping across the bed to the balcony, but I feared he'd catch me.

And that balcony is so high—four storeys above the ground. I couldn't have got down safely. I thought about screaming for help, to the people standing in the street ..."

She meets the detective's eyes.

"Did you say anything to him?"

She shakes her head. "I was frozen. It was like a terrible dance. He moved then I moved, like hunter and prey." She shudders again, and Doug strokes her fingers.

"Hunter and prey? So, he seemed set on hurting you?"

Damn. She feels her colour rise. "I don't know. I think he was scared of me too, scared of being caught."

"But you clearly did not have a mobile phone on you. And he was the one with access to the staircase?"

"Yes. But I saw his face. I could identify him."

He nods. "And we will be asking you to come to the station, to try and identify him. Did you notice if he was wearing gloves?"

She frowns, pretends to think. An assassin would wear gloves, a regular robber might not. "No, I don't think so."

"What else can you tell us—his age, hair colour, eye colour? Clothing?"

"He was bald," she says. "Early middle age, about 40, getting a bit heavy. And he wore a denim jacket, pale denim, and jeans. His eyes were pale blue, I think."

The detective nods. "Getting heavy? So, he did well to scale the garden wall."

Marilyn flushes. "I guess."

"You stared into those eyes?"

"Yes."

"How did you get away?"

"I pretended to move backwards to the bathroom. He leapt toward me and I made a wide arc around him and ran for the stairs." She feels her pulse and temperature soar at the memory. "I flung myself down. I reached the landing. Ran down the hallway, threw open the door." Her voice catches. "I hoped the dogs might attack him, slow him. I could hear him behind me. I needed to get down the next flight of stairs, to the front door. If I could get into the street, there would be people—at the bus stop and taxi stand—they would help me." She stops, surprised to feel tears on her cheeks.

"Take your time, Mrs. Brooks, take your time."

"Finn charged out. He leapt on the man, grabbed his arm. But the man, he transferred the knife to his other hand. He brought it down." She turns and glances at the blue blanket, at the mound of Finn. "He killed Finn. Winston was there too, barking, trying to help. But the man was by the stairs. I couldn't get down. I froze. I grabbed the Chinese lamp and smashed it on his head. He ... he was stunned. Then he recovered a little, stumbled to the garden door, got it open, disappeared. I locked the door."

She blinks, breathes. "I couldn't stay in the house. I ..." She glances at her husband. "I needed Doug. I feared the intruder might be in the street, hiding among the people, so I went into the garden. I jumped. I ran to Doug."

She grips her husband's hand so hard she feels the bones in his fingers. She feels that the bones in their hands might meld together. If only they could. If only she could meld with Doug and be safe, from the world, *from myself.*

"I ran. I knew Doug would be walking on the inland route." In her mind, she congratulates herself. She'd said 'route' the American way, not the British way, route like root. "I saw Doug coming toward me in the darkness, and I knew I was safe."

DC Wallace gazes at her. "I am sorry you had to go through this, Mrs. Brooks. I assure you, we citizens of Portsmouth usually treat foreign visitors more kindly." He turns to the young officer, "Don't we, Kate?"

She nods, her eyes touch Marilyn with sympathy. "Yes, sir."

"Oh, we've had a fine time till now," Doug says, "awesome city." He sighs. "We'll have to tell the homeowners." He glances at the blue blanket. "I'll call them in the morning, if you think that's okay?"

The detective nods. "Of course, I'll interview them when they return."

Doug frowns. "This might sound greedy, money-minded, but I hope they don't decide to come back early. It'll be expensive if we have to change flights, stay in hotels."

Marilyn feels her lips tighten. *Shut up, Doug.*

"We'll manage," she says, although she wishes she didn't have to spend one more night in Warhol Way.

Doug glances toward the garden door. "I presume the door will be safe tonight?"

"I'll send a team around," the detective says. "Tonight. They'll swab for fingerprints, other DNA evidence." He turns to Marilyn. "You say he wasn't wearing gloves? So, there will likely be evidence. Maybe Finn even drew some blood when he grabbed his arm. Did you see if the attacker bled, Mrs. Brooks?"

She shakes her head. Damn. The lack of fingerprints will lead him to suspect she lied. Never mind, the intruder could have been wearing transparent cleaning gloves. They're hard to see and very common.

"Will you have a police line up?" Doug asks. "To see if Marilyn can spot the attacker?"

DC Wallace shakes his head. "We don't do that anymore. We'll ask your wife to look at photos of suspects—men of similar age and race—to see if she can spot the perpetrator. It's less distressing for the victim."

Marilyn stiffens. Victim—there's that word again, applied to herself again.

"Could I see your passports, please?" Marilyn feels her heart alert. "It's just a formality," the detective says. His eyes pass between them. "I have to confirm that you are who you say you are."

"I'll get them," Marilyn tells Doug. It's probably a mistake to seem keen to leave the room, but she needs a break from the detective's razor gaze.

"Are you sure?" Doug's eyes shift to the blanket.

"I'm okay. I have to go to the washroom." He nods. "Won't be a minute," she tells the officers.

She steps wide around Finn's body. She doesn't look at it, sees it only as a terrible mound at the edge of her vision. She realises she doesn't yet fully believe it, cannot believe that Finn will never again stride bedside her along the waterfront.

It's hard to walk up to the bedroom. She glances around the room as she enters as if the attacker might have returned. She finds the passports in her suitcase behind the cold weather clothes she hasn't needed. She takes them out, opens hers to the photo page, stares at her picture as if confirming it is herself, and glances at her biographical details. Born in Bangor, Maine.

He can't argue with that.

She rests the passports on the suitcase and moves to the bathroom, closes the door. She walks to the window, opens it and breathes in the damp night air. If only she could pull herself up and through this window, escape across the rooftops. But she's not an acrobat and she cannot desert Doug. Instead, she flushes the toilet, washes her hands and towels them to create a sense of verisimilitude for herself. She longs for a beer. She picks up the passports, walks down the stairs, hands them to the detective.

"Thank you." He takes his time over each document, passing his eyes over their photos, checking the digitised images with the living ones before him. Marilyn sits beside Doug.

This will be over, soon.

"Thank you." The detective hands the documents to Officer Hussain and she writes down the information, takes photos of each passport with her phone.

Doug grins. "I feel like we're the suspects."

"Just dotting our Is and crossing our Ts."

"What will happen to Finn?" Doug glances toward the doorway. "Should I call the vet?"

"The crime scene investigators will examine his wound," the detective says. "It will tell us about the weapon used. We'll remove his body. I presume the attacker bent down to retrieve the knife, Mrs. Brooks?"

"Yes, he did." She breathes deep. "I need to say goodbye to Finn," she says. "Before you take him."

"Marilyn, are you sure?" Doug's voice rises. "Are you sure you want to see him ... now ...?"

She turns to her husband. "Yes Doug. I need to say goodbye."

She looks at the blanket-draped body in the doorway. Finn saved her. She should be brave enough to pay her respects.

Doug glances at the detective. "Did you ... Did you notice if Finn's eyes were closed?"

"I closed them." Officer Hussain nods.

"Thank you, Miss," Doug says, and he turns to Marilyn. "I'll come with you. I want to say goodbye too."

She feels a moment's irritation. There's no rest from her husband's concern. Why can't she have a few moments alone with Finn?

I was closest to Finn, spent the most time with him.

"Okay," she says.

They get up, walk together to the blue blanket. Doug kneels and gently lifts it. "Oh Finn." He sighs.

Marilyn kneels, and slowly places her hand on Finn's dear face, strokes his elegant snout. She doesn't look at the dried blood that matts at his neck, that has darkened the fur along his flank, that is giving off a sour, metallic odour.

She lowers her face to Finn's, puts her hand on his sleek skull. She feels the soft fur and shuts her eyes. In her mind, she thanks him. She tells him she loves him.

I will never forget you.

"Marilyn?" She ignores Doug. She blocks him out. She feels the seconds pass. She must get up. She must pull back Finn's blue shroud and return to the living room. She opens her eyes, drops a soft kiss on his snout, strokes his dear head one last time. "Goodbye Finn. Thank you, my friend."

She gets to her feet. Tears come, and Doug leads her to the sofa. There's a long silence. Marilyn hears her sobs rise and fall. She longs to stop crying and she longs to keep on until all her grief is gone, until she's empty.

Then maybe I could finally start again.

"It's okay, it's okay." Doug's arm surrounds her. He hands her a tissue. "Let it out."

"I am so very sorry about what has happened here, Mrs. Brooks," the detective says when she has managed to quell the tears, when she is wiping her eyes, sniffing into the tissue.

"I am also very sorry," Officer Hussain says.

Marilyn nods. "Thank you."

"You get so attached to these animals," Doug tells them. "It's amazing." He pauses, his eyes fill. "You're only with them for a short time but when you leave, you're always sad because you will likely never see them again."

The detective nods. "I can imagine." He gets to his feet, gazes down at them.

Doug stands, extends his hand. "Thank you, Sir." He turns to Officer Hussain. "Thank you, Miss. You've both been so kind." He looks down at Marilyn. "Can you believe you didn't want to talk to the police, Marilyn?"

"Really?" The detective's eyes rotate. "Why is that, Mrs. Brooks?"

She feels her face flush but meets his eyes. "I'm not good with stress, Sir. I suffer severe anxiety. I just wanted it all to go away …"

He nods. "I see." His eyes sink into hers. "I'd be grateful if you could stay here, in the house, this evening. A team will be a around shortly to do the forensic work and remove the body of this heroic dog."

"Of course," Marilyn says. She glances down at Winston and bends to stroke his fat baby face. He stares up at her, as trusting and loving as his dead friend. She gazes back, and thinks how this is all wrong. Winston shouldn't trust her. Finn shouldn't have trusted her. No one should.

The detective doesn't.

Chapter 31

Paula wakes to a text from Marion.

I was attacked, a man with a knife, Finn is dead. Can we meet?

Paula, sits up in bed, re-reads the text. Husky stirs and she reaches out, rests her hand on his belly. She shivers, cold to her core. She replies: *Murphy's on the waterfront at ten.*

Everything feels different. It wasn't that she didn't believe or empathise with Marion before, but now everything the other woman has said has fallen into a weighty, terrifying order.

I've been naïve, a fool, to doubt that violence would occur.

She walks Husky and texts the wife of the cheating husband. They arrange to meet in the afternoon. Then Paula receives a call from Rob.

"You're not the only one interested in Marion/Marilyn Brooks," he says. "The mayor's man was inquiring, asked if she's acquired weapons."

"Who's the mayor's man?"

"Big guy, Dennis."

"What did you tell him?"

"Said I'd never heard of her."

"Thanks."

"I'll be in touch if I hear more."

"Thanks Rob. You're a pal."

When it's time to meet Marion, Paula walks fast, her collar high, hands in pockets, head down. There are a lot of people about although the day is cool with a drizzling rain. She pauses often to check her shoulder. Sean knows that she found Marion. She sent the email confirming Marion's identity and location. She cashed the cheque Hugh gave her. Sean likely doesn't know she knows about the rape, but he might fear she does. The mayor might decide to get her out of the way too. How would they conceal her murder? They'd make it look like suicide probably. People would believe that—a disgraced cop, abandoned by her spouse. People would believe she'd been that depressed, that desperate. Her former colleagues might recall the old, bolshie Paula and wonder, but they'd likely assume life had weakened her. She'd like to think that a respectful hush, a sombre stillness for a fallen comrade would fall over the station at news of her death, but would anyone really care? Paula thinks of Neil, her mum and Husky.

They're all that matter now.

Marion is sitting in a far corner of the café when Paula arrives. From the doorway, Paula sees that her face is even paler than usual. She crosses to Marion's table, canvassing the room as she walks. It seems to be a café full of retirees chatting out of the cold.

"How are you doing?" She sits down. Marion looks terrible. The doll mask is gone and she looks utterly, appallingly, human. This is the first time Paula's seen Marion without Finn. Paula hasn't brought Husky either, although the café is dog-friendly. Bringing Husky would have been cruel to Marion.

"I'm all right," Marion says. She falls silent as a waitress approaches the table. Paula orders a coffee, strong and black. She hasn't taken off her jacket, she's still freezing. "I'm so sorry," she says. "It must have been terrible."

Marion's eyes gleam. She glances down, twists her hands on the tabletop. "I can't believe it. I keep looking for Finn. Winston, the other dog, does too." She pauses, drags a tissue from her pocket and rubs her eyes. Paula wants to reach out and hold her hand, but Marion would not like that.

"Doug has told the owners." Marion takes a gulp of the tea that sits before her. "He put them on speaker. They cried. We cried. They apologised to us. They said they were so sorry I had such a terrible experience in their house, that nothing like this has ever happened." Her eyes meet Paula's. "Doug told them I'm okay, that Winston is okay, that they don't need to come back early." Paula nods. Marion sounds Californian again. Is she distancing herself, moving back to the refuge she's created?

Paula's coffee arrives and she wraps her hands around the tall, warm mug. The café is humid, foggy with breath and condensation, but she's still chilly. She's seen a lot of violence, deaths. But there's something so coldly brutal about this case—about Marion's vulnerability, about a perpetrator piling fresh terror on old, the injustice, the power imbalance. A spurt of anger heats her body.

When will it end? Conviction rates for rape are pathetic. What are they now, one or two per cent?

"You leave soon?" she says.

"Yes, but the next few days won't be easy. I have to go to the police station, look at photos of suspects."

Paula nods. "I presumed you'd call the police—your husband would, if not you."

"Yes, Doug did. So many questions, fingerprints." She sighs. "They took Finn's body away."

"Can you tell me what happened?" Paula asks. "No worries if not. I know it's hard."

Marion nods and haltingly recounts the events of Thursday afternoon.

Paula feels her own eyes brim. "Poor Finn." She shakes her head. "I can't imagine if it were Husky ... Who's the investigating officer?"

"He's CID—DC Wallace. And a young police officer—Kate Hussain. She recorded the interview, took notes."

Paula nods. She feels a moment's nostalgia. Dare she risk calling any of her former colleagues, suggest a drink? It would be good, comforting, to catch up. But no.

I don't want their curiosity, pity.

"I lied to the police, about the attacker. I said he was middle-aged and bald. In fact, he was dark-haired and young, a white guy, thin, not more than 25, 30." Marion stares at Paula. "I saw him before too, several times. He was outside at the bus stop, staring up into the kitchen window. His stare was ... threatening. He didn't look away when I stared back." She shakes her head. "I told myself he was just a very rude man. You see all types on that street."

Paula nods. "You couldn't have known."

"Why did he do that?" Marion asks. "Stare up? It was a threat but ..." She frowns. "Why bother?"

"I don't know," Paula says. In fact, she has her suspicions. Some violent attackers like to taunt their victims, to toy with them. The people who employ thugs to commit violence likely don't know about their extra-curricular cruelty. After all, being seen makes the criminal more likely to be identified and caught. Who'd suspect they'd be careless with their own security? But the monsters want to drag out the infliction of pain and fear. They are sadists.

Marion shudders. Paula sees it ripple through her body as her thin shoulders hunch deeper in her coat. "When I saw him—in the bedroom—he said, 'Hello Marion.' He said, 'You should have stayed in San Francisco.'"

Paula reaches out and grips Marion's cold white fingers. Marion doesn't respond but she doesn't pull away.

"You didn't tell the police that?"

"Of course not."

Paula sighs. "DC Wallace is a good detective—solid. But he can't act on false information. That wasn't wise, Marion. It's not too late to go to the police, say you were terrified and in shock. Tell them you want to tell the truth, the whole story."

Marion withdraws her hand, tucks it under the table, glances from the foggy window. "Paula, I lied—to the police. It's not even the police I'm worried about. It's my husband. I told you, Doug knows nothing."

Paula shakes her head. "Marion, Doug won't blame you. He'll be angry *for* you."

Marion takes a sip of tea, which is cooling, the surface congealing with the settling milk. She grimaces, puts the cup back in its saucer, stares into Paula's eyes.

"I am so upset, distraught about Finn. I feel sick, so sick ..." Her hand caresses her chest. She shakes her head. "I can't believe how much I miss him."

"Of course, you miss him. He was your friend. He was fine, a special animal."

Marion nods. "And underneath I'm furious." She shakes her head again. "I thought I was angry before ... but I really need revenge now. It's eating me—the desire, the hunger ..." She stares at Paula. "I'd planned to kill Sean, you know. I mean I wasn't sure, one hundred per cent, but ..."

Paula frowns. "Murder ... It's not something most people can do, Marion. It's just an idea in your head."

"I was going to. I had poison ... I was so upset about the new victims, those girls ... But then ... Doug and I ... we're ... happy. I had hope for the future. I wanted to forget, return to the US with my husband."

"Marion, please. ... Tell the police the truth. I've been in law enforcement a long time. It's the only way." She watches Marion. The other woman hasn't registered that Paula might also be in danger. She's thinking only of herself. Perhaps that's not surprising.

Marion frowns, makes a scoffing sound deep in her throat. "Yes, the police would believe me, wouldn't they? Everything would be just fine. I don't think." Her eyes gleam. "Think of all the women, Paula. If Sean dies, his future victims will be spared. Think of how much damage he could do if he gets elected, in London, with more power."

Paula nods. "I get that, but murder is murder. DC Wallace is sharp. He probably doubts your story. This was an unusually brutal attack with no obvious motive. You say he asked to see your passports?"

Marion nods. "That worried me, but he said it was a formality."

"It is, but ... I doubt it was only a formality."

Marion says nothing. The silence drags on. Paula finishes her coffee. "How do you feel being in that house now?"

"I hate it, but Doug changed the locks—the owners said he could." She smiles. "Doug's very handy. This morning, David, my brother, was standing outside the window, looking up. I had to run down and tell him Doug was there and he mustn't ring the bell." She frowns. "Do you think David was involved in the attack? Should I be afraid of my brother?"

Paula shakes her head. "I doubt it." But she too feels a pulse of alarm. She thinks back to her meeting with David. Did she let slip that she knew about the rape? David had been convincing as a concerned brother, owning up to his part in Marion's tragedy.

Was David involved in this?

"Marion, do you recall anything else about the attacker? You say he was white, young, thin, dark-haired—anything else?"

Marion turns her head, her eyes gaze at the condensation coursing down the window. Paula is reminded of bored school-days, watching the weather, studying trails of condensation on classroom windows.

"Yes," Marion says. "His voice was very soft—light. And his accent, it wasn't Portsmouth, not south coast, maybe Liverpool, somewhere up north. He sounded a bit like the Beatles to me. I hit him over the head with a vase. I hurt him. He was stunned, staggered away."

Paula nods. "Thank goodness you reacted fast. If he didn't wear a mask, conceal his identity, he meant to kill you. Be careful, Marion."

Paula looks out of the window, past the condensation, to the grey day beyond, and considers going to the police herself. But it would feel very wrong to betray Marion now. Marion will soon be gone. Then Paula will speak up. She'll say she only just found out Marion lied. She'll say Marion confessed after she left, sent an email. The authorities won't try and get her back from America, not when they know what Sean did. Her eyes flicker to her phone as she suppresses the impulse to pick it up, take action. Impatience has always been her worst fault. Wait, she tells herself. Wait.

Chapter 32

Marilyn congratulates herself on how she deals with the police photos of suspects. She studies each photo, says several suspects do resemble the attacker, but no, she's sure none of them actually did break into Warhol Way. Doug stands tight by her side, his hand in hers. She thinks how he would likely remove his warmth forever, if he knew the truth.

DC Wallace is disappointed. "So, none of these men could be the culprit?"

Marilyn shakes her head. "No."

The detective frowns. "We didn't find any fingerprints at the scene. Are you sure the intruder wasn't wearing gloves?"

Marilyn glances down, pretends to think. "He could have been wearing those see-through cleaning gloves ..."

"We did find one very short dark human hair on the upstairs carpet. It was over by the window." The detective glances at Doug's short grey hair, at Marilyn's blonde bob. "It didn't come from either of you." He stares at Marilyn. "Are you sure the attacker was bald?"

Marilyn feels herself blanch. She breathes, lowers her shoulders. She can cope with the detective for a short time, but then his astute eyes begin to get inside her.

She lifts her head and feels the bones in her neck click. A sharp pain cuts the muscle above her shoulders. Her tension is getting worse. Her shoulders and hips have begun clicking too. People will soon be able to hear her click when she moves, perhaps they already can. She's becoming like the Tin Man in that old movie.

"Yes, he was bald," she says. "Maybe the hair came from one of the homeowners. We didn't meet the people who own the house. They had an early flight and left before we arrived—that happens sometimes, with pet-sitting."

"Really?" DC Wallace frowns. "People jet off and leave their homes and pets with people they've never even met?"

"We do have excellent reviews online," Doug says. "All five-star."

The detective smiles. He finds Doug amusing, Marilyn sees. Doug maybe seems like an American in a movie. Enthusiastic and sunny. Perhaps he seems ... naïve, silly. Marilyn suspects the detective is looking down on Doug in that patronising English way. It makes her feel protective of her husband. English people are so superior. It's just because Americans are more open, more optimistic.

I would be optimistic if I could.

"I doubt many of these trusting pet-owners work in law enforcement," the detective says to Doug.

But Marilyn is remembering the photo on the pet-sitting website that shows a smiling young couple posing with Finn and Winston: a man and a woman, the man with blond, collar-length hair, the woman with a spectacular red short cut. How long will it be before the detective checks out the website and finds pictures of the homeowners?

"We'll find out who this creep is," the detective tells her. "We always find out what's going on. Well, usually."

"Do you think he'll try again?" Doug rests his hand on Marilyn's shoulder. "It could be something about those houses? The owners maybe seem rich, worth robbing?"

"Yes," the detective agrees. "But I doubt he'll return soon. He's more likely to try his luck elsewhere."

"That's what I thought." Doug smiles at Marilyn. "I just wanted my wife to hear it from you, and I did change the locks."

Marilyn smiles back and wishes her loving husband would shut up. She must escape DC Wallace before one of them—probably Doug—says something incriminating, before her heart starts churning her blood through her body and her ears scream with tension-induced tinnitus.

"I think you're unlikely to encounter more trouble in Portsmouth," the detective says. He glances at Marilyn. "Please do keep your eyes peeled for your attacker. And we'll continue to search for a suspect who matches your description."

Marilyn nods. The detective senses she hasn't divulged the whole story. She can see it in his manner—courteous, but watchful. Maybe he wonders if she was cheating on Doug with a local guy who turned out to be violent. Nothing could be less likely but he can't know that. She hopes this is what he suspects.

"You officers do great work." Doug's voice is rich with gratitude. "You've been awesome. My father was a police officer, in San Francisco—forty years service. My poor mom was so relieved when he finally retired."

The detective raises his brows. "That's impressive. I'm not quite at forty years myself ..." Marilyn smiles, relieved for this genuine connection with the officer.

"It's a shame Marilyn's attacker wasn't in one of those photos, but thank you for your work, Sir," Doug continues as DC Wallace walks them to the exit. Doug turns and offers his hand as they stand in the doorway.

The detective shakes Doug's hand. "Just doing my job. When did you say you are leaving?"

"Next Thursday," Doug says. "Early from Heathrow."

"Thank you," Marilyn tells the detective and meets his eyes.

"What is the name of the pet-sitting site you use?" he asks her.

"Loyalpetsitters.com," Doug says, although he is already turning toward the steps and looking out at the busy street. He longs to go running. Marilyn can sense the need, the physical and mental tension in him.

"Thank you, I'll be in touch." And the officer bestows his cautious smile on each of them.

As they walk back to Warhol Way. Marilyn only half listens to Doug talk about the things they never got to see in Portsmouth, how there's no time now because they must stay home and comfort poor Winston. Doug says they'll have to return one day and explore the south coast. Marilyn nods and smiles.

I will never return.

Doug makes lunch—a low sodium vegetable soup with granary bread that Marilyn struggles to eat. Even before the meeting with DC Wallace, she'd been exhausted. The previous night, she kept imagining she heard footsteps in the house. Her mind had swung back to the attack. She saw the attacker's face, pale and menacing, watched him slip from the shadows, heard his feet swipe the stairs, his soft voice. "You should have stayed in San Francisco, Marion."

"Come on, Marilyn, eat," Doug says.

"I am." She stirs the soup, brings the spoon to her mouth.

Damn Sean. Damn him. And she remembers the day he attacked her when she was child. She remembers it again, coldly. She goes through each heart-spinning detail. She's terrorizing herself with the memory, stoking her fury to find the courage she needs. And for a moment, she longs for the emotional numbness she lived in for decades after the attack, the numbness that wrapped her in a soft, muffled half-life. Doug walked into her ward, smiled his kind smile, and began to make her whole and real. That has brought joy and hope but also a resurgence of pain. She breathes, tries to settle her shoulders, but she won't let her rage dissipate. She feels the anger circling, sharp-clawed, in her gut and knows that, finally, there's nothing she won't do.

She glances at the patio, to where the koi fish swim—how strange that they have no sense of what's happened here. She wonders if the ghost knows, if that poor tormented girl witnessed her terror and poor Finn's murder.

You could have materialised and scared the thug to death. She smiles at the thought.

Her eyes graze the orchids on the windowsill. She must water them before she leaves. Her gaze moves to the doorway, to where Finn's blood still stains the pale floorboards. She hadn't been able to get the stains out. Doug scrubbed the wood but didn't make an impression either. "Leave it, Marilyn," he'd said. "Don't Google it. It doesn't matter if we don't get a five-star review."

Now he reaches across the table and takes her hand. "Marilyn, don't look at Finn's blood. Eat your soup."

She moves the spoon to her lips but pauses. "I'm going out this afternoon," she says, "with Karen—the woman we met at the *Mary Rose*."

"Great!" Doug grins. "I'm glad you're going out—a distraction."

"We're going to look at the charity stores, maybe get some bargains."

"Great," Doug says again. "I'll stay with Winston, sit with him on the sofa."

"Thank you." It's good of Doug not to mention that he sorely needs a run. Marilyn intends to meet her brother at Salty's. She'll ask him outright if he knew Sean sent someone to kill her.

She will see through David's pale eyes to the truth. She will poison Sean with Doug's pain pills and her own Xanax. Research has taught her that it's impossible to know how many OxyContin might kill a person, but, blended with a benzodiazepine like Xanax, the sedative effect of both drugs is magnified, the depressive effect on breathing heightened. And, if Sean should have a drink—even better. Even one alcoholic drink and one OxyContin can depress breathing.

"I'm going to bake some muffins—carrot," she tells Doug after she's forced down some soup and bread. "A gift for Karen."

Doug beams. "I'm happy you feel you can bake again. Maybe I could have one, just one?"

She shakes her head. "Sorry, Karen volunteers at a youth shelter, the muffins are for the kids."

He nods. "Right."

She reaches across the table, grasps his warm, kind fingers. "Could you take Winston out in a bit? It will do him good."

"Yes. You want me to grate the carrots first?"

She smiles. "Sure."

They move their plates to the kitchen. "Those will be the kind of muffins I like," Doug says, glancing at the pan she's bought, "Big and fat and moist."

Marilyn grins and gathers flour, butter and sugar. She watches her husband grate thick wedges of carrot into a bowl with his dear, warm, sexy hands and smiles. "Thanks for helping me. I always catch my knuckles or nails on the grater." She grimaces. "No one wants to eat shaved skin and nail."

Doug chuckles. "You just need patience." He grins. "Maybe we should get a blender. It's fun to be working together like this, isn't it?"

She nods, smiles into his eyes, imagines the children they might have had if only they'd met when they were young. If only she'd been Californian, one of those tanned, confident girls.

Silly to think that.

She tips flour into the old-fashioned weighing scale she found in a cupboard. "A cup is eight ounces, I think?"

He snickers. "How would I know British measurements?"

She shrugs. She doesn't know either. She left England before she became a baker, but she'd looked it up one time in Maine, out of interest.

Doug puts down the grater and remaining piece of carrot, wriggles his fingers to loosen the tension. "Maybe you could take up baking again, for real?" he says. "Start your own business?"

She grins, delighted he has faith in her. "I don't know ..."

He nods. "Only you can decide."

"I would like to create something new, something of my own."

"Good." He puts down the grater again, brushes shredded carrot from his fingers.

Marilyn gazes at the bright mound of his work. "You did that fast."

"Strong fingers." He waves them at her. "My fingers are good at many things—lifting gorgeous women onto beds, and ..." His eyes turn to the love seat, "sofas."

Marilyn feels herself blush. "Doug, stop. I'm baking. ..."

He chuckles. "You're so cute when you're embarrassed. Later then, waiting is good."

She nods, glances at Winston, who's standing by the dining table, studying them intently. Anxiety has made him more active, restless.

"You going to take Winston out?" she asks again. "He could use a long walk. Take him to that derelict house on the next street they're going to knock down."

Doug moves to the sink and washes the carrot from his hands. "Yep, I will. Poor old Winston doesn't sleep like he did." He dries his hands then strides over to Winston. "Come here, old guy." He kneels, pulls Winston close, strokes his round skull. He glances at Marilyn. "God, I hope he gets back to normal, becomes himself again."

"Me too." It's hard to look at Winston. His trauma and his presence evoke Finn's absence.

Even dogs suffer in this world, even animals feel pain.

"I'm glad we're going home," she says.

Doug nods. "It'll feel good to sleep in our own bed and see some sun. Come on then, old guy. Let's see if we can make you feel better." He leads Winston to the door. "See you in a bit, hon."

"Yes. Don't rush. Lock the door."

"Yep, of course," he says as he descends.

Marilyn waits until she hears the door click then crosses to the window. She fears seeing the gaunt face of her attacker in the street. But it's just a line of regular folk, weary and laden with bags, bodies tensed against boredom and damp. She runs upstairs, goes to Doug's suitcase and removes his painkillers. She takes three from the package then removes three Xanax from her own case, then runs back down to the kitchen with the pills. She tips them into the pestle and mortar that sit by the kettle and grinds them very small. Her hands feel strong, determined. She enjoys watching her wrists and palms pressing down, her fingers pushing.

My hands are strong, I am strong.

She grinds until the pills are reduced to a fine white powder then carries the bowl to the flour and buries the crushed pills. She seasons the mixture with blended cinnamon, nutmeg and cloves and tosses in a few currants. She adds softened butter, blended eggs, milk, a splash of brandy, then inserts her finger into the doughy mixture and tastes. Mm, delicious, fruity and warming.

Her heart is starting to leap, her nerves buzz. She moves to the fridge, takes one of Doug's beers, pulls the tab and feels the cold liquid slip down her throat. The relief comes fast as the alcohol hits her almost-empty belly. She finishes the can, buries it at the bottom of the recycling bag.

Then she returns to the counter, tips the batter into the greased muffin pan and puts it in the oven. She washes the mixing bowl before Doug can get back and demand to lick it clean.

Then she turns to the door to go upstairs to clean her teeth. She needs to brush away the alcohol, freshen up. Her nerves are still churning, and she can't drink another beer, can't.

The front door clicks and opens, and she hears Doug moving into the house with his customary energy. She hears Winston's shuffling gait.

"Hello Babe," Doug calls.

"That was a good, long walk," she says as she leans over the banister to see the two of them begin to climb the first flight of stairs.

Doug grins, red-cheeked. The scent of salty Channel air reaches her. I'll miss the Channel, Marilyn thinks, I'll never see or smell it again.

"Yep, Winston got all the way to the derelict house. He said hello to lots of dogs. Then we walked a good long way along the waterfront." Doug sniffs the air. "Those muffins smell great. Sure I can't have one?"

"Next time, promise," and she recalls that she didn't clean her teeth or suck a mint and must have beer on her breath. She moves into the kitchen, to the counter, takes a piece of chewing gum from the drawer, inserts it in her cheek as Doug leads Winston to the sofa, helps him jump up, settles down beside him.

Marilyn goes to the sink, finishes the washing up then, surprised by Doug's silence, looks over at her husband. He's nodded off, his head fallen back on one of the bulldog-themed cushions. He's snoring softly. Love and guilt dampen Marilyn's eyes.

Poor Doug, this has been no vacation.

She makes the kitchen spotless, and soon the muffins are ready. She smiles when she sees that they're well-risen and golden. Who wouldn't want one? She slips the muffins from the pan and onto the cooling rack. When they're sufficiently cooled, she takes several of the roundest, most well-risen and attractive muffins and slips them inside the cute little cake box she purchased at the bakery then she places the box in a wide Waitrose carrier bag.

She throws the rest of the muffins into a garbage bag and tucks them in her purse. She will toss them into the public bin on her way to Salty's. Nerves are dancing within her again, and she steals another of Doug's beers and sneaks upstairs to the bathroom. She paces and slugs the beer then swills mouthwash and hides the can in her toiletry bag. She slips downstairs, and writes Doug a note: *Back soon. Love you.*

Then she puts on her jacket, grabs her purse and slips the bag containing the muffins over her arm. She checks the kitchen window before going downstairs. Her attacker is not at the bus stop. She breathes deep, lowers her shoulders.

Downstairs, she closes and locks the door. Her eyes scan the street then she turns right, crosses the road, and sees Salty's on the corner, its windows both foggy and attractively bright. She smiles. It feels good to have a plan, to be taking action.

It's time.

Chapter 33

Paula walks Husky. She's cautious, watchful for the thug who attacked Marion. She avoids the nearby park and the waterfront. She sticks to the busiest street and takes Husky home sooner than usual.

"Sorry, old boy," she says, as she hangs up his lead and bends to stroke his dear head. "I know that wasn't much of a walk. I'll make it up to you." She grins. "You don't need to talk, do you boy? That face says—I've been short changed and don't think I don't know it." She gives him a few of his favourite beef chews, distracts him with his squeaky pig, Oinker. He'll have to suck it up. She doesn't intend to risk meeting Finn's killer.

She walks to meet the cheater's wife and again sticks to busy roads. They've arranged to connect at the fancy hotel that sits on the Common, *The Victoria.* Paula sees its bountiful white façade with the big red lettering, and grins. It's three pm. The hotel will be serving its famous cream tea—scones with jam and clotted cream will be good.

The client, Mrs. Wilson, is already seated at a small circular table by one of the restaurant's many wide windows when Paula arrives.

"Hello, Ms Moore!" Mrs. Wilson calls and waves across the busy room. Paula is surprised she's being so open about their meeting. People might know who Paula is. They might have seen her ignominious exit from the force on the news. They might know she's now a P.I. But perhaps it's not surprising, Paula reflects as she crosses the floor. Mrs. Wilson has probably already decided what she's going to do. Soon everyone will know about her bad marriage because when she's seen the pictures she will chuck her man out. She's going to throw shit at the fan, Paula thinks as she walks beneath the elegant brass-armed ceiling fan twirling above the room.

"How are you?" Mrs. Wilson rises to her feet as Paula reaches her. "Thank you for meeting with me."

She puts out a manicured hand. Paula shakes the fingers with the seriously red nails and feels her body loosen. She's grateful for the warm welcome. She hadn't realised just how wound up she's feeling about Finn's killer. At least the abusive texts have diminished in number since her confrontation with Sue, although she'll likely still have to go to the police.

She lowers her bottom carefully onto the insubstantial-looking gilt-edged chair then pulls the chair and herself toward the slender table. She admires the smooth white table cloth and gleaming silverware. The elegance cheers her—the cream tea will be good. She drops her bag beside her feet, feeling glad she's dressed in black shirt and trousers, nice and smart, and teamed with a small heel. She's been missing her police uniform, missing its reliable formality, even the weight of it. Relax, she tells herself as she tucks her jacket over her chair and glances about. It's nice here, spacious and classy. This is a boring case, but it pays and this woman needs—deserves—your attention.

"So, you have some photos for me to look at?" Mrs. Wilson rests her expensive hands on the table and gazes at Paula with artfully magnified eyes.

"I do." Paula retrieves her phone from the bag at her feet. She punches in her password and pulls up the images she took in Eastbourne then slides the phone across the table. "I'm sorry," she says.

Mrs. Wilson picks up the phone, swipes through the pictures. When she hands the phone back to Paula, her eyes are sad but her voice is steady. "This is no surprise," she says. "I was hoping there might be some innocent explanation but I know that woman. Pamela Hawkins. She's been after my husband for years." She runs a hand through her shoulder-length blonde hair. The colour contrasts with the strong black of her brows. Paula senses her client's colouring is natural and she finds it attractive, intriguing.

"I'm going to lose friends over this." Mrs. Wilson shakes her head and her hair swings. She's wearing a silky teal blouse that drops into a long V at the neck. Paula sees the outline of small breasts, a suggestion of nipples, and feels a tremor of arousal.

She looks away, relieved to be distracted by a server, clad in pristine black trousers and white shirt.

"Have you ladies decided what you'd like?" the pretty youngster asks.

Paula fumbles with her menu and wishes she could ask for a beer or glass of red. This is what it's going to be like from now on, she thinks. I'm going to have to be a marriage counsellor. I'll have to listen, sympathise. Hopefully there will also be unfaithful wives to pursue. If all the miscreants are male, the sad sack wives will get depressing.

"I'm ready to order." Mrs. Wilson flicks her menu shut. "I'm going to have the full cream tea." She smiles. "Fuck my waistline."

Paula grins. "Same for me, please." Mrs. Wilson is nice, fun. Paula almost feels bad for charging her £100 a day more than she charged Hugh and David.

Her client frowns and leans across the table. "He's denied it, of course. Lied to my face."

Paula shakes her heavy white napkin and drops it in her lap. Can she just nod and stay mute? *I can do mute.*

Mrs. Wilson waits as the waitress delivers two large white pots of tea to the table. "He's not that good in bed," she confides.

Paula pours milk. "Heterosexual women tell me I'm lucky to be gay." Gay. Why did she say gay and not bi?

Am I flirting with Mrs. Wilson?

Her client laughs, deep and rich. "Well, lucky you ..."

The waitress brings raspberry jam, cream. Paula eyes the cream's yellow richness. She hopes the scones are fresh with lots of raisins. It's good the girl has brought each of them their own little pyramid of cakes and sandwiches. She doesn't want to share.

"It's partly my fault. I haven't been any fun since the kids went away to university," Mrs. Wilson says as she picks up an egg and cress sandwich. "I hate being an empty-nester." She frowns, puts down the sandwich. "It might be my fault he's cheated. Do you think it is?"

Paula shakes her head. She's decided to leave the ham sandwiches and the meringues on the cake stand. She can't eat everything. She must make a good, professional impression. This woman might recommend her to wealthy friends. Hopefully, Mrs. Wilson will get teary and need to go to the loo then Paula will extract the ham from the sandwiches and slip it in her bag for Husky.

"But isn't this a good time for you?" Paula leans forward. She genuinely wants to be supportive and she hasn't been out with an attractive woman in ages. "I mean, with your kids grown, it's time for you again?"

Mrs. Wilson sighs. "That's the theory. ... I am lucky to have my health, money. But life will be even lonelier, at least for now."

"Yes," Paula says. "I've just split with my wife. It's tough."

"Well, I don't suppose you have to be heterosexual to have a marriage go bad."

"No. But I did expect marriage to be easier for two women." Paula's surprised to find herself opening up. "My parents divorced. I feared divorce for myself. But, of course, there are always problems in any relationship, and it turns out they're not so different."

Mrs. Wilson nods. "I'm sorry to hear that, Ms Moore."

"Call me Paula," she says. "Why are we Brits still so formal?"

Mrs. Wilson chuckles. "Linda." And she reaches a hand across the table. Paula takes Linda's hand, feels the supple strength of her skin and bones. As Linda pulls away, she lets her fingers rest on Paula's wrist. Paula's pulse jumps with surprise. Linda is gazing at her with deep, suggestive eyes.

She's coming on to me!

But then the client's fingers dart away and Paula's not sure, although the touch of Linda's skin lingers on hers. She feels her face heat and picks up a neat square of salmon and dill. She bites and avoids looking at the other woman for a moment. Is Linda also bi, or seeking a little experimentation, a diversion? Paula's heart pulses hard.

I'd be good with that.

She looks up, intending to convey that information with a deep stare of her own, but her eyes falter. Can she really embark on another relationship, however casual? I'm still out of shape, she thinks. And my confidence is shot. It's the lack of confidence, of course, that's the real problem.

But I have to start to live again sometime ...

"What work do you do?" she asks.

"I was a doctor, a GP," Linda says. "I retired early, but I might go back to work now, at least part-time." She smiles. "I did love it."

Paula nods. "Good for you. There's something about public service, isn't there? I loved my time as a cop—most of it. I hate that it ended so badly." She stops as tears threaten.

Bloody hell, Paula.

"Yes, it's important to make a difference to your community, a privilege too." Linda has obviously seen Paula's distress as her voice is soft and warm.

"Well, I have an appointment to get to, but it was lovely to get together." Linda reaches into her bag and brings out a card, which she slips across the table. "I'd love to see you again, Paula," she says. And she extends her hand again. When Paula grasps it, Linda smiles into her eyes, lets her fingers linger then stroke—a tender, tentative touch. Yup, no doubt what she's conveying. Paula feels her skin tingle with combined excitement and apprehension.

"Please send me your final bill, Ms Moore. And I'll pay for our tea on the way out," Linda says. "I've enjoyed your company."

"Me too." Paula, feeling nervous, makes her gaze mingle with Linda's. She wonders if Linda has experience with women or if she's leaving early because she's also nervous. Paula wonders if she's up to taking the lead if necessary. And maybe Linda is too like Jane—that slim, athletic, classy type Paula's always liked. It's a date, she reminds herself. Just a date.

She sits, her pulse beginning to calm then she reaches out and removes the ham from the sandwiches, wraps it up in tissues she's got in her bag. Linda has left ham and salmon. Paula reaches for Linda's leftovers too, and wraps them. She grins as she tucks the food away. At the very least, this is a step away from Jane, toward new experiences, a new life. And Husky is going to be a very happy dog.

Chapter 34

Marilyn shuts and locks the bathroom door. She crouches, opens the cupboard under the sink, reaches her hand in and back. Her fingers search for the bottle she tucked behind the curve in the pipe and find it. She pulls out the vodka and takes a long, soothing gulp, then another. She stands as the alcohol slips down and waits for the radiating, embracing glow. Kneeling, she reaches for the knife she tucked beside the bottle. She feels the rough kitchen towel she wrapped around the knife, senses the slim wedge of the blade within, then pulls it out and stands.

Carefully, she unwraps the kitchen towel. The inner layers of paper are stiff and stained with Finn's blood. Grief fills her throat, blurs her eyes but she keeps unwrapping. The towel gets stiffer and darker the closer she gets to the blade. The last layer sticks to the metal. With her free hand, she turns on the tap and lets the water run hot. She drops the knife into the sink and watches the blood begin to soften, to liquefy and fall from the blade. It dissolves, blends, tinges the water pink, flows.

She tears the stained paper towel into pieces and throws the bits into the toilet bowl then flushes with her elbow and turns and places her hands under the tap. She's trembling, the faint pink of Finn's blood stains her fingers. The last of Finn's blood will not leave the knife. She has to snatch toilet paper from the roll and wipe it across the blade before it's fully clean.

Picking up the bar of soap, she washes her hands again and again.

This is Finn's blood. Finn's. And this is Sean's fault.

Anger froths, heats her. Finally, both the knife and her hands are clean beneath the running water. She stares at the gleaming, curved blade in the sink. The blade is thinning, curving like a hook. It's been used and sharpened often. She dare not touch it, yet she picks it up by the handle, dries the tip on a bath towel. David had a Swiss Army knife as a kid and this is similar. The blade lies tucked inside the handle until released. She holds the knife in her hands and feels her lips lift.

She pushes the blade back inside the handle, then presses the button and watches the blade spring out again. Perfect. Tucking it inside her jacket, she thinks how she must carry it with her. Finn's killer could return, Sean might send someone else.

She arrives at the café before David and snags a table at the back of the room. It's a snug spot, the only table off by itself, under a slant in the roof. She needs privacy for the coming conversation. The table is surrounded by paintings of Portsmouth waterfront and historic ships. Marilyn's eyes rest on *HMS Victory* and she glances away.

Don't think of Daddy.

No, she tells herself, *do* think of Daddy. Be strong and brave, like him. She watches the door, intending to see her brother enter. She needs to see his face before he sees her, needs to see if his expression changes, if guilt slides from his features and hides behind his eyes.

People hurry in from the cold, stamp their feet on the wide, bristling doormat. Marilyn sees how the trusting ones, or the ones with little money and cheap clothing, hang their jackets on the coat rack, how others carry their expensive coats with them to a table. She observes what people buy. Tea and scones, Victoria sponge and flapjacks. She feels at home, in tune.

I know what Portsmouth people want, how they behave.

Among the mingled aromas, she discerns the deep, fragrant scent of the baking that's sitting in the bag at her feet. Her creation is filling the room with deliciousness. No doubt her baking is prompting the café's clients to buy more cakes and biscuits than they otherwise would.

She doesn't feel guilty about waiting at a table without food when the café is crowded. She ignores the searching gazes of other customers. Order or move on, their eyes say. But she needs this table for a very important conversation—one of relevance to everyone in the room.

I'm saving our town from the criminal you keep electing.

She waits. David can order for them both when he arrives. He'll have to go to the counter. The single server is rushed.

Maybe Doug is right and she should start her own baking business? She's weary of working as a supply teacher between pet-sits. It's not rewarding. There's no depth to the work because she doesn't get to know the children. Doug's nursing money is not much and the inheritance his parents left won't last long. Impatient, she picks up her phone and checks the time. Where is David? News flashes onto the screen: *Another Woman Accuses Mayor.* Marilyn stares at the words.

"Marion!" David is smiling and walking toward her. She breathes deep, drags down her shoulders. She rises as David reaches the table then she leans in, kisses his cheek.

"Hello." He flushes with the surprise of her warm greeting. "Good to see you, Marion." He sits. "How you doing?"

"Let's order first," she says. "I have a lot to tell you."

"Of course." He takes off his jacket, hangs it on the back of his chair, and gets up. "I'll go to the counter. What would you like?"

"Just tea, please."

"Share a flapjack? They're good here, crunchy, lots of fruit."

"Okay." He can eat the flapjack.

"So, how are you?" he says when he returns with the teas and the flapjack, all balanced on a small circular tray. "I'm really glad to see you." His eyes are so warm, she feels bad. "I didn't want you to leave with, you know, after what happened ..."

"Me neither...I'm okay. You?" she asks, as he settles himself opposite her.

"Yep, okay. ..." He's brought two plates for the flapjack. He empties the tray, cuts the cake—his piece is slightly larger. Marilyn watches as he rests his arms around his plate. He will study the cake before bringing it to his mouth. She suppresses a smile. He treats his food with such affection, reverence. He puts his head down, studies the cake, takes a big bite. Half his slice disappears. She watches him bite again. It does look good.

"You can have my half." She pushes the plate toward him.

"You sure?" She nods.

He takes her plate, studies her slice. It's amazing, his scrutiny. Does he think this piece will taste different? He eats, and she waits and breathes.

"David, something terrible happened. A man broke into the house. He had a knife. He tried to kill me. Finn—one of the dogs we care for—protected me, he ... The attacker stabbed Finn in the throat, killed him."

"Oh my God, Marion." David reaches out, grips her fingers. She wants to pull back but doesn't.

Let him hold your hand.

"Are you okay?"

"As well as can be expected. It was Sean, David. Sean must have hired the ... killer."

David pales. "You don't know it was Sean."

"Who else?"

He takes back his hand and rubs it across his face. "I don't know. Maybe the homeowner is involved in drugs or something, maybe it was mistaken identity. You don't know these people whose house you're in, do you?"

"No. And your theory is unlikely. If someone was after the people who own the house, he would know what they look like."

"Not necessarily. If you're living in a house, people assume it's your house."

"No. He came after me, David. He waited till Doug left. He said, 'Hello Marion. You should have stayed in San Francisco.'"

David sinks his head to his hands. When he glances up, he looks exhausted, older. He didn't know, she thinks, he didn't.

"To be honest, Marion, I feared something bad might happen. But that was my worst nightmare. I didn't actually believe ..."

"So, you didn't know about this attack? Didn't ... sanction ... it?"

"Hell, is that what you think of me?"

"I don't know what to think, who to trust ..." She studies his shocked face. "Okay, I believe you didn't know. But he's not getting away with this." She glances about, lowers her voice. "Sean must be stopped." She breathes deep. "I want him ... dead ..." She jerks her head at the TV screen, picks her phone off the table, brandishes it at him. "Have you seen the news? Another woman ..."

"Marion ..." David's eyes are wide and alive in a way she's never seen. "Do you hear what you're saying? You don't know

Sean ordered that attacker into the house. You don't know the accusations are true."

Marilyn gulps back tears. "David, I have ..." She taps the tabletop with her phone. "Had enough. It's my mission to stop Sean. Dad would have stopped him. Someone must, and it seems it has to be me, and you ... you will help. Together, we will finish the man who's ruined our lives."

"Me?" David's astonishment is almost comical.

"Yes, David. I've baked muffins, very special and beautiful carrot muffins. I want you to deliver the baking to Sean, as a gift, a treat, from one friend to another."

"Carrot muffins?"

"Poisoned muffins, David. I put pills in the dough." A smile arrives, she doesn't quell it. "For Sean."

"What's in them?"

"Xanax, OxyContin." She leans across the table. It actually feels good to tell her brother how clever she's been. "A lot of both. I'm hoping—expecting—that you will deliver them to him, one friend to another."

David frowns, smiles ironically. "I don't bake."

"You can say you bought them as a gift. I've packed them in a cake box. Sean's had to cancel another engagement. He's been sick for ages. Good. This is a cheer-you-up gift. Thoughtful. All men feel sorry for themselves when they're sick."

David shakes his head. "Sean's very health-conscious, he won't eat cake."

"Say they're full of healthy ingredients, say there's a little alcohol to taste, brandy, so he mustn't share with his kids. Say you bought them because the bakery advertised them as healthy."

"And which bakery shall I say made them?" David is mocking her.

She shrugs, irritated. "I told you—you decide. Say you took a drive along the coast and went to a market. Make something up, David."

He sits back, studies her. She stares back.

He has no idea what I've been through.

"So, you want me to act like some kind of crazed Judas? By the way, he's really not a well man, Marion. This flu thing? He can't shake it. He's been tested for laryngitis and pneumonia. He's losing hair, but they don't know why. Anyway ..." David spreads his hands. "What's likely to happen if I actually deliver your creation? I'll tell you—Sean will eat one very small piece, a small bite—he wouldn't have more, and maybe get a bit sick. But he probably wouldn't link it to the muffin. He's unlikely to die. Worse, his wife and kids will finish them off." He frowns, purses his mouth. "Maybe you'll kill a child, Marion. How would you feel then? Like you'd really made things better?"

"David. I told you—say there's alcohol and they're not suitable for kids." Anger froths in her veins. "David, you have to do this. You owe me ..."

Why is everything so hard? Why am I so alone?

"This is your chance to make up for what you did, to finally make things better for me."

Her brother leans in. "Marion, I do owe you, but this is insane. And don't talk about Dad. Dad was a military hero not a self-appointed assassin."

"Self-appointed?" She glares. "You think I chose this role, David? No, you and Sean, Mum—you chose for me."

He flushes, pushes his chair back, crosses one leg, very carefully, over the other.

Tears fill her eyes and spill down her face. "David, I'm leaving for San Francisco soon. ... And I can't get close to him. He has security people. They know what I look like. If you do it, if you keep the muffins in the fridge then take them to him, in a little while, I can get away, back to America, before the cops get suspicious."

"Why would the cops suspect you?"

She frowns. "The attack in the house was so savage they think there's more to it than a burglary gone wrong."

He nods. "Even more reason not to do this. ..."

"David please ..." She fingers her tears away. She must not create a drama in the cafe. "Don't you care that Sean sent someone to kill your sister? Don't you care that he's still harming young women in our town? Are you gay because you hate women David, because Mum was ... cruel?"

His brows rise and he produces a chuckling, dismissive snort deep in his throat. "Marion, people don't *choose* to be gay. They don't decide to be gay because they dislike a parent. And yes, I do care that someone, maybe Sean, tried to kill you. I'm sorry about the dog. I'm sorry about the other victims. But you're asking me to become a murderer." He raises his hands, lets them fall. "That's … preposterous … I feel terrible about what I did. You want me to make myself worse? Go to the police, Marion."

She stares. She'd known he wouldn't help, but she still feels a coursing disappointment swirl through her. "You never cared about me." She leans across the table, rises up into his face. "You've never been any kind of brother."

He pulls back. "Marion, are you drunk? Are you on pills or something?"

She feels her face flush. "I am not drunk."

"Well then …" He pushes back his chair. "Yes, I've been a bad brother. But … I've tried to make amends recently, am trying."

He studies her as she sits and wipes her eyes, as she tries to put on a face that will enable her to walk out of the café and back into the world, to cross the street and be natural with Doug.

"Is your husband a good man, Marion? You said he's a nurse?"

"Don't bring Doug into this."

"What would he say, Marion? What would your husband think you should do, if you told him the truth?"

She glares. David nods, gets to his feet. "Goodbye Marion. Enjoy what remains of your time in Portsmouth."

She watches her brother leave. Damn him. She has the attacker's knife.

I'll find a way in to his house. I'll do it my goddamn self.

Chapter 35

Paula goes online and looks for thugs who match Marion's description of the man who killed Finn. It's a shame she no longer has a password to access the police databank of known criminals, but Marion said the scrote had an accent suggestive of the Beatles so Paula Googles *Liverpool, youth knife crime suspects/attacks.* A series of news articles scroll across her screen but the pictured perpetrators and suspects don't match Marion's description. Maybe it wasn't Liverpool. Manchester maybe? She tries again. No. Newcastle? No. Leicester. An article about a knife attack pops up. The story is a few years old but the face of the young thug in the photo is unusually gaunt. Trevor Chisholm grew up in care and knifed another kid at the home. The victim survived. If the kid in the article is the youth inside the house on Warhol Way, he's still only 20.

Paula stares at the menacing face on her iPad. Perhaps he was feigning the accent. He's likely one of those kids who never had a real chance, like the young men she's arrested in Portsmouth and those she encountered in San Francisco. It's a type of youngster she first met in English literature class among the pages of Graham Greene's novel *Brighton Rock.* She smiles, recalling her teacher. Mr Hindley always taught curled up on his desk, his long legs tucked under his body, his wide expressive hands darting and gesticulating. He adored sharing his love of literature with his 13-year-old students, and they responded to his passion and the way he treated them as equals. He was the only teacher Paula liked. She didn't like the book though. Greene's Pinkie, a soft-spoken, skinny, teenage thug, was the stuff of nightmares and her subsequent career. She'd hated Pinkie's viciousness, the book's nihilism. Perhaps she'd been sad about her parents' divorce at the time, and the boy's lonely fury resonated with her. Maybe.

It's interesting to see how far Sean's men may have reached in their efforts to find a scrote who wouldn't be on the radar of local police. She wishes again that she could contact her former colleagues and let them know about him but there's Marion's need for secrecy. Anyway, none of her colleagues have contacted her to see how she's been doing since she left the force. She sighs, feeling her professional isolation like a physical pain. If only she could go to the station, tell them they're looking for the wrong man.

Call them when Marion's gone. In the meantime, keep your eyes peeled.

She takes a photo of the kid's image with her phone and sends it to Marion: *Is this him?*

Her phone rings. It's her mum's care home.

"Hello, Paula here."

"Paula, it's Daphne." Daphne is the staff nurse. Paula knows her mostly by sight. Paula tenses.

"Paula, you might like to come in. I'm sorry to say Lorraine's taken a turn for the worse. She may not have long left."

"Right." Paula hears her voice sounding small and far away. "Thanks. I'll be there soon."

"Good, see you soon." Daphne hangs up.

Paula ends the call. She's been waiting a long time for this summons, yet she can't believe it.

Half an hour later, she's sitting in the comfy armchair beside her mother's bed, listening to the clock on the wall fill the room with precise, irrelevant sound. Her mind is stilled by a new kind of fear. Her mum's death, so long awaited, has arrived, and Paula's not ready, not ready at all.

Her mother lies asleep, her skin deeply pale. Paula longs to reach out and wrap her arms around that tiny body and hold on. At the same time, she longs to leap up and flee the hospital.

Instead, she sits and gazes at her mum, at the morphine drip feeding into Lorraine's arm, at the bland hospital tiles and the grey, vacant day beyond the window. She ponders the fact that Jane has declined to visit —"Sorry Paula, it would be weird." How could Jane not say goodbye to the woman who was a loving, constant part of her life for more than fifteen years? Jane's indifference reminds Paula there's no hope left with her wife and that's a good thing. The hope is Neil. Soon, her son will bring his youthful kindness into the death chamber. She smiles. Who would have thought a fifteen-year-old could be so patient and wise around death? Maybe it's God in the young man. Maybe it's evolutionary, some genetic reason for the young to know how to care for their elders at the end. Paula doesn't know. She only sees that Neil is calmer and braver than she is.

He gives us strength

Her thoughts turn again to Marion's attacker. She feared she'd glimpsed him the previous afternoon, standing like a bad mood at the end of her street. She'd flinched and halted in her stride, jerked Husky on his lead. Husky had looked up, questioning, waiting for direction. And Paula had smiled down and strode on, towards the youth, filled suddenly with anger and rebellion.

Why should I hide?

You know how to defend yourself, Paula, she'd reminded herself. Don't run. And her mind filled with memories of damp darkness, of the sound of her own pounding feet. As a rookie cop, she'd regularly chased down knife-wielding scrotes. One kid led her down a blind alley, at night, and she'd kept calm, called for back-up and subdued him. That's who you are, Paula, she thought as she stared at the menacing young figure at the end of her road.

It's wise to be wary of a knife, of course. The swift, efficient cruelty with which the thug finished poor Finn had played in Paula's mind as she walked toward his killer. The youth watched her approach, scowling, until she was almost upon him, her eyes meeting his vacant stare all the way. Finally, he crept from her, around a corner. And she was left, her heart panting.

It wasn't even him, a home-grown lout, maybe someone I put away. But I should have turned the other way, not tried to face him down.

Later, she'd Googled Leicester news again and again found the face of the Leicester thug, even younger and more angular, glaring from another newspaper article. Trevor Chisholm was now a car mechanic and was suspected of being involved in the recent stabbing deaths of two Brighton drug dealers. Paula skimmed the details of the murders and frowned. Both victims suffered multiple wounds. The bodies showed evidence of malicious, pain-inducing injuries. Chisholm was believed to have fled the city. Someone with a close resemblance to him had been seen striding, seemingly carefree, along Portsmouth's waterfront.

Her phone vibrates and she looks down. Marion has finally got back to her about the photo of the thug she sent. *It's not him*, Marion has texted.

Don't lie, Marion. I'm trying to help you. She doesn't send the thought.

She looks up and around the bland but cheerful little room that has become her mother's last refuge then turns again to her mum and winces. Lorraine always was petite but cancer has winnowed her to her essential essence. Only the core of her body remains, the nub of her.

Paula remembers when her father was dying, also of cancer. He too had been whittled, reduced and refined. His death had been less emotionally painful than her mother's—his earlier desertion diluting Paula's affection—but, at the end, he'd become her father again, and she his daughter.

Now, her eyes snag on the bag of golden morphine slowly dripping mercy into her mother's arm.

Thank goodness for painkillers.

Perhaps Chisholm left DNA evidence at Warhol Way? His blood could be mingled with Finn's. There are likely stains that could be examined, could convict him, if only the police knew who to look for. Paula sighs. This inactivity is so frustrating.

Marion will soon be gone.

"Hey Mum." Her lovely boy fills the doorway. He walks in, and she feels the room lighten.

"Hi love." She lifts her face for his kiss. "How was school?"

"Fine. ..." He settles himself by his grandmother's feet, moving so softly the bed barely shifts.

"You have much homework?"

"Nope." He drops his schoolbag on the floor.

They're whispering, but Lorraine senses their voices. She stirs, wakes, sees her grandson by her feet and smiles.

"Hello, love." Her head turns slowly to Paula. "You here too? Hello, my girl."

Lorraine's smile is enormous. There's such a feeling of closeness in the room that for a moment everything feels wonderfully okay. But reality creeps back.

"Hi, Gran. How you doing?" Neil gets up, kneels by Lorraine's side, drops a kiss on her face.

"Oh, you know. ..."

Again, Paula looks with gratitude at the morphine drip. Her mum does seem okay although she is groggy. Paula wonders if it would be preferable for her mum to be more alert. She hopes for some final intimacies, some words to carry with her into the future.

Neil takes his gran's hand in his. Lorraine has been a good grandmother, present and loving. Neil's memories of his gran will always be with him. Lorraine's eyes rest on her grandson's face. Paula sees a tear slide down her cheek.

"Oh Mum!" Paula rushes to her mother.

"I'm ... I'm ... all right. I'm just ... sad." Lorraine's voice is a rasping whisper. "I'm sad I won't see Neil when he's grown, won't be at his university graduation or his wedding, won't know his children." More tears come. "I won't even see him graduate from school."

"But we're together now, Gran." Neil leans close, strokes her cheek. "I'll never forget you, Gran. Never."

Lorraine nods. "Bloody cancer. You look after your mum for me, won't you, Neil?"

He grins, glances at Paula, standing trembling and uncertain on the other side of the bed. "I will."

Lorraine chuckles. "Your mum acts all tough but ..."

Neil nods. "I know..."

Lorraine grips his hand, her eyes close, and she drifts back to sleep.

"Here, you have the chair," Paula tells Neil. "Let me lie by Mum for a bit."

"Okay, don't wake her."

She grins at this shift in their relationship. She already knows these shifts can be stark, sudden, and they can also be gentle and imperceptible as a summer tide. "I won't. You get on with your homework."

Paula slips onto the bed and lays her head near her mum's. She almost falls asleep, is musing that she must get home to walk Husky, when she realises she's painfully thirsty. A dehydration headache is tapping at her left temple.

She sits up. "I'm going for a coffee," she whispers. "You want anything?"

Her son looks up from his books. "A Diet Coke."

"That stuff'll kill you."

"In seventy years, maybe." He grins, and she marvels how smiling makes him look older. It creates lines not yet there, tucks a crease of skin beneath his chin. Foreshadowing. I hope I'm still here, she thinks, when his wrinkles are real.

In the white corridor she stops for a moment and breathes deep, feels her chest loosen, then takes the stairs that lead down to the hospital's vast canteen. She finds the canteen surprisingly empty and pays a bored cashier for the drinks. Needing a longer break from the sick room, she takes the coffee and Coke over to a table by a large rectangular window, and stands, gazing down on the car park, sombre in a misty light.

She cups her hands around her coffee and sips. The drink is bitter and tepid, but the small warmth seeping through the paper cup is comforting.

She finishes the coffee, drops the cup in a bin, picks up Neil's Coke and walks across the empty room toward the stairs. Her feet slow as she walks, and she thinks of her father. What an intense man he was, always in the grip of some passion or other—cathedrals, stately homes. ... He adored historical re-enactments. How odd he'd looked dressed up as one of Henry VIII's warriors, the bulky chain mail accentuating his thin bookishness. So many affairs. What did the girls see in him? Was he an abuser? Did he threaten his female students with poor grades?

No, don't think that!

"Paula?" It's a voice she knows but can't place. Turning, she finds herself looking into the face of a former colleague, Sergeant Ian Wilson.

"Ian!" She's so glad to see this officer with whom she trained as a rookie, this colleague with whom she shared long years of friendly rivalry, that she almost reaches out and hugs him.

"It's good to see you, Paula." Ian's face glows. He never could hide his feelings. "How you doing? You're a private investigator now?"

"Yes. It's early days."

"We often talk about you at the station, wonder how you're getting on. I was sorry to hear about ... everything. ... You should come out with us. We still do Friday nights at The Helmsman."

Paula feels herself warm. Gratitude prickles her eyes. She glances down, blinks.

God, don't cry.

"That would be good, thanks Ian. Right now, I'm here with my mum, she's very sick ..."

"I'm sorry to hear that. I remember your mum, a great lady. Well, I'd better get going. I'm here with a scrote." He turns, glances down the long, white corridor. "Got himself locked in some offices during a robbery, injured himself when he tried to escape from an upstairs window."

Paula's eyes graze the uniform she wore with such pride. "Familiar tale."

He reaches into his jacket pocket. "Give me your contacts. I don't want to lose you again."

Paula smiles as she gives him her phone number. Has she let shame, pride, get in her way? Has she kept herself lonely? Not everyone's like Sue, she thinks, two-faced and deceptive.

"Good to see you, Ian."

"You too. Don't be a stranger. You know where we are, Paula."

"Yes." She smiles.

I do.

Chapter 36

Marilyn watches the blade spring from the handle. She tucks it and slips the knife inside her jacket beside a pair of transparent cleaning gloves. She stares at herself in the bathroom mirror above the sink and feels a surging sense of power in her chest and limbs.

I'll be at Heathrow by 8am tomorrow.

Sean has cancelled another public meeting due to ill-health. He's resting at home, the news said. Marilyn will return to his street, wait until his family leave, and find him. Sean has been sick for a while. He'll be weakened.

Walking in to the bedroom, she goes to her suitcase and pulls out a cap she bought in the Oxfam store across the road. The cap is black, the peak pulls forward and shadows her eyes. With her hair under cover and her big sunglasses on, she may not be instantly recognisable. Going downstairs, she finds Doug sitting with Winston on the sofa.

"I'm going out, hon. Karen and I are getting together one last time."

"That's nice," Doug says. "I like your cap."

"Thanks. I got it in the Oxfam store." Marilyn's heart lifts with love for her husband. He's tired. Unusually, he hasn't been sleeping. He's holding a mug of coffee and his other hand rests atop Winston's broad back. Marilyn walks over and gives Winston's head a deep massage. He grunts, relaxes under her fingers, looks at her with those big eyes. She smiles. *Dear Winston.*

"Winston will miss you when we go," she tells Doug. "You're always together."

"I'll miss him too. Won't I, fella?" And Doug scratches Winston's neck. The dog shifts his gaze from Marilyn to Doug. His eyes look a little doubtful, unsure. He's learned he cannot trust the world. Finn's absence fills the room.

"I'll see you later." Marilyn drops a kiss on her husband's forehead.

"Bye Winston," she says. "See you later, honey."

Outside, the morning is turning sunny. Spring is coming, and for a moment Marilyn regrets they won't be around to see it.

It's 8.15 am when she reaches Sean's street. As she passes his home, she notes that the red VW that ferries his wife and children about is still in the driveway. There's no sign of the security guard. Hopefully, the wife will soon emerge and take the kids to school. Then Marilyn will make her entry. Sean may be sick enough to have hired a private nurse. He may not be alone. The security guard may be with him. Finn's killer could be with him. Marilyn has looked for news of a young man, injured with a head wound, going to the hospital. But there has been nothing.

He could have recovered.

The thought doesn't deter her. She's filled with a driving emotion that feels like determination but could be recklessness.

She walks the entire street, wastes time at the far end where she can't be seen but is close enough to observe when the VW leaves. She grows impatient. Sean's kids will be late for school. She heads back up the street and sees them emerging from the austere white house. They clatter down the steep stone steps. The mother is there, and the big security guard. He was in the house with the family. They must like and trust him.

As long as he gets them out of my way.

Marilyn watches them get into the car then recalls that last time she was here, their car reversed and drove down this end of the street. She retraces her steps, lowers her cap, puts her head down as the car drives by. It doesn't pause, no eyes appear to be watching her from windows or mirrors.

Keep going, drive on.

She watches the car disappear around the corner then turns once more and heads back to Sean's house. She crosses the street, to his side, intending to dart into his garden, head round to the back to break a window for access. But she doesn't have to. As she arrives in the peaceful, manicured rear garden, she sees that a kitchen window is open. It's an old-fashioned window, secured by a latch, and it's a few inches ajar. Marilyn feels a moment's surprise at the window's lack of sophistication. It's a reminder of the home's age, of all the lives lived here. She can slip her fingers inside, loosen the latch, climb onto the sink. *No problem.*

She slips the cleaning gloves over her hands and they slide over her skin, cloaking, empowering. Easing the window back, she levers herself onto the windowsill, then down from the draining board adjacent to the sink, and on to the floor. Her arms are steady, her body light and limber. She feels a rush of confidence.

I'm healthy and fast. Sean is sick.

She removes her sunglasses, slips them in her pocket, and glances around the kitchen. It's spacious and full of family life. Colourful childish drawings are fixed to the fridge and a pinboard on a wall. There's a smell of coffee, toast. There are breakfast dishes on the smooth wooden table, a patch of milk under a spoon, scattered cereal flakes.

Marilyn passes through to the door at the far end. This door must lead into the hallway, to the staircase and the upper floors. Sean will likely be in bed.

The door leads into the elegant hallway behind the front door. Marilyn sees the stairs, stretching high and white at the far end, but pauses to check each room she passes. Sean could be at work on a sofa or sleeping in the sun by a window. She sees only an old tabby snoozing in a patch of light.

As she nears the staircase, her hand tightens on the knife in her pocket. At the foot of the stairs, she stands gazing up. A large stained-glass window sheds a soft light down the carpeted steps. There's a deep blue shield adorned with a gold star and crescent inlaid in the window. It's Portsmouth's coat of arms. The image feels like a warning, as if the citizens are protecting the man they elected. Breaking in has been too easy.

A trap? Should I turn back?

"Don't be ridiculous, Marilyn, Sean put that window in. It's his self-importance." She hears her voice sounding small and tense in the still hall and pauses, afraid she's been heard. She wonders if there might be security cameras and pulls her cap low. Her body feels heavier as she lifts her feet and begins the climb upward.

Sounds reach her—soft, classical music. Perhaps it is soothing the patient. It does not soothe her. Her heart accelerates as she moves higher. She feels as if her body is protesting, but she must avenge Finn and all Sean's victims.

The music is masking her approach. She recognises it as Handel's Water Music Suite, the dropping, fluid notes are unmistakable. David used to play it. He was an accomplished pianist when he was young. She wonders if he still plays and if it comforts him.

The music is coming from a room at the far end of the hall. Light spreads from the door. It's that special morning light, rich and soft, filled with a hopefulness that fades as the day moves on. Even in hot California, morning light has that luminous optimistic quality, and Marilyn thinks of her new home, the home she's made with Doug.

Soon, we'll be home again.

She crosses the landing with soft-footed speed, glancing into each room she passes. There are tossed sheets, scattered clothes—Sean's children, on their way to school—now already there? She moves faster at the thought of the wife's return.

At the threshold of the music room, she peers around the half-open door. Sean is lying beneath a large window on a chaise longue. He's resting in the warmth of the sun, propped up on pillows, a baby blue blanket draped across his legs. He's facing away from her, toward a fireplace. She notices the lovely patterned ceramic around it. She sees a sofa, a small TV mounted on the opposite wall, side tables and stacked bookcases. The walls are a subtle peach tone. The wooden floorboards gleam. There's a sumptuous rug. It's an elegant, beautiful room.

Sean is holding a document with one hand and making notes on it with the other. She sees a fat briefcase on the carpet, resting against the chaise longue. He's lost a lot of hair at the back of his head. There are patches of scalp beneath dark strands. She's surprised by Sean's ugly hair, and by the fact he has not turned around. He should have been able to feel her fury burning the back of his head.

She waits, and when he keeps reading and annotating, when he flips up the page and moves on, she steps into the room. As she moves, the music grows louder in her ears and she feels a spurt of panic, as if she is an actor who must now take centre stage and control the action. She doesn't know how to do that but feels sure that if she keeps moving forward, it will come to her. She pauses, breathes deep, lowers her shoulders, and walks toward the man who made her difficult life almost impossible.

The music, his focus on his work, mean he doesn't hear her. She must attack him while he lies on the chair. She imagines his shocked eyes as they focus—in death—on her vengeful face. She sees his blood seeping over the chaise longue. She moves forward, into his line of vision, but doesn't take out the knife.

He glances up. He's expecting someone else—his wife, his guard, a nurse. Marilyn sees that expectation fall, and surprise, uncertainty fill the eyes behind the reading glasses. A swift frown as he takes in her face, her jacket, the cap pulled over her eyes. His eyes do not move to her hands, do not register the near-transparent gloves. His slowness is unexpected. She pushes back her cap. "Hello Sean."

He knows her at once. She sees alarm spark in him, but it's not yet fear. She's just Marion. He might fear her tongue, her public accusations, but he doesn't fear her. She's just silly, neurotic Marion. There's contempt in his eyes. What harm can she do?

"Marion." His mouth twists. "You've finally decided to come in out of the cold." He glances back, toward the door. "Where is the dog, that lovely collie you're always walking up and down?"

Anger heats her, but it's slow. She's not lit up, consumed and impulsive. "You know what happened to Finn."

He doesn't reply. There's a blankness in his eyes, a hiding, that makes her think of David—David as he used to be. She stares. Sean looks old, older than when she saw him at the *Mary Rose*. His face is sunken, as if the flesh has dropped away too fast. Like coastal erosion after a storm, she thinks, leaving just the bones of the cliff. His voice is weaker too and slightly slurred. She glances at the little circular table that sits by the chaise longue. It looks attentive, the way it is poised by his side. She sees black coffee, half-drunk, in a rose-patterned cup.

He puts down the document he's reading, pulls off his glasses and places them on the table. "What do you want, Marion?"

What do you want, Marion?

The question surprises her, and she realises she's never heard it before.

That's because I've merely existed, snatched what I could. I had no plan for my life.

"I want, I wish, it had never happened," she says. "I wish you'd never raped me. I wish I could go back to being a girl of 13 and start my life again." The words sound ridiculous, but they are true.

He looks so exhausted. He's been ill, of course, and she hopes the many allegations against him, all the bad press, have been disturbing his sleep. Is he going to deny he raped her? She puts her hand in her pocket, feels the wedge of the knife's handle, envisages the sharp blade curling inside, ready to spring at the command of her finger.

"Marion, we are ... middle-aged." He sighs, disdain filling the sound. "We all have things we wish we'd done differently."

She stares. "Are you sorry you raped me?"

His hands rise and fall. "Is that what you want—an apology? Okay then, Marion, I apologise." There's a long, stretching pause. She doesn't believe him, doesn't forgive.

"But you women, you bitches ... You can't blame me for how your life has gone."

"I also blame my mother. You, and her, you ... submerged me." Tears fill her eyes. "I have survived, not lived."

"Marion, it's time for you to go." He pushes aside the blue blanket and lifts his legs to the floor. He's wearing a blue housecoat with pale blue pajama legs and navy slippers. She thinks of Finn, lying beneath the blue blanket.

"I've been patient, but you need to take your accusations and leave." He stares up at her and contempt hardens his eyes. "Go and walk a dog or something. There's still one to care for, I believe." He puts his hands on the chair, slowly levers himself up. He stares down at her. "Go, Marion."

She stares back, almost cowed by his height, his coldness. "You killed Finn. You wounded those girls. You sent that thug ..."

He shakes his head. "You're wrong, Marion."

Still denying!

She steps forward. Instinctively, he moves, but the chair is against the back of his legs. She sees his feet, in his slippers, and thinks how vulnerable he is. Human vulnerability, it's unavoidable. If he would only admit what he's done, if he'd apologise, really apologise, she might yet be able to forgive him. She thinks of her brother's brooding shoulders and lonely beer belly.

But Sean's disdain ... Anger heats her. She pulls the knife from her pocket, thumbs the button and the blade springs out. She glances at the silver threat in her hand. This blade will do anyone's bidding. She fears the knife, loathes it. But cutting is its nature, and that's why she's here.

Sean's eyes drop to the blade. He moves back, but there's still nowhere to go. His hands come up and reach for her. She shoves him, tries to get him down on the chair. She will finish him.

But Sean doesn't fall. His hands remain on her shoulders. His fingers dig in. He's trying to push her over. His force causes adrenaline to shoot through her limbs. Male strength. Even a sick man can't be counted out. But she's not sick. She's fit and fast.

She ducks, wrenches her body away, leaps to one side, but strikes the table. The coffee falls. Dark liquid. She raises the knife. He lunges at it, and she darts into the middle of the room as he comes at her, staggering, furious.

She watches him come, watches his slippers, and she puts out her foot and trips him. For a moment, he's suspended in air, like a cartoon character. He lands hard at her feet, and gazes up at her. He twitches, tries to move, but does not. She sees pain travel through his face, a grimacing twist of the mouth that reminds her of the thug after she dropped the lamp.

Is he having a fit?

She stares into eyes that are morphing from wary to fearful. She must crouch and stab him, slit his throat before he finds the strength to rise. It will be cleanest and quickest, although he's managed to lift one arm to his face. She raises the knife, and her hand pauses. Fear clouds his gaze. It's not an emotion he's familiar with.

I've taught him fear. Contempt washes through her and it's mingled with something else. Pity? Empathy? Her hand stills. Was Paula right—she can't do it?

Marion. Do it. For Finn, for all of us.

His eyes are desperate, yet ... detaching. Is he dying? Has she killed him without the knife? She has a vision of herself in a few hours' time, sitting alone in a police cell, mourning the happiness with Doug that she's sacrificed. There must be cameras in this house. She'll be caught.

So do what you've come to do.

Again, she raises the knife and again she feels that suspension of time, and the sinking that tells her she can't do it.

"Are you a victim or a slut?"

She thinks the words have come from her own mind, from the desire of her feet to flee, from her growing awareness of the incongruous sunlight filling the room, of Handel's gentle water music.

But the voice isn't hers. "It doesn't matter. Get out."

Marilyn glances toward the door. Sean's wife, Janet, stands there, smart in grey pants and white blouse, her hair is spiky, pixie-like, around her face. It's a new style. She looked different online and on previous sightings.

Marilyn is suspended, the knife in her hand. She hasn't used it, but Sean's wife sees it. She sees Marilyn threatening her husband. At any moment, his wife will pull out her phone and take a picture, call the police. Why hasn't she done so already?

"I haven't touched him." Marilyn glances at Sean. His eyes have closed.

He can't be dead. I've done nothing...

"I don't know what's wrong with him." Panic grows in her and protest, returning fear and self-doubt, self-preservation. "Honestly, I don't know." She lowers her hand, brushes the button on the handle of the knife. The blade retracts and she slips the weapon into her pocket.

"Your husband raped me." She stands. "When I was a girl, 13. I came here today..." She glances at Sean's motionless body.

"He threatened me. I had to defend myself."

"He's sick." Janet walks into the room. Marilyn feels herself flinch as Sean's wife moves closer, but Marilyn refuses to move. She clenches her fists by her sides, grips the weapon.

She's not getting the knife.

"He's sick," Janet says again. She looks down at her husband's lifeless body. She stares at Marilyn. "I saw you," she said, "In the street. I wondered if you were a victim or a slut." Her mouth is a slash of pink, her lips a sneer. "I see you are a victim. Oh, don't assume that all the women who have sex with my husband are unwilling. Powerful men attract the worst kind of woman." Her eyes—green, like Sean's and David's—challenge Marilyn. "I heard you and Sean talking," she says and she nods at the door.

"He raped me. You believe me? It's the truth."

Janet gives her an assessing stare then looks down at her husband. She reaches into the pocket of her sleek pants and pulls out a slim grey phone. She turns her gaze on Marilyn, and Marilyn sees eyes filled with emotions she can't identify. Marilyn feels a tremor run through her body.

"Get out." Janet's voice is calm and firm. "Get out while the security guard is picking up my shopping. Get out before I change my mind."

And Marilyn, her head so full of questions she is mute, nods and flees.

Chapter 37

Several days later, Paula is resting at home when her phone vibrates inside her jacket. It's a text from Marion: a smiley face. Paula frowns and deletes it, puts the phone back in her pocket.

The woman is driving me crazy. She needs a therapist. She needs to help herself.

She sighs and looks out of the canteen window, down into the hospital car park. There are so many vehicles. Will she ever earn enough to buy another car? Does she want one? She used to enjoy driving, but ownership is a hassle and there's climate change.

She startles, jerks her coffee as the phone in her pocket rings, the sound harsh and alarming in the empty canteen. She glances at the name and number: Marilyn Brooks. She takes a deep breath. "Hello."

"I didn't do it, Paula." Marion's voice is firm and clear. Her accent is English, just a little Transatlantic, although Paula knows she must be back in America by now.

"Didn't do what, Marion?"

"Didn't kill Sean Adams."

Paula pauses. Carefully, she turns and places her coffee cup on the nearest table. "The mayor is dead?"

"Yes. He died suddenly at home. It's in the news."

"I'm supposed to believe a man, still young, health-conscious, just dropped dead, Marion?"

"Yes. And Paula, I didn't do it."

Paula hears the silence stretch. Her gut twists with shame.

I should have stopped her. I knew and did nothing.

"I didn't do it, Paula. Please believe me."

"You don't want me to go to the police."

"Of course, I don't. I also want you to know I didn't do it."

Paula doesn't know what to say. She would have expected Marion's tone to be more timid, fearful. Marion should be scared, remorseful. Paula's intrigued. This is partly what's kept her involved, of course—curiosity and compassion, both likely born of boredom and loneliness.

"It felt weird, leaving again," Marion says. "San Francisco will never be home like Portsmouth is, but I have more chance of being happy, normal, here. I'm going to be happy." Marion is smiling—Paula hears a lightening, a lifting in her tone. "Come and stay with me, Paula? We have a nice apartment in a great place called Dogpatch." Her voice rises on the invitation. "I'd love to see you, anytime."

Paula is surprised by the invitation and, despite her anger and fear, touched. "If I ever make enough money to travel again, maybe I will. Thank you." It sounds like Marion is being genuine—there's something bright, like hope, in her voice.

"There's a ghost, you know, in that house," Marion says. "A young girl, pregnant...I think my own trauma called to her...Such sad eyes..."

Paula doesn't know how to respond to this.

Poor, mad Marion.

"I know you don't believe me," Marion says. "About anything, but you'll see. Goodbye Paula."

"Good bye, Marion. Sorry, I mean Marilyn. And remember Marilyn, none of it was your fault."

"Thank you. I will. Goodbye," Marilyn says, the smile back in her voice.

Marion/Marilyn hangs up, and Paula stands, not knowing what to think. She slips the phone away. Marion is back in Dogpatch. Paula imagines how she travelled to Heathrow, while she herself was preparing to spend more time at the hospital, while she was steeling herself to contact Linda, to suggest a date; just a drive along the coast, dinner maybe. It's taking her a while to find the confidence to call Linda. She picks up her coffee, forces down the drink which is now cold and even more disgusting. But it's liquid and caffeinated. She'll need both while she sits by her mother's bedside. Her mother has rallied again.

Maybe she's immortal?

Paula ponders what to do about Marion. If she's going to report her to the police, she must do it soon, obviously. Marion has already left the UK. Paula frowns. There should be no doubt in her own mind. She should be dialling the station right now. But Marion was grievously wronged and is a sick woman. Sean Adams was a bad man. And there's her own involvement. Questions will be asked, judgements cast—again. She thinks of Jane's disapproval, of Neil's disappointment, the social media mob.

And Mum is dying.

She finishes her coffee and bins the cup.

The mayor can't hurt anyone now.

Chapter 38

Marilyn struggles with jetlag when she returns to San Francisco, and is standing on the balcony of her apartment very early in the morning, her hands resting on the night-cold railing, when she feels her husband's arm snake around her waist.

She startles. Doug had looked deeply asleep, his mouth open, his arms flung, when she left the bed. And she has been so immersed in watching the dark waterfall in the courtyard below, so keen to lose herself in its soothing sounds, she has not heard him approach.

"Are you happy to be home, my love?" Doug murmurs against her ear and holds her body against his. "I am."

"Yes, it is good to be back." She is reluctant to talk, to lose the night's stillness.

Doug withdraws his arm, puts his hands on her shoulders, and slowly turns her to face him. "You seem calmer since we got back," he says softly, and she knows he doesn't wish to disturb their sleeping neighbours. "It was rough on you, wasn't it in England, being surrounded by news of rape, of abuse of power?"

"It was, yes."

Her husband nods, his kind nurse's eyes deep with sympathy. Marilyn knows he is hoping she will finally open up, tell him about her own experience with rape. All Doug knows is that some man, sometime, someplace, raped the woman who became his wife.

Doug has been so patient, so loving.

And Marilyn feels a warm rush of optimism, the belief that she can finally tell Doug the truth, and have him love her as he does now. Her lips actually open to confess her bitter, ugly story. But she closes them again.

It is too late. And too great a risk.

Maybe she should concoct some tale, about a rapist in her former life in Maine? But no, she might forget the details, give herself away.

No more lies.

"Perhaps we should stay here, in San Francisco, for a good, long while," she says. "After all, we have a lovely home in a wonderful city, one of the best cities in the world. Travel is tiring, stressful." She turns to the waterfall in the courtyard below, now partially gilded with rising sun. "Home is good."

"Home is good, but we talked about more pet-sits, maybe going to London in the summer, to Europe." Doug's eyes search her face. "But yes, we can stay here for now."

Marilyn reaches out, takes Doug's hands in hers. "I want to get to know your city," she says. "The place that made the man I love."

He smiles, and his eyes moisten. "That is so sweet, Marilyn. Yes, let's stay here. I do have a lot to show you."

She nods, relieved. "I want to put down roots with my new husband." It is the right thing to say, and she means it.

He pulls her to him, hugs her tight against his chest.

"We are going to be happy here, Marilyn. We are."

And Marilyn breathes in her husband's deep, familiar body scent, and something loosens inside her breast. The new sensation lifts and warms her like sunlight.

It is hope, she thinks. No, it is trust.

I trust Doug.

"Yes, we will be happy," she says.

Chapter 39

Several days later, Paula wakes, wanders into the living room and turns on the TV. She's hoping for some early-morning trivia to distract her from the prospect of another day at the hospital. Her mum is hanging on. No doubt she's sustained by the fact Paula is going on a date. Neil has agreed to sit with his gran while Paula and Linda get out of town for a few hours. Paula has bought herself a gorgeous, multi-hued top that brings out the shades of her eyes and skin and skims her breasts in a subtle, sexy way. She's bought new lingerie, although she does not expect to use it anytime soon. Just having the lingerie is confidence-building. And she does look good in the slinky bra and knickers.

I'm lucky I got Mum's genes.

She grins. *Yup, I can see why someone—Linda— might fancy me.*

Linda's going to pick her up and the two of them are going to drive along the coast and find somewhere good to eat, Brighton probably, a little out-of-town anonymity would be welcome.

Paula grins; her heart beating a little harder than usual. It's just a date, she reminds herself. But hope lifts her lips.

Does Linda like dogs?

She's about to switch from the news channel to the celebrity chat when she hears: "The mayor's wife, Janet Adams, has been arrested for his murder." Photos of the mayor scroll across the screen—the mayor speaking before the crowd at the *Mary Rose*, the mayor cutting a ribbon at the dockyard, the mayor shaking hands. The images are followed by shots of his slim, elegant wife, handcuffed, being led away from their expensive, white-faced home.

Paula sits abruptly, reaches to stroke Husky, who is hovering, anticipating his morning meal. She has the strangest feeling—a sinking sense of recognition. She should have seen it. It was always the most likely explanation. Sean has been ill, sickening for some time and no one knew why. Of all the women with reason to hate him, who might be expected to hate him more than his wife?

Still, it's shocking news. Paula recalls seeing Sean's pale face, his body contorted with coughing at the *Mary Rose*. Could it be that all the time Marion was obsessing about revenge, his wife was slowly taking it? What did his wife use? Did she think she'd get away with it? Maybe she was so crazed with distress and fury she didn't think about the consequences to herself, her children.

She just wanted him gone.

Paula reaches for her iPad. Online, she finds speculation about the fact Janet grew up on a farm. Her parents still live on the farm, and she's visited recently, took her kids to spend time with their grandparents. Did she steal something from her childhood home, chemical fertiliser maybe, something deadly but slow-acting enough not to arouse suspicion? An old jar of rat poison, pre-1970s, might have contained thallium, which is the most obvious explanation for the mayor's symptoms.

How was the crime uncovered? Paula's professional curiosity is aroused. An autopsy, probably, toxicology tests. She wishes she knew the details. Her former colleagues will be discussing it at the station. She stares at Janet's features on the page—an attractive face, minimally marked by time, nothing apparent on the surface. Had she feared for her kids?

Paula feels her shoulders slump. The kids always suffer. She recalls the day she trailed Marion and Finn to the mayor's house, recalls the delicate, athletic girl and the sullen boy standing on Sean's steps. His wife—seemingly content, privileged...

A breaking newsflash appears on the TV: a body has been found in Southsea, in a house awaiting demolition. The victim, a young man, was discovered by a contractor visiting in advance of the work. The youth appears to have been dead for some time, of a head injury.

Paula recognises the house as being near Warhol Way. The camera closes in on the home and garden. A lovely old property. No weapon was found at the scene.

She strokes Husky's neck. He is growing impatient, nudging her arm with his snout. "I know Husky. You need food and a walk, I need coffee."

A headshot of the dead youth appears, and Paula gasps. The lad has an angular and menacing face. Dark hair, pale skin. He is believed to be Trevor Chisholm of Leicester, aged 19. Anyone with information is asked to contact police.

Paula's mind spins. Did Chisholm die of the head wound Marion inflicted? She sighs, sad for a youth who never had a chance, who died alone and un-mourned.

She sits, until stirred to life by Husky's hunger. "Okay, boy, come on," she says as she lifts her body from the sofa. She moves toward the fridge and Husky's food. How did Marion react to the news about Sean's wife? Hopefully, she's not too disturbed, not empathising too much with the disgraced wife.

As Paula spoons wet food over Husky's kibbles, she hopes Marion is happy in her peaceful, secluded home in Dogpatch. She and Doug will have unpacked their clothes, filled their fridge. They'll be getting back to normal life in that beautiful, sad city.

She puts Husky's bowl on the floor and wanders to the sink, fills the kettle—coffee will clear her mind and warm her before she walks Husky and leaves for the hospital. She reaches for a mug, and thinks about her mum's ancient china doll, Ee-bord—Edith. Today, she'll get the doll out of the cupboard and get her fixed up. One of those clever, craftspeople in Southsea will restore her battered face and body. Paula's heart quickens with anticipation of her mother's delight, followed by a swift fear—she should have done this earlier. She will ask the restorer to hurry.

Hearing a sudden rush of sound, Paula glances up, from her narrow window, and watches a fighter jet soar across the city. It turns, spins out over the distant, bleakly grey Channel, leaving a plume of exhaust, visible as a darker grey against the sea and sky. The plane is joined by another military plane and another, and another. They roar in, meet, dance together, light-hearted and dangerous, in the clouds.

"It's all right, Husky," Paula says, turning to him. "It's just a coupla military planes." But Husky remains engrossed in his food, and Paula turns again to the window. She feels the planes' speed, their power, vibrate in her gut, her blood, and she smiles, stirred by some deep, surprising pride, a sense of familiarity and belonging.

She thinks of Marion and feels a rush of warm kinship with the woman who lost her father so horribly, who lost her city, her country as a child. Paula cannot imagine such rootlessness, such a lack of belonging. She cannot help but wish Marion peace in California. If only the news about Sean's wife had come earlier, she would have been able to say a proper goodbye to Marion, to wish her the best in her life and marriage.

She puts up her hand and draws the outline of a fighter jet, lean and aggressive, in the morning condensation still coating her window. Then she grins and adds a smiley face. She watches the plane and face fade, drip, blur. Inexplicably, Paula feels her eyes fill and she moves to Husky, leans down, and strokes his warm, reliable back. He looks up from his bowl as the jets again roar and drench the city in sound, as the planes torment and delight the citizens of Portsmouth.

"Goodbye Marion ... Marilyn," Paula says as she returns to the window. "Good luck." And she feels another surge of physical warmth that is something like joy, release. She raises her voice above the planes' din as if hoping to be heard in far-away California.

"Take care of yourself, Marilyn Taylor."

Chapter 40

Acknowledgements

Getting a novel from an idea to the finished page is a long, often lonely, slog. This novel deals with some tough subject matter so I was particularly glad of the support of my writing buddies: Susan Church; Jill Hamilton; Mary-Lou Petersen, and Cheri Wilson. Warm thanks also to Brian Parsons for sharing his time and expertise on military aviation. And love and gratitude to my husband and main editor, Peter Moreira, author of The Haight Mystery Series.

Printed in Dunstable, United Kingdom

65716436R00191